True Hope

True Hope

FRANK MANLEY

CARROLL & GRAF PUBLISHERS
NEW YORK

TRUE HOPE

Carroll & Graf Publishers
An Imprint of Avalon Publishing Group Incorporated
161 William Street, 16th Floor
New York, NY 10038

Copyright © 2002 by Frank Manley

First Carroll & Graf edition 2002

Library of Congress Cataloging-in-Publication Data is available.

ISBN: 0-7867-1020-9

Printed in the United States of America
Distributed by Publishers Group West

FOR CAROLYN

True Hope's a glorious Huntresse, and her chase
The God of Nature in the field of Grace.

— *Richard Crashaw*

True Hope

1

It was a cold day for South Georgia, and I was out in the yard sitting with my back to the wall trying to get warm. The sun was bright, but the air was so cold it canceled it out, and I was just sitting there picking at the grass and drawing in the dirt with a Popsicle stick, thinking about how funny it was that this was the first time I knew where I was since before Kate died, and it turned out to be Reidsville. It could have been anywhere else in the world and it would have been better.

That night I was laying up in my bunk studying the ceiling and listening to this song on the radio all about how a man loved a woman and lost her. The tears rolled down the side of my face, and I didn't even bother to wipe them off. It was like hearing my own heart singing the song. It wasn't on the radio. It was inside.

One time we went to Florida. Kate had never seen the ocean, and when she did, she couldn't believe it. She kept saying it reminded her of God, which, of course, I didn't want to hear. I told her, "Forget it." And she said, "I can't. As long as I'm here, that's all I can think of." So I took her into town. This was in Apalachicola, and the town's on the river, back from the ocean. We went shopping. There was this store that had seashells and orange nets hanging in the window and souvenirs of Apalachicola. The souvenirs were mostly little bales of cotton with pickaninnies sitting on them dangling their feet. Apalachicola used to be a big port for cotton, shipped it downriver before they had roads. Along with the pickaninnies they had little rows of air conditioners set up like toy cars, and on top of each one a label that said, "Souvenir of Apalachicola, Florida." I asked the man what that meant, and he said there was a doctor there, lived in Apalachicola, invented air conditioning. I didn't know that before. I was still talking to him about it when Kate came up with a conch shell in her hand.

"Listen," she said, and put it up to my ear.

It was cold and hard like a piece of stone that had been polished smooth for thousands of years. I listened, but I didn't hear a thing.

"Listen harder," Kate said.

It sounded like she was far away.

And then I heard it.

I said, "Put that goddamn thing away!"

It was the ocean, of course. I could hear it roaring inside that conch except it wasn't just the ocean. It was the salt of my blood and the tides of my body, rising and falling, and the sound of a drum like the sound of a clock beating time to the roar of the waves. It was inside me, and the way Kate was looking, she knew it was inside her, too. The only difference between her and me was that she wanted to hear it, and I didn't.

It's all right to think about God when you have to, like before a ball game or when things aren't going good and you lost your job or at weddings or funerals. Things like that, where God's important. But I didn't want Kate messing up her personal life thinking about it. I look back from where I am now, and I wonder how I could have ever thought that. It seems like a joke or a whole different person. But I swear to God that's what I thought.

One reason was, she already thought about God too much, and I wasn't jealous exactly, but we were just married, and I didn't want her getting distracted thinking about death and dying and how unhappy some folks are and how she ought to do something to help them. Somebody's got to think about things like that, but I figured it was preachers and politicians, not young folks like us, just starting out. I wanted her to spend her time with me. But it's like she was already marked by God. I look back, that was one of the main reasons I loved her. She had this kind of sadness in her that cut through the fun like light through the shadows. She was all lit up with something inside her I didn't know a thing about, and I resented it, I suppose. I was attracted to it in a way, but mostly I resented it. I couldn't understand it. That's how come I found it attractive. But something made me afraid of it, too. I was afraid I might lose her. It's like she had a fatal disease, and I kept trying to cure her of it. I knew if she got to thinking too much about all that stuff, it might claim her or something. And finally it did.

I used to tell her she was too young to think about dying. She had her whole life ahead of her yet. But she said it wasn't dying she thought of. It was living eternal life. I told her that was the same damn thing. You had to die to do it, I said. "Why don't you pay attention to us?"

And she used to pat my cheek and say, "I do, honey. I think about you all the time. I sleep, I even dream about you. You're all I love and all I live for. I wouldn't know what to do without you."

But I didn't believe her. It seemed to me then that any time you think about God—I mean really think about Him when you're off somewhere by yourself, not what you do on Sunday at church—it was bound to make you unhappy and get you to wondering about what it all meant and what you're supposed to be doing here and how come there's all this death and dying and people suffering right and left. I knew enough about my own family to keep me depressed the rest of my life.

They say you shouldn't have regrets, but that's one thing I can't help regretting. But then I think, maybe Kate knows. I don't think I ever lost her. After she died, I used to pray and ask her to help me, and I could feel her in the room. I'd be so drunk I wouldn't know the way to the bathroom, but there was still one part of me sober, and I used to pray to get it drunk, too. I wanted to forget, but I couldn't do it. No matter how hard I tried, I wasn't able to get drunk enough. That's why drinking's so pitiful. The part you want to get drunk never does.

I used to wish I never knew Kate. That way I wouldn't miss her so much. I used to wish she was never born. I thought if I could just quit missing her and forget what she was like, if I could just get drunk enough to do that, I'd be all right. I could make it.

It was my soul. That was the part I couldn't get drunk. And Kate was all mixed up with that. I couldn't forget her any more than I could forget myself. She was like something young and innocent in me. Our whole life together was always there from beginning to end, pure and untouched, and I wanted to kill it and get rid of it somehow, just like I wanted to kill myself. But it was the only thing I had left that was still decent. And then when I finally got out of prison and she was still with me. . . .

But I'm getting too far ahead of my story. Whenever I get to thinking about Kate, I always get carried away like that. I can't seem to help it. She's this one bright light in my life, and everything else is a kind of a shadow.

One time I was at the Grand Canyon, going cross country in a truck, and they had this clock called The Clock of Time. You turned it on, and it showed how old the earth was. It had these lights that clicked on. It started with the Age of Man and showed you how long that was. It was over in a flash—one or two seconds. Then it showed the animals, and they were a little longer, and then the dinosaurs, and then the fishes, and each one was a little longer until it went back to before there was any life at all, when there was just this empty ocean covering the whole face of the earth, and that was the longest one of all. It lasted hundreds of millions of years. I couldn't believe it. There wasn't another thing in the world except the ocean and the waves roaring in the wind, and under the surface, in the depths, just a sort of quiet and stillness. And that was the origin of life. That's where it started. Everything we know on earth came out of that ocean, and that's what I was listening to when I was laying in my bunk with the tears rolling down my cheeks. I didn't know it when I was first married, but after Kate died, I knew it then. Your life's not your own. It comes out of that ocean. Nobody knows how or why. And it goes back into it again, like Kate. You're just swallowed up, and nobody knows why that is either. And all the time you carry it in you if you listen hard enough. You can hear it surging and singing inside your blood, in the roar in your head, if you get distracted enough like I was, or desperate enough. That's when you hear it at night when you're sleeping or when you just wake up in the morning and you lay there real still and listen, and there it is like distant traces, like some kind of music so far away you can't even make out the tune.

Something in me broke when Kate died, and I wasn't any good for the world anymore, and what I got was this instead, and it wasn't exactly a fair exchange. The only one I belonged to was Kate. This other just had me like it had her, and it took her, and it was going to take me, and there wasn't a thing I could do about it except drink and try to forget it. The only difference was, when I was laying in my bunk at Reidsville, I didn't have anything to drink and knew I wasn't going to get any. That and the fact that there was this song about a man who lost the only woman he loved.

If you were to ask me what I was—I don't mean my name or what I looked like or what my I.D. number was or what I was in prison for or what I was going to do when I got out, what my plans were, if I was like most folks and had any plans—I mean what it was like to be me, what I thought and what I felt and what I lived with from day to day—I would have had to say that was it. The sound of the ocean.

2

After I got out of Reidsville on October 22, 1972, in one year and ten months with fourteen months off for good behavior, they gave me a ticket for the bus and a new set of clothes and fifty dollars. They put my old clothes in a grocery sack and handed them to me. I told them, No, thank you, I didn't want them. But they said it was regulations. I came in with them, I was going to have to go out with them on my back or under my arm, it didn't make a goddamn bit of difference to them. Outside the gate they had a van that was going to take me down to the crossroads so I could catch the bus out of there. They said a guard had to go and flag it for me or else it wouldn't stop.

We got there early. The bus wasn't there, so we stood around waiting. I didn't want to talk to the guard. I never saw him before in my life, and I was just beginning to feel my freedom and wonder how I could have stood being locked up in prison for nearly two years, and I didn't want anything reminding me of it. I just wanted to see the pines and smell the turpentine in the bark—a little whiff of vinegar in the air—and feel the sun on the back of my neck and look at the sky with nothing in it, not even a cloud, and think about how empty it was. That just goes to show you, I thought. Anything's possible.

All of a sudden the guard said, "Hey, what's your number?"

I said, "I don't have a number. I just got out."

He said, "Well, what's your name, then?"

I said, "Al."

He said, "Al what?—goddamn!"

I said, "Al Cantrell."

He said, "That ain't much of a name, is it?"

I said, "Suits me. What's yours?"

He said, "Captain Bilbow."

I said, "I see what you mean. I'm going over here."

He looked at me and said, "How come?"

He was a little skinny fellow about sixty years old who looked like he might have been a hard drinking man himself. That or a house painter. He was from town. He wasn't from the country. He didn't have that country look, and he was a little too high strung and edgy.

I said, "What's it to you? I'm a free man now. I go where I want to."

He said, "Not till you get on that bus."

I said, "How come?"

He said, "I got a wife and children to think of. I need this job."

I said, "You're too old for children."

He said, "Shit you say. You ought to talk to my wife about that."

I said, "First wife or second?"

I was getting kind of interested by then. I wondered who would marry him.

The guard looked at me, then looked away like he saw something far off down the road. The roads in South Georgia are as flat and straight as the roads in Florida. They keep on going as far as you can see through nothing but woods and swamps with black water running along on the sides of the road in the drainage ditches and a cow or two, maybe, browsing on the right-of-way or standing in the middle of the road looking surprised like it was wondering what the hell you're doing there. It's the loneliest place there is. The cows are so wild, they got to have special people to catch them. I mean professional cow catchers. Say you're a farmer down near Reidsville, and you want to round up your cattle for market, you get hold of the county extension agent, and he makes arrangements with one of those cow catchers to come out with a team of horses and dogs and drive your cattle out of the swamps onto high ground so you can try to fatten them up and get some meat on them instead of just sinew and gristle, bones and hide, before you can sell them.

At first I thought he was distracted by something walking up out of the swamps dripping black slime and water, or buzzards congregating on something, flapping their wings and walking around pushing each other to get at it better. Or maybe the bus was finally coming off in the distance. But it wasn't that.

He was just standing there thinking or something. I don't exactly know what he was doing. Sometimes a man just stops like that and starts thinking about something, and all of a sudden he forgets what he's doing. He might have even been thinking about how that road looked like the rest of his life, if he was lonely enough to think things like that. A man with a dead wife and nothing much of interest around him except woods and swamps and sometimes a cow looking up with a mouthful of grass, or cars whizzing by at sixty or seventy miles an hour full of people going to Florida on a vacation—families with children and old married couples—a man like that might look at the road and start wondering about it. One way's about the same as the other. You might as well be going backwards as forwards for all the good it does to the landscape. Might as well just stay where you are.

That's what he *might* have been thinking about. That guard was a prisoner just like I was except I was inside and he was out, and you might think that'd make a whole lot of difference, but at Reidsville it doesn't. There isn't any outside or inside there. It's all the same. Some are guards, and some are prisoners, but they're all locked up in prison together. The only difference is the prisoners get out, and the guards stay on from year to year. I was fixing to get on that bus a free man. It was going to take me away from Reidsville, back to the known world, and he was going to get in that van and go back to prison because I just had a three-year sentence, and he was in there for the rest of his life.

We were doing like that, staring off down the road, thinking about one thing or another, when all of a sudden the guard said, "Third." He didn't even turn around and look at me. He just said "Third" real slow like he was talking to himself.

I said, "Third?"

I didn't know what he meant for a minute, and then when I did, I couldn't believe it. No woman in her right mind would marry him and move out to Reidsville, let alone three of them. There wasn't another human being within fifty miles of Reidsville except prisoners and black tenant farmers running tractors for rich men in town and living a mile or two apart with a family of children crawling around on the bare dirt under the chinaberry trees. I figured he must have had some sort of special supply, like a woman's prison or an insane asylum.

I was amazed. I said, "Where'd you get them?" I meant out there.

He said, "I contracted for them."

That got my attention. I'll say that for him. He was what Kate called a man of surprises. "I'd rather meet a man of surprises," she'd say, "than the president of the United States." I'd say, "Some of them are men of surprises." And she'd say, "That's not the kind of surprises I mean."

I had to take a pee real bad, but I didn't want to stop talking to do it. That's what Kate meant. If it was the president of the United States on TV talking about something, I wouldn't have a bit of trouble. That's the main difference.

I said, "*Contracted*? What do you mean? They ain't cases of Coca-Cola."

He said, "I mean Filipinos. I was in the Philippine Islands."

He was talking about the Second World War. That's how old he was. He said his first wife was a Filipino, and after she died, he sent for her sister and married her, and after she died, he sent for another, but by that time all his wife's sisters were married. They promised him a cousin of hers, but she was still underage. She was something like eight or ten years old, and they wanted to wait till she was a woman.

"Them Filipinos," he said. "They got their own ways."

He said he married three of them, and they might as well have been peas in a pod. That's how alike they were. Pure Filipino. He could hardly tell them apart. They never did learn to talk. He'd have been willing to teach them, he said, but they wouldn't do it. They never could carry on a real conversation. Just pass me this and pass me that, pointing at things.

I said, "What about contracting for them?"

That was the part that interested me.

He said it was because of that cousin. They wanted him to wait two years, and he wouldn't do it.

"A man can't go that long," he said. "Not in this line of work."

He was reading a magazine one time, and it had this section after the pictures advertising mail-order brides. You could get Indians, Chinese, Filipinos—whatever you wanted. The way it worked was you sent them ten dollars, and they sent you these pictures and vital statistics.

I said, "What vital statistics?"

He said, "How old they are and how much they weigh and how big their titties are and if they know how to talk yet or not. Things like that. Of course, Filipinos don't have big titties. That's one thing about them."

I said, "Then what?"

I was more interested in contracting for them than I was in the titties.

"Then," he said, "you take your pick. You tell them which one you want to marry and send them the air fare and five hundred dollars, and a few weeks later you pick them up at the airport. That's all there is to it, except marrying them, and they already got that arranged."

I said, "How's that?"

He said, "By proxy. They do it before they even come over. Otherwise, they wouldn't let them in. They don't want Filipinos coming in here except if you marry them."

I said, "How dark are they?"

This was way down in South Georgia, and I was wondering how that worked.

He said, "Not as dark as you might imagine. They look a little like Mexicans. That's what most folks think they are. They don't mind."

I said, "How about you?"

I kept thinking about those Filipino women and what they thought when they got to America and he took them to Reidsville and if they ever got out of the place and what they died of and how come there were so many of them. I mean how come they died so fast?

He said, "How about me, what?"

He looked suspicious like he didn't like the way the conversation was going.

I said, "How did you feel about them looking that dark?"

He straightened up like I just hit him with an electric wire, looked me right in the eye, and said, "I'm from Akron."

I said, "Akron?"

Kate was right. He really was a man of surprises.

He said, "Akron, Ohio."

I said, "Is that right?"

I knew where Akron was. I passed through there once on the way to Chicago. I was just waiting to see what he'd say.

He said, "I ain't got a prejudice bone in my body."

I liked him a little better for that. I figured his principles were all right as long as they didn't touch him in person. I couldn't condemn him. I'm a little like that myself. But those Filipino women, they're the ones that suffered out there.

He kept going on about how good Asian women are if you're from Akron like him and don't mind the prejudice. He said they treat you like a king. The one he was married to now, he said, wasn't more than eighteen, nineteen years old, and she was prime. She was just prime.

I said, "What did they die of?"

But he wasn't interested in talking about that.

I said, "How many children you got?"

I figured they might have died giving birth.

He said, "Two. Two boys. Sons of bitches, I haven't seen them in seven years. Gone to Alaska. Ever hear of that? Half-Filipino bastards, gone to Alaska, freezing their balls off."

I said, "No wonder you haven't seen them," when all of a sudden I saw a blue dot coming out of the line at the end of the world, moving toward us through the heat, coming on down the road like it was gliding through pools of water.

I said, "What's that? Is that the bus?"

He looked and said, "Yeah."

Then he kept on about his wives.

"You know what they do with the dishes?" he said. "Scrub them with sand! And toilets? They don't even know what a toilet is. You got to show them. They don't come with American ways in every little thing they do. Take this one I'm married to now. You know what she does? Washes her twat every time she takes a shit."

I was thinking about Kate and those poor, sad, foreign women having to live with someone like that. But I didn't have time to argue about it. The bus was coming, and I had to take a leak real bad.

I said, "Listen. I'll be back in a minute" and started running toward the woods.

I got to the first line of trees and started unzipping my pants. I was happy I made it that far and was just about to commence when all of a sudden here comes the captain pulling up beside me yelling, "What happened? What happened?"

He must have thought I was bit by a snake or stepped on a yellow jacket's nest. Or maybe he thought I was escaping. A man like that, guards other men with a gun for a living, you never know. Those Filipino women prove that.

I was trying to turn my back to him, but he kept following me around saying, "What happened? What happened?"

I said, "I'm trying to take a piss!" just about that time he looked down and saw what I had in my hand. He didn't even say a word. He just turned around and walked back to the road. Before he got there, he yelled, "I'll flag it for you." But I was already pissing by then, and I didn't care one way or the other, it felt so good.

That was the first time I pissed outside. My first free piss in a while, you might say, except for that guard checking it out, and it was like saying good-bye. I knew I was leaving Reidsville behind me.

I zipped up my fly and started to pick up that sack of old clothes they gave me. It was a pair of dirty white boxer shorts, a summer shirt, a pair of straight leg jeans, and a leather belt with a turquoise silver buckle I got from an Indian worse off than I was for a bottle of Southern Comfort in Tuba City, Arizona. That buckle was one of my real prize possessions. I can't tell you how many times I had it in and out of pawn. I looked at the buckle, and it gave me a start. I felt my heart turn a flip. It was like seeing myself in a mirror. That whole other way of life came back in a rush like they say when you're drowning and your whole life flashes in front of your eyes. I wanted to put it on again and get back to where I knew what I was. But I was afraid to. I didn't want to go back to drinking. I hadn't had a drink since I was in Reidsville, and the funny thing was, I didn't miss it. I could sleep at night, and I didn't regret the past or fear the future like they say in the Program. I truly believed my Higher Power took the craving away from me. But seeing that belt buckle brought it all back, and I knew if I was ever going to be free, I'd have to leave all that behind me.

I turned around and looked for the guard. I couldn't see him, so I took the clothes out of the sack and spread them out on the ground like a body—the shirt here, the trousers there, socks on the bottom. Then I took the buckle off the belt and put it where the head should have been and ran the belt down the middle like the backbone. Then I covered it up with pine straw. I mounded it up so it looked like a grave. Then I took the grocery sack and put a rock in it and balled it up and threw it as far as I could in the woods.

Then I just stood there. At first I thought if somebody found it, they might think it was a murder. Then I started hearing the wind. It's like it rose up in the pines, and they were all swaying and moving around. It looked like the whole world was moving, bending this way and that, and I could hear the wind in the branches swishing like the sound of a woman's thighs when the tops of her stockings are rubbing together. It was rich and full like that. The wind wasn't blowing up on the road. It was just inside the pines. And all of a sudden I started praying. I don't know what else to call it. I was thinking about Kate when I thought about the sound of the stockings. I used to love to walk beside her and hear how she did. It was like knowing a secret, something nobody else in the world ever knew—like what her skin smelled like or how she tasted. I thought about Kate and then went on past her. It was the first time I ever did that.

I said, "Deliver me, Lord, from this body of death."

That's all. If I could have thought of something else to say, I'd have done it. My heart was full of pain and sorrow. I'd have knelt down right there and prayed for forgiveness, but I couldn't do it. My heart was too hard. I wanted salvation. I wanted freedom. And I was a free man already. I just that minute got out of Reidsville. I wanted my whole life to live over, and there it was more than halfway past. I wanted Kate dead and forgotten, but that was the problem. I couldn't forget her. I loved her too much. I wanted my old life back again. I wanted her to rise up from the grave. That's what I meant, "Deliver me, Lord, from this body of death."

I said, "God, You laid in the tomb three days and three nights, and then You got up and filled it with light, and before that You did the same thing for Lazarus, and I don't even know how long he was dead. You picked the worms off him and took him by the hand and led him out of that place of darkness, and he stood there blinking, he was so blind, and by and by he found his way home. I know You can do it. Give her back to me, O Lord. I love her too much to lose her forever. Death is a long, long time."

And God heard my prayer—the first prayer I ever prayed in my life where I really meant it. It's like I was sick and longing for something, and God heard my prayer and gave it to me except it wasn't what I wanted. It wasn't what I even meant.

3

All of a sudden I heard the air brakes on the bus, slowing it down. Then the guard started yelling, and the bus started honking, and I came scrambling out of the woods. I was already climbing on, handing the driver my ticket, before I even got a chance to say Amen. I bent down to wave good-bye to the captain, but he wasn't paying any attention. He was already walking back to the van like I was a load of chickens he just sent off to the processing plant.

And that's how I left Reidsville prison. In fact that's how I left most places I stayed at the last ten or fifteen years.

Besides the fifty dollars in my pocket, I had the address of a house in Decatur where the social worker fixed me up with a job and a place to stay. It was in what you might call a mixed neighborhood. There was a white woman living with two or three black men a couple of houses away, and the rest of the neighbors were all black. The man that owned the house was black, and he was the one that gave me the job. He was a painting contractor and preacher who used to be in Reidsville himself for armed robbery and extortion before he got into AA and changed his whole life. He used to come down to Reidsville sometimes and lead the Meetings. Most people wouldn't go to them. They said it reminded them of church. But I went with Palermo just to have something to do. I never liked the preacher too much myself, and it wasn't just because he was black. He talked too loud, and he laughed too hard about nothing, and you couldn't have a conversation with him. He talked and you listened. That was his style. He might have done a lot of good for people. I'm not saying he didn't. All I'm saying is the ones he did it to didn't much like it. Doing it made him feel real good and made you feel like shit.

But I didn't know that at the time. I was a house painter by trade. That's what I took up after Kate died. Before that I wasn't much of anything. I was too young. I hadn't settled into my life real good when she was taken, and after that I didn't much care what I did. House painting's the only thing I found where they'd leave you alone. I'd get up on a ladder painting the side of a big old house, I felt just like a kite, the way you hold it in your hand and feel like you're flying. Besides that, they couldn't tell if you were drinking. Smell something, they thought it was paint. Most house painters I knew smoked dope or drank whiskey, depending on how old they were. So I more or less fit right in. It wasn't like a regular job where you went to the same place every day for fifty years. Paint a house, you're through with it and move on someplace else. Each job is different.

This preacher I'm talking about heard I was a house painter. One of the rehab officers told him, and he came walking up to me one night after a Meeting and asked what I was fixing to do. I didn't know what he was talking about, so I said, "The Fourth Step." That's one of the Twelve Steps in AA. Taking a personal inventory.

We just finished what they call a Step Meeting, where everybody sits around and grumbles about how hard it is to take one of the steps and how rewarding it is when you finish. So that's what I thought he was talking about. Other than that I wasn't fixing to do anything except go back and listen to Palermo talk about his days in the army, and I don't hardly call that something. But the preacher meant when I got out. Was I any good as a painter? I said No. I just did it to keep from drinking. I wasn't any good at it.

He grinned, and I could see the pores in his nose and the way his nostrils flared out when he smiled. They looked like gills.

He said, "Not anymore. I'm going to fix it up where you love it."

I said, "You got a job ahead of you then because I purely don't like it."

He said, "You ain't ever worked for me."

I said, "Who are you, anyway?"

He said, "Bubba Jones, the B and O Construction Company. I'm the biggest minority painting contractor in the city of Atlanta. You know my motto?"

I said, "No, I don't."

He said, "There's no telling the amount a good man can do if he don't care who gets the credit."

I said, "Is that right?" I didn't give a shit what it was.

I started to walk away. I figured he was fixing to tell me about how important he was and how many contracts he got because he was a minority and the city administration's mostly all black and the federal government said that so many percent of all government contracts have got to be minorities, and so on like that, when all of a sudden the preacher said, "You want to get out fourteen months early?" And that caught my ear.

He took me over and gave me the details. If I agreed to work for him for about two-thirds of my regular pay, he agreed to fix me up with a place to stay and tell the parole board I had a regular job. All I had to do was sign a contract. I figured it was something like that. I had to work for him for a year and a half. That was the fourteen months I still had to serve plus four more for his trouble. And I couldn't argue with that. It was a good deal for him. That's why he did it. Preaching is preaching, but business is business. And it was a good deal for me. So I signed up, and they let me out early.

I lived eight months in that house in Decatur, and every morning Bubba Jones would pick us up in a truck with a camper top—he called it his personnel carrier—and take us to the job site. We were all indoor men. The kind of contracts he got were mostly all government buildings, and the painting work was indoors. The outside was usually unpainted concrete. The house I lived in was full of wallboard men and tapers, stipplers and painters. I was the only white one there except for this one boy. I don't know where they got him. He was the cook, they called him Cookie, and the rest of them did what they wanted to with him, the ones that got a taste for that in prison. I never did like it. I'd just as soon use my fist. It seemed less unnatural. But some of them said they liked the fit. The boy had a room to himself off the kitchen, and they went in there.

I don't blame the boy. He couldn't help it. I blame the others for doing it to him. A man got a taste for something like that when there're women around, I figure there's got to be something wrong with him. It wasn't my business, but I couldn't eat there.

Over the front door of the house was a sign in blue letters on a white piece of plywood that said, NO ALCOHOL BEVERAGES ALLOWED ON THE PREMISES. BUBBA JONES HOUSE OF HOPE.

That's the kind of place it was—reformed drunks humping the cook in a room off the kitchen and working six days a week to mainline it. That's what they called the end of the contract. Bubba would say, "You got three more months to mainline it, boy. Don't blow it now."

I usually ate at a place on College Avenue beside the railroad tracks called IT'S GOOD. They sold barbecue mostly and Brunswick stew and ready-made sandwiches wrapped up in pieces of cellophane. Brunswick stew was their specialty. They had a sign out in front—one of those signs on a trailer you hook up to the back of your pickup truck, got a hitch at one end and two wheels on the other and movable letters in slots on both sides. And every week they'd tell about how many gallons of Brunswick stew they sold just like the sign on Peachtree Street that tells how many people there are in Atlanta down to the last baby just born across the street in Piedmont Hospital. When I was eating there at IT'S GOOD, they'd been in business eight years and were up to around fifty-three, fifty-four thousand gallons of Brunswick stew. I forget the exact figure, but it was enough to fill a good-size pond. And it was good. I'll say that for it. That's how come they sold so much. Every night I went up there, I had me a bowl and a sandwich of whatever was left over from lunch. I liked to see the numbers change on the sign. It made me feel like part of the neighborhood. Looking back, that don't seem to make a whole lot of sense, but you got to take me as I was. That sign and IT'S GOOD, where I ate every night, were things I could count on. It was warm in there, and the folks were friendly, and it smelled of Brunswick stew simmering on the back of the stove, and the windows were all steamed up, it was so cold outside, and sometimes it felt almost like home.

I was what you might call a token. Bubba needed a white man or two in his House of Hope. But that was all right with me. I don't have a thing against Bubba except that white boy in the back room. He was from a little town called Dacula and couldn't have been more than twenty years old. He told me he quit school in the eleventh grade because he didn't fit in there. I could see why. Not many folks could unless they chewed Red Man Tobacco and drove a Ford pickup truck with oversized wheels and worked in the chicken processing plant cutting up parts and got married and lived in a mobile home in back of their daddy's place in the country. He was just different. Bubba and the other men in the house were using him three or four different ways, not the least of which was he was white.

That's the kind of man Bubba was. Nothing was simple, least of all him. That's how he got where he is today. When I knew him, he was driving the personnel carrier, doing good three or four different ways at once. And now he's in a three-piece suit sitting on the City Council. It was like destiny. He was heading there all the time and didn't even know it. He was a natural-born politician and rose to his own level just like a cork.

I was in the House of Hope three or four months when one night I was sitting on my bed listening to them going on in the kitchen, laughing and joking, and I thought about killing myself. It was the first time I ever did that. It seemed like such a good idea I couldn't believe it. All the trouble I'd been in and all the mornings I woke up and wished I was dead, I never once thought about killing myself. I look back at it now, it seems just like a miracle because I might have done it. If I thought of it before, I might have been drunk enough to do it, but I never did till I was sober.

I sat there and thought about ways how to do it. This was on a Friday night, and I thought about waiting till Monday morning and going to work and jumping off the top of the building. Then I figured I couldn't wait that long. I had to do it now. So I thought about jumping off a bridge on the interstate highway in front of a truck. Then I thought about the driver and how he'd slam on the brakes and start skidding and what he was thinking about when he hit me, and I couldn't do it. I couldn't have it on my conscience, him thinking about me all his life and wondering what he could have done to stop.

Then all of a sudden I started praying, and after a minute it just came to me. I thought about General Lee. My daddy told me his daddy told him—or his daddy's daddy, I forget which—that if General Lee had got up in the mountains instead of trying to join up with Johnston, they might have still been fighting the war. "The Blue Ridge Mountains," my daddy said. "General Lee could have got up in there and fought the Yankees the rest of his life." That was the only story he ever heard firsthand about General Lee, and he used to tell it every so often, whenever somebody was talking about mountains. I'd ask him how come General Lee could have held out in the Blue Ridge Mountains. And he'd say that's the nature of mountains. You get up in there, they can't get you out.

The reason I got thinking about General Lee—I mean besides praying—is that I was looking at a postcard I stuck on a nail in the wall where somebody used to have a picture. That card was the only thing I got in the mail the whole time I was in Reidsville. The rest were just bills I didn't pay and wasn't about to when I was in prison. I don't know how they got my address. The card was from Tom, Kate's father. I wrote him and told him I was in prison so he could get hold of me if he had to. My momma and daddy are both dead and all my brothers and sisters are scattered from here to California, and they wouldn't want to hear from me anyway. They have troubles of their own, and besides I was always borrowing money. We lost touch over the years, and I wouldn't even know where to find them. Tom's the only one I kept up with, and I wouldn't have done that except for Kate. She was an only child. Her momma died when she was a girl, and Tom raised her. He was the only parent she had, and I tried to keep in touch for her sake. He was the only one in the world that knew her like I did. I used to call him up long distance and talk about her, and when I didn't have the money for that, I'd write him letters. Finally I quit doing it. He wouldn't answer. But I kept up with where he was, and as soon as I got sent to Reidsville, I wrote him, and by and by, a couple of months later, here comes a card.

On one side was a picture of the town square in Etowah, Georgia. That's what it said. But it didn't look like a town square to me. It looked more like a parking lot. There was a patch of ground about forty foot square with a monument on it I took for a gravestone. I could see some writing on it, but it was all blurry so I couldn't be sure. The whole picture was kind of blurry. They must have printed it two or three times to set the colors, and each time was a little off, so everything looked a little fuzzy like it was made out of wool. Next to the gravestone there was a flagstaff and what looked like an American flag. I couldn't be certain, but the colors were right. They were just fuzzy. All around the gravestone were cars. I say cars, but they were mostly pickup trucks. In back of the cars was a patch of asphalt and then a row of stores on three sides. They were all brick, two stories high with false fronts made out of lumber with signs of some sort on most of them I couldn't make out. The whole thing might have been in Alaska or out West a hundred years ago except for the trucks where you might expect horses. The picture had a mean, pinched look about it even with all that frizzing and fraying to soften it up. In the background, over the tops of the buildings, you could see the humps of the mountains. They were the only things that were clear. The colors were all right on the mountains. They looked like blue drifts of smoke or banks of clouds laying low on the horizon. On top of the picture it said, "Town Square. Etowah, Georgia." Then on the next line it said, "And in the Distance the Blue Ridge Mountains." That was on the side I had showing.

On the other side was the message. It said, "Wish you were here." Considering I was still in prison, I thought at first it was some kind of joke. Then I got to thinking about it. I might make a joke like that. But not Tom. Tom don't joke.

Seeing that card and thinking about what my daddy said about General Lee and the Blue Ridge Mountains, it seemed to be some kind of message. I wasn't thinking about either one, and all of a sudden there they were both together just like they fit. I figured God had answered my prayer. I quit thinking about killing myself and started thinking about what to do next.

4

The next morning was Saturday. The first thing I did was get my money out of the light fixture. I had it hid in the overhead light behind the insulation. That's where I always hide my money. Thieves don't ever look in there any more than they do in the plumbing. I counted it, I had six hundred and seventy-eight dollars. I put the seventy-eight in my wallet and got some toilet paper and wrapped up the six hundred and put it in the bottom of my right shoe. At first it was folded, and that made it too high. It felt like one leg was taller than the other. I took it out of the heel and unfolded it so it went the whole length of the shoe, and that was all right. I could walk from here to New York with that six hundred dollars in my shoe like that. Then I went up to IT'S GOOD for breakfast and had some bacon and grits and biscuits and gravy and three cups of coffee to clear my head. I had a lot to do that day, and I didn't want everything looking frazzled like that postcard of the town square in Etowah, Georgia.

* * *

A little ways down from IT'S GOOD was a sign that said, SAM BROWN USED CARS, EST. 1912. There were about twenty cars among the weeds in back by the railroad tracks and a few more up front along College Avenue. The ones in front were on gravel mostly with some grass growing up in it, and all of them had signs on the windshields saying things like, BUY ME. $75.00. NO CREDIT? NO CREDIT CHECK. EASY TERMS. OWNER FINANCED. SAM BROWN SPECIAL.

What caught my eye was that 1912. If it was Sam Brown and he started the business in 1912, he'd have to be at least eighty years old. A man in his eighties in the used-car business might have a lot of experience, but it isn't much help. He'd be too slow. That's what I was counting on. I already picked out the car I wanted. It was back in the weeds near the railroad tracks. But I didn't want to tip my hand, so I started checking the ones in front, pretending I was interested in one of them. I opened the door to the first one I came to, and there was this man sitting in there staring at me. His eyes were wide open, and I thought he was dead.

I said, "Good God!" and slammed the door.

As soon as I did, the door popped back open, and the man jumped out like he was hooked onto it with a spring. He was saying something as he came, but I couldn't hear him. I was too startled. The first thing I made out was, "Son of a bitch!"

I said, "What?"

He said, "You heard me!"

I said, "Me?"

He said, "You liked to scare me to death."

I said, "What are you doing in there?"

He said, "It's damn cold, you notice that?"

I noticed. I also noticed he didn't have an office. Established 1912, and he didn't even have an office.

I said, "How come you don't have an office?"

He said, "What do I need an office for?"

I said, "To do business."

He said, "I do business. I don't need an office. Offices are needless overhead. That's why I sell cars so cheap. I pass it on. The money I save, I pass on to the customer. You interested in buying a good used car?"

I was more interested in him at the moment.

I said, "How old are you, anyway?"

He wasn't eighty. He didn't even look to be ninety. The more I looked at him the more I was revising my estimate upward. The sun was shining on his face, and his skin was transparent. It looked like you could see clear through it.

He didn't say how old he was.

I said, "*Established 1912.* What's that mean?"

He said that's when he was born.

I said, "It usually means when you open for business."

He said, "That's right. Now how about you and me *doing* some business."

He slung his arm over my shoulder. It felt like somebody dropped a stick on it. Then he took me straight to the car I already picked out and said, "There it is. That's the one. Looks like it got your name on it, don't it?"

I couldn't believe it. I figured he must have read my mind.

He said, "You like it?"

I hardly knew what to say.

He said, "That's the perfect car for you."

It was a 1965 Ford sedan, painted yellow, but it had been rolled two or three times, and most of the paint had come off the top. The rest of it was all right. The odometer said 74,280 miles. The frame wasn't bent, and it hadn't been chopped. The engine looked clean. The head was in good shape, and the belts and hoses were all right. It had antifreeze, and the tires were good. That's what surprised me. They were a brand-new set of tires. There couldn't have been more than a couple of thousand miles on them. The only thing the matter with it was the body, and the only thing the matter with that was the roof. It looked like something squashed it flat and they got up inside and beat it out with a sledgehammer.

I said, "This car?"—playing along. "This car looks like it's been in a wreck."

He said, "Wreck? Hell, no!"

He said that car belonged to his aunt. She was a widow and bought it with the insurance money and drove it to church and the grocery store and back again. That's all. It was a one-owner car. He said he was with her when she bought it.

I said, "What happened to it, then?"

He said, "Something fell on it."

I didn't say a word. I couldn't believe it. That car had been rolled on a regular basis.

I said, "What fell on it?"

He said, "A dead body."

I said, "A dead body?"

He said, "That's right. A suicide victim. Jumped out a fifty-story window."

That got me to laughing. I couldn't help it. I knew he was trying to soften me up, telling me that so I'd buy a car from him. That way

I wouldn't be looking when he hit me upside the head and stole all my money.

But it wasn't that. At least I didn't think it was because all of a sudden he slammed the door and said, "Forget it. You don't want it. That's a death car."

He started walking back to College Avenue.

I said, "Wait a minute." I ran after him and said, "How much?"

He said, "How much you got?"

I felt my pocket. It was still buttoned. I already put the money in there so I wouldn't have to take off my shoe.

I said, "Four hundred dollars."

He said, "That car'll cost you six hundred dollars."

I didn't even stop to think how he knew. It's like he had X-ray eyes or something like that. I told Tom about it later, and he said we ought to tie him up and take him to Las Vegas and make a million dollars on him. But I figured it must have just worked on cars, or else he'd have already done it himself.

I said, "All right. Let's hear it."

We went on back and tried to crank the engine, but it wouldn't turn over. The battery was dead, so we got one out of another car. He said he'd throw in the battery for ten more dollars, but I wouldn't do it. I told him if I buy a car for six hundred dollars, I expect it to have a battery already in it. He said it had one. I told him I meant one that works. We went round and round about that. We both knew what car. We both knew how much money I had. The only thing holding us up was the ten dollars extra for the battery.

Finally I said, "I'll tell you what. I'll owe you for it."

That seemed to soothe him. He took me back to what he called his office and opened the trunk and got out the papers. He had a whole file in there in a cardboard box. Then he signed the title and said, "Where's your insurance?"

I said, "I don't have any insurance. I can't afford a six-hundred-dollar four-door Ford sedan and insurance, too."

He said, "Six hundred and *ten* dollars. Don't forget that battery. And watch your ass on that insurance. They ain't going to give you a tag unless you got no-fault insurance."

That was news to me. They must have put that in when I was in prison, but I didn't say anything. The tag on it still had a couple of months. By that time I figured I might be dead or it wouldn't be running.

He said, "Here's my address." He got out a pencil and wrote it across the top of the title. "I'm trusting you, boy. Don't disappoint me."

I thought in a pig's ass I won't. But as soon as I got working, I sent it to him. I don't know why. I kept thinking about him sitting in the front seat of that car looking like he was ninety years old, trying to keep warm, and I couldn't help it. I got a ten-dollar bill and wrapped it up in a piece of toilet paper.

Tom said, "What you writing on it? What's the message?"

I told him, Nothing. I was just sending the money. He'd know what it was.

Tom said that didn't seem likely. There's always a message. "Give me the pen."

I gave him the ball-point pen I was using, and he wrote on the back of the toilet paper, "Try Las Vegas. Wish you were here." And I mailed it to him.

* * *

After I bought the car, I drove back to the House of Hope and started packing. I took Tom's postcard off the wall and went in the kitchen and got a couple of grocery sacks and put my clothes in them. Then I went back and got some apples. I carried it all out to the car and went back in and looked around. I didn't even have enough to fill the backseat. I figured Bubba owed me something for all the back pay he was holding out on me. I thought of the color TV set, but if I took it, Bubba might not buy them another. I thought of the sign over the door, but it was too big, and I wouldn't want it all anyway, just the part that said, HOUSE OF HOPE. I thought I might give it to Tom. But he probably wouldn't know what it meant. Tom don't hope.

So I took a picture. There was one over the fireplace, must have been there since the house was built. There weren't any colors. It showed this road going off in the distance. It was early morning, foggy or misty, you couldn't tell which, and the road ran straight out the back of the picture. Up front you could tell what it was, but the farther it went, the dimmer it got until finally it just disappeared. There was a barbed wire fence running along one side of the road and nothing but woods on the other. The trees were so dark you couldn't see through them. There were mountains all around coming down on the road, squeezing it in. They weren't mountains like you see out West hundreds of miles off in the distance with the bright sun shining on the snow on top. These were mountains that come down on you like a fist with no flat land to set them off, just hills and coves and deep-sided valleys. You could see that in the picture. If you lived at the bottom where that road ran along, the sun wouldn't get there till ten in the morning, and it'd set at four in the afternoon.

I never noticed that picture before. It was just there. But as soon as I did, it felt like I'd already been there before. I didn't exactly know where it was, but it looked so familiar, I almost even knew where it went. But I couldn't remember. It was like the road to the future. Anybody looking at it, that's what they'd think. That's how come they had it up there. It looked like the road of life. Except in my case it was going back to somewhere I'd already been. That's what I couldn't figure out. How come it looked so familiar? How come I was going back?

I'd just climbed up on a chair and was taking the picture off the wall when Cookie came in and wanted to know what I was doing. He was eating a banana, so I didn't answer. I just kept on with what I was doing. I got the picture and put the chair back, and he threw the banana peel in the fireplace. That's when I told him I was leaving and was taking the picture with me. He wanted to know how come. And I showed it to him and asked what it looked like to him, and he said, "The Road of Life."

I said, "That's right. That's how come I'm taking it with me."

He didn't give a damn. It wasn't his picture. He flopped down on the sofa and put his feet up in a chair. The cushions on the sofa were soft, and he sunk down in them till he looked like he was planted there. His head was all pink and white and rubbery like one of those flowers you see on a houseplant that looks like human flesh. And all of a sudden I felt sorry for him. It was just like that man who sold me the car, sitting in one of them all day trying to stay warm. He bought cars and sold them and traded them every day in his life and didn't go anywhere except in and out of that one car he called his office. He might have been dead in there after all. He was at the end of the trail. And so was Cookie except he wasn't eighty or ninety years old. Cookie wasn't even twenty. Other people came and went, seeing if they could make it this time, but Cookie stayed on in the House of Hope, screwing and cooking. He was like a rock in a stream. He didn't have a future. All he had was what he was doing.

I said, "You ever think about the future?"

He said, "What future?"

That's what I figured.

I said, "You're only twenty years old. What are you going to do?"

He said, "Do?"

I said, "With the rest of your life."

He started laughing, and it kept on getting higher and higher like it was skittering out of control.

He said, "My! My! Aren't we being serious, anyway!" He said it like it was a proposition. "What got into you, sweetheart? You sound like you're nervous. You sound like your nerves are all a-frazzle. What you need's a little fun in your life. You don't get enough relaxation."

I said, "You finish high school?"

He smiled like he felt sorry for me.

He said, "What do I need high school for? I'm fixing to have a good time. That's what I'm fixing to do with my life."

I said, "Cookie, I'm leaving here. You want to come with me and start a new life?"

He shrieked and said, "What is that, a proposition?"

I told him Yeah. It was a proposition.

I didn't know what I'd do with him, but I'd figure out something. Tom wouldn't mind. He might be surprised at first, but that's one thing about Tom. He's what you call adaptable, meaning he don't give a shit. Something bothers him for a minute, then he forgets it.

Cookie was sure to get on his nerves. He'd get on anybody's nerves. But after a day or two Tom would forget it.

Cookie didn't seem to care one way or the other. He was like a man drowning at sea. I was standing on the beach, and I could see him, but I couldn't reach him. Nobody could. I looked at him laying half in and half out of the cushions, and I couldn't help but feel sorry for him. I went over and shook his hand.

I said, "Cookie, I'm going to miss you."

He said, "How come? You hardly know me."

It was the first sensible thing he said all day. He rose up halfway out of the sofa and said, "What I mean is we're hardly friends. You know what I mean. You hardly paid me any attention."

I said, "I'm going to miss you anyway, Cookie. You sure you won't come?"

He said, "Of course not!"

He said it real snippy like a woman aggravated at the store.

I said, "You know, you remind me of something."

He said, "What's that?"

I said, "Me."

He started shrieking and rolling around. I put the picture under my arm and went to the door. What I meant was when I was drinking. I'd be laying there like that, drowning inside. But it wasn't just that. It was like those old clothes I laid out at Reidsville and prayed God to deliver me from the body of death. I knew what that meant now. Cookie was the body of death. The road ahead was clear to me. It was just like in the picture I had in my hand. I was going back in the mountains to find something important I lost, and I was so grateful, my whole heart swole in my bosom, and I almost choked on it. I got in the car, I was still shook up, I was so full. It's like I was reborn. I could feel it rise up in me like a flag, straining and popping. It was like God finally answered my prayers. I don't know why. After all those years of doing nothing, all of a sudden I could feel Him there just like Kate laying beside me, whispering in my ear that she loved me. God was delivering me from the body of death. He was delivering me from the House of Bondage. I turned on the ignition and started to drive off. I knew now where I was going.

He was leading me into the wilderness.

5

The first few miles there was nothing but filling stations, furniture stores, ball bearing factories, Ford dealerships, fast-food restaurants, and houses scattered in among them and patches of red clay with bulldozers in them crawling around like lost bugs, getting ready to build something else. Then it started thinning out till it was just woods and pastures and in the distance the humps of the mountains coming on fast. I was driving through a wilderness of pine trees and hardwoods, stag horn sumac, red on the tip like fists of fire, and dried-up honeysuckle on fences. Every now and then there were patches of kudzu, brown in the winter like some kind of fungus eating the woods and climbing up barns and deserted buildings. It looked like a cobweb or a tangle of twine.

I had on a country music station, and they were singing about lost loves as usual, and I was beating on the steering wheel in time to the music and feeling pretty good about myself considering I didn't know what I was doing or where I was going or what I was fixing to do when I got there. I was just following the signs on the highway. Marietta, Woodstock, Canton, Jasper. I went through one town after another and hardly even knew they were there. I'd come up on a bunch of houses looking surprised at having a road cutting across the backyard and some brand-new businesses sitting on raw dirt, clotted up on the sides of the ramps. They'd started thinning out just about the same time I got to them, and pretty soon it was woods and overgrown pastures again. That's how I knew it had been a town. The businesses were kind of like billboards. You saw them a minute, and then they were gone.

All the while I was watching the mountains. They kept coming on, getting bigger and bigger, till I could see the trees on top of the ridges like bristles of hair on the back of a hog. The mountains were blue at that time of year with shadows of clouds drifting across them, turning them black. They looked like something I might have dreamed and then woke up and not remembered till all of a sudden I saw them again. There was something I did or was fixing to do— I couldn't remember. It was like going back to something I'd already forgotten, and I hadn't even got there yet. That's how bad off I was. I could see from where I was there was nothing on them. I mean no sign of human beings. No houses, no roads, no fields, no pastures.

I said, "God, it sure is empty."

I didn't like them. I wasn't used to them. I never did get used to them. They weren't ordinary.

I said to God, "That's a real wilderness You got out there."

What with singing and praying and thinking about all that, I was already ten miles past where I was going before I knew it. I pulled off the road and checked the oil. It was down a quart. That old man who sold me the car knew what he was doing, all right. It wasn't as good a deal as I thought.

I drove across the median and headed back to Etowah, listening for knocks in the engine. If it got real bad, I figured I'd walk. But it was all right. I drove it real slow and looked for the town.

There were some houses sitting on hills. Most of them were old, beat-up places with white paint peeling off the siding and tin roofs bleeding and streaked with rust. They were all facing away from the highway. The porches on back were either broke down already or sagged like they were fixing to. That's where the people who lived in them stood to throw out the garbage. The backyards were full of trash and piles of stove wood, engine crossbeams nailed on trees, and wrecked cars and pickup trucks with saplings growing out of the windows.

The only other thing besides the houses was a filling station and a couple of fast-food restaurants—a McDonald's on one corner and a Burger King on the other. Across the street from McDonald's was a ten-acre field of mud filled with machines building a motel. I got some oil, then pulled across the road to McDonald's and drove to the window.

A woman said, "What'll you have?"

I said, "Is this Etowah?"

She said, "Yes, sir."

I said, "Where is it at?"

She said, "Right here."

I said, "I mean the rest of it."

She said, "Over yonder on Route 5."

I said, "Where's that?"

She gave me directions, and I went over a hill with a couple of houses stuck to the side and a green metal building that looked like an airplane hangar. A hardtop road cut straight across it like a knife through a melon.

On the other side, I came out on a river. The town was stretched out along that. There were cornfields and pastures and a tractor dealer and a grammar school. Up from the bottoms were two or three roads, and most of the town ran along them. All the stores and businesses. The houses were mostly up on the hills, some of them halfway, some of them all the way to the top. One of the hills had a graveyard on it. The slope was so steep it looked like the graves were fixing to slide and head straight into the center of town. The whole side of the hill was in grass, and it looked like a ski slope except for the tombstones. It was the only town I was ever in where the main thing to see was the graveyard.

As soon as I got to the center of town, I knew where I was. I saw the tombstone in the middle, and when I got to it, I could read the writing cut in the marble. It said, "In loving memory of all the boys of Beaufort County who died in foreign wars."

I'd looked at that postcard so long and thought about Tom walking around in it so many times that after a while it didn't seem real. It seemed like someplace I might have dreamed about or imagined. Like Kate. Half the time I couldn't even believe in her. It was so long ago, it seemed like I must have made it all up. It was the same thing with that postcard. But there I was, driving around in it. It looked just like the picture except the colors were sharper, and the stores and trucks were dirtier, and it had people and the other one didn't. All it had were trucks and stores and in the distance the high blue mountains hanging in the sky like clouds.

On one side of the town square was the courthouse. That's where the picture was taken from. There was a terrace in front and some benches with old men sitting on them, talking and spitting. The ground at their feet was covered with amber.

I drove up and stuck my head out the window and said, "Hey, there."

One of them spit. The other ones just looked at me.

Then one of them bent his head like he was praying and spit down between his feet. It looked like an oyster except it was brown. Then he took the sole of his shoe and mushed it up.

One of them said, "You looking for something?"

I said, "Yes, sir. Information."

He said, "We don't got none."

He started laughing and looking around to see what the others thought about that. They started laughing, and he kept it up.

He said, "We're fresh out of information."

There were three or four of them, and they were all chuckling and laughing like that was the smartest thing they ever heard.

I said, "You know where I can find Tom Forrest?"

The funny one said, "Who's that?", looking around at the others again.

Nobody laughed, and one of them said, "Tom Forrest. Is he from Florida?"

I said, "No, sir. He's from right here."

He said, "What's he do?"

I said, "He used to be in the army."

He said, "He the one killed all the Germans?"

"He was in Korea," I said.

He said, "Damn right. Chewed his ear off. You hear about that?"

I knew one of Tom's ears was gone. Or mostly gone. There were some fleshy parts to it left, but it didn't look like an ear. It looked more like a belly button the way it was all puckered up. Kate said he lost it in an automobile accident.

I told them that, and one of them said, "No, sir. It was a dog."

I said, "A dog?"

He said, "Yes, sir. In Korea."

I wasn't going to argue the point. Tom's awful bad for lying like that. Always has been.

"That's the one," I said.

"Well, shit," one of them said. "Why didn't you say so? Go out Gum Springs Road about nine miles. Just keep your eyes open."

I said, "What for?"

He said, "His mailbox."

I said, "It got his name on it?"

I didn't know if it just had a number.

He said, "No, sir."

I said, "How am I going to tell it, then?"

He said, "He got it painted like an American flag."

It took me almost two hours to find it. I'd stop at a house and ask, and they'd say, "Go back," and I'd go back and stop at another, and they'd say, "Too far. You've gone too far."

I finally got it narrowed down to about a mile. I drove it real slow, looking on both sides of the road, and pretty soon, there it was, up in the woods. It wasn't on the road like a regular mailbox. It was up in the driveway. I asked Tom about it later, and he said people were stealing his checks. He got an army check one week and a Social Security check the other, and they were getting both of them on him.

As soon as I saw the mailbox, I turned in and drove up the driveway. I call it that, but it was just a road through the woods. The gravel was about as big as your fist, one layer spread thin, and most of it was already gone. The curves were all rutted and filled with water, and the uphills were slick. I hardly made it. One time I lost my traction and had to back up and hit it again. I saw a road go off to the right, but that wasn't it. It was too overgrown. Pretty soon I came to some piles of trash in the woods. Cans mostly and plastic milk bottles. I knew I was getting close, and sure enough I turned a curve, and there it was.

Aquamarine blue. That's what the man who sold it to him said it was. Brand-new color. Looked like the inside of a swimming pool with the sun shining on it, flashing and popping light in your eyes. I could hardly bear to look at it sometimes, it was so bright. Not only that, it had Florida windows all over, meaning they were little slits, cranked out like Venetian blinds. There was a car, a big old '68 Ford LTD with the hood up, and off in the woods a couple of trucks. They were a good distance away from the trailer.

The driveway went up to the front door and stopped. The rest of it was mostly all mud and tree stumps except what looked like logging pallets. There was a sawmill down the road cutting railroad ties and lumber for logging pallets, and Tom got some and made what he called a patio. Sometimes he called it that and sometimes a deck. What it looked like were logging pallets running off in the woods thirty or forty feet with a couple of aluminum chairs with plastic webbing sitting in the middle of it looking lost. There was a stovepipe sticking out of one window and stovewood piled up on the edge of the woods beside the driveway. The rest of it looked just like it did before Tom got there. The trees were mixed hardwoods, and it must have been timbered ten or fifteen years ago. They were about six to eight inches thick. Behind the trailer about fifty feet was an old rock chimney and a pile of mossy timber from where there used to be a house. You could see the old road going on where the driveway ended, or what used to be a road, and a couple of boxwood trees nearly about as high as the chimney on either side of where the front porch used to be. Coming around from the back of the house was a bold spring branch. It went along beside the house and crossed the road between it and the trailer.

I pulled up in front of the trailer, I could hear dogs howling inside. They were like ghosts, they sounded so mournful. I cut off the engine and listened to them. There's no sweeter sound in the world than a hound singing about pain and sorrow. Just being that close to Tom reminded me so much of Kate I almost turned around and drove off, and I probably would have if that wasn't the reason I was there. I was drawn to him like a moth to the flame. I couldn't help it.

I sat there and listened to the dogs for a while. Then I got out.

6

I went up to the door of the trailer and beat on it with the side of my fist. The door sounded hollow. It was like beating on the side of a car. I was afraid I might put a dent in it, so I looked in the window and started yelling, "Tom! Tom! Guess who's here!"

I heard a voice say, "I already know."

It was behind me.

I turned around, and there he was, standing on the edge of the woods.

I said, "What the hell are you doing out there, Tom? I thought you were inside the house."

He said,"I heard you coming and ducked out to see who it was."

I said, "You haven't changed much, have you, Tom? Who'd you think it was, anyway?"

He said, "I didn't know. I heard a car."

I said, "Well, how about inviting me inside the house?'

The dogs were still howling.

He said, "It's full of dogs."

I said, "You still hunt coons?"

He didn't answer.

I said, "You keep them for hunting?"

He said, "You coming in?"

He started walking toward the door.

I said, "Yeah, I'm coming. How often you hunt them?"

He said, "I don't hunt them."

I said, "How come?"

He said, "I'm too damn old. My legs gave out. I can sit by the fire and drive the roads, but I can't keep up with them in the woods."

I said, "How come you keep them, then? I wouldn't keep dogs if I didn't hunt them."

He said, "That's what you know."

He opened the door, and the dogs came boiling out. Two blue ticks and one black and tan. They hit him and bounced off and came at me, jumping and licking.

He said, "I told you they ain't worth a damn. A total stranger, and look how they're doing." They were running around in circles, barking and howling and wagging their tails and their whole behinds. "You come here to kill me, they'd help you to do it."

The dogs were already back in the house before we were.

Tom shut the door on them and said, "Get on in there, you sons of bitches."

He was pointing down the hall, and they ran off somewhere.

"They're good company," Tom said. "That's one thing. And I like to hear them. They hunt by themselves, and I sit out on the patio and look up at the stars and thank God I'm still able to hear them. I'd miss them if I didn't have them with me. What do you want?"

I said, "Hell, Tom, what do you think? I've come to see you."

We were still standing, and he said, "Sit down, sit down," and waved his hand at some furniture.

There was an imitation leather sofa and a couple of imitation leather recliners and a plastic coffee table and a couple of dinette chairs dragged out from the dinette table that were all full of old clothes and newspapers. One of them had a car battery on it.

I said, "You mean here?" and cleaned off one of the plastic recliners. I ended up with an armful of clothes and said, "Where you want me to put it?"

Tom didn't answer. He just brushed some old newspapers out of the seat of the other recliner and sat down. A couple of beer cans came out with the papers and rolled across the floor. I sat down with the armful of clothes in my lap. It felt like I was holding a baby, so I put them down on the floor. Tom was rocking back and forth, humming something.

I said, "It sure is good to see you, Tom."

He quit rocking and said, "How come?"

I said, "I don't know. I missed you, I reckon."

It was like coming home again and seeing Kate wrecked and ruined like the story of that frog in the fairy tale. I looked in his eyes, and they were the same blue as hers. It was almost like seeing a ghost. I could hear something in his voice that reminded me of her. It was like echoes. Like being in two places at once. I hardly knew what I was saying, I was so busy thinking about Kate and wishing I had her.

Tom didn't say anything. He just kept on humming. Then he said, "What do you want? You looking for money?"

I said, "I don't want any money."

He quit rocking and looked at me.

He said, "What do you want, then?"

I said, "I don't know."

I grinned at him. I couldn't help it, I was so happy.

I said, "Seeing you . . ."

I didn't know how to say it.

I said, "Seeing you—it's like coming home."

He started rocking and humming again. This time I could hear the tune. Kate used to sing it. All about how we'll never grow old. Then he quit and looked sideways at the door like he was expecting somebody to open it in a minute and he had to talk fast before they came in.

He said, "How long you fixing to stay?"

That almost got me to laughing. I hadn't even got there good, and he was already trying to get rid of me.

I said, "Hell, Tom, what's the hurry? I just got here. I might get the wrong impression, you keep on going on like that."

He said, "Like what?"

I said, "Like you aren't glad to see me."

He said, "I'm not."

I said, "Of course you are."

He said, "That's what you think."

I said, "Tom, how come you told them a dog chewed your ear off?"

That pulled him up short.

He said, "What?"

I said, "I met a man in front of the courthouse said a dog chewed your ear off."

He said, "That's right."

I said, "In Korea."

He said, "That's right."

I said, "How come you told them that?"

He said, "Hell, I was talking." He stood up. "Where are your things? You got your things out in the car?"

I said, "Yeah. I got something for you."

He was just like a child. That got him to grinning, and he was out at the car opening the door before I even got down the steps.

He said, "What the hell you got in here, groceries?"

He got out one of the sacks of clothes and started dragging things out and dropping them on the ground.

I stooped and picked them up and said, "Hold on, Tom. You're getting them dirty." He was already through one bag and starting in on the other when I said, "Hold on. It isn't in there."

He dropped the bag and said, "Where is it?"

I got in the car and pulled out the picture. I held it out to him, but he didn't take it.

He looked at it and said, "What's that?"

I said, "A picture."

He said, "What of?"

I said, "A road. Look at the mountains."

He said, "I see them. What's it mean?"

I said, "What do you think?"

He looked at it one way, then turned around and looked at it the other and said, "Nothing. Not one damn thing."

That's the way it is with Tom. Half the time you don't even know what's going on, and the other half you can't believe it.

I said, "How about that road? Where's it going?"

He said, "Nowhere. That's the problem. What it needs is a house at the end or a man on a horse or a woman waving."

He went up to where I was holding it and pointed his finger. "Right there." He made a grease smear on the glass. "Standing right there. If it had a woman standing there waving, it'd be all right." Then he said, "Hell, boy. What the hell we standing out here for?"

He turned around and carried the picture in the house. I picked the sack of clothes off the ground and got the others out of the car. By the time I carried them in, Tom was already sitting at the dinette table, staring at the picture. I could see his mind was on fire. I didn't want to interrupt him, but I wanted to get settled. I had a lot of catching up to do. So I said, "Where do you want me to put my things?"

He said, "Down there," and waved his hand down the hall.

I said, "What about the dogs?" They were so quiet I almost forgot all about them. "They're down there." But he didn't answer.

I picked up my things and went down the hall. There was a red shag rug on the floor, but it was so matted and stuck with trash it didn't have a whole lot of shag left except on the edges.

I went in the first room. There was a double bed with blankets piled up in the middle, and on either side of them was a dog. They looked up from where they'd been sleeping and wagged their tails—thump, thump—on the mattress. One of them growled and showed his teeth. Then he yawned, and I could see clear down his throat. His tongue looked too big for the rest of his mouth. Then I started yawning, and the other one took it up. Then I heard something thumping behind me. I turned around, and there was the black and tan under the dresser, half in and half out. It was so big and its legs were so long, it couldn't get much of itself up in there. Its head was somewhere in the back. All I could see were his legs drawn up where he was stretching. They moved together all in one piece like they were wired.

I said, "Tom, there're dogs in here."

He didn't answer.

I stuck my head out and said, "Where the hell you expect me to sleep?"

He said, "Anywhere you want."

I said, "I'm not sleeping with dogs."

He said, "Nobody's asking you to."

I said, "Dogs sleep outside."

He said, "It's too cold. They'd freeze overnight."

I looked over my shoulder at the dogs on the bed. They looked just like a nest of babies, they were so peaceful. They had their heads down and their yellow eyes rolled up in that other eyelid they got. It looked like a film of spit over them. I could see their loose lips flap when they breathed. I didn't care if they froze or not, I wasn't about to sleep with dogs.

I went down the hall to the next room. It was a bathroom. I knew that as soon as I got there. I didn't even have to open the door. The next room had a card table and five or six folding chairs. There was a pack of cards on the table and a hubcap full of cigarette butts.

I stuck my head out and said, "What's this?"

Tom said, "Bathroom."

I said, "I'm not talking about that. What's this other one?"

He said, "The game room."

I said, "The game room?"

I looked back at the table and chairs. There might have been a game in it, but it wasn't ever what you'd call a game room.

I said, "Where am I going to sleep?"

Tom said, "The chairs fold up."

I said, "Then what?"

He didn't answer.

I pulled out three chairs and lined them up against the wall. Then I set my sacks on them. That was the dresser. Then I got another chair and put it near the door. That's where I put my shaving things and my comb and brush. There were two windows, and outside, there was nothing but woods all the way north as far as Canada. I thought of myself laying there, listening to nightingales. Then I picked up the hubcap, and it made me sick. One thing I did when I was in Reidsville besides coming back to life was to quit smoking, and I couldn't stand the smell of it. There was a mound of cigarette butts as big as my head. I took them to the bathroom and flushed them down the toilet. I washed out the hubcap and set it in the tub to dry. Then I went back and folded the table and set it in the corner. That left me with a real big room. I stood there and looked around.

My own room.

Say what you want, it was better than Reidsville.

That night we just sat around. I made a fire in the stove. Tom hung the picture on the wall. Then he got the dogs and kicked them out. Most of them didn't want to leave. It was getting cold, and they hung in the door like they were stuck. Tom was cussing and pushing at them, and the dogs kept trying to circle back on him. Finally he got the door shut on the black and tan. He was the last. I told Tom they were worse than cats.

He said, "Is that right?" But he didn't want to talk about that. What he wanted to talk about was how long I was fixing to stay. I didn't want to mention any definite dates. He was thinking about a few weeks. I was thinking about the rest of my life. It wouldn't do to tell him that, so I laid low and asked him what he had for supper. By that time the dogs were back at the door pawing and whining to get in. I told him they sure were fast. They must have peed on the door going out to be finished already.

I said, "Look at your shoes. You sure they ain't wet?"

He said, "What the hell are you talking about?"

I didn't know what to make of that. At first I thought he was putting me on. But it wasn't that. He couldn't hear them, not unless they started howling. Then he'd get up and let them in. He could hear voices most of the time, but I wasn't ever certain about that. He might have read lips and filled in by guessing. Most of the time he seemed to know. Then sometimes the gears would slip, and he'd do something, and I wouldn't know if he was crazy or if he just hadn't heard a word I said the last three or four days. Something was missing. He looked the same, he talked the same, but it wasn't him exactly. Not like he used to be. He was more like a child. But he didn't know it. That was the difference. Children know what they are. But Tom was crazy or old or something, and he didn't know it. He was like some child I never knew. I learned to love him just like a baby.

I never had a child of my own. Kate died too soon. I thought we had the rest of our lives, and I didn't want to lose her that quick. I knew how she'd be if she had a baby. She'd love it so much, she might not pay enough attention to me, so I wouldn't let her. That's the worst thing I ever did. I used to get drunk and think about that. All she wanted was something to love, and I wouldn't let her. I think sometimes that's why she died. I was too cruel. I knew that. I was cruel to the only one I ever loved. I could have done the only thing she ever really wanted to do and not let her die thinking she wasted her life.

She was laying in the hospital and told me she was an empty pot. I asked her what she meant by that, and she said, "A broken vessel."

I said, "What?"

She said, "I haven't fulfilled myself, Al."

I told her we were married, weren't we? What about that?

I thought she meant being a virgin. Fulfilled herself that way, being a woman.

She said, "That's right," and squeezed my hand. I was sitting there holding it, and she said, "I got that to be thankful for."

I think of that I almost cry, I was so stupid.

But now all of a sudden I'd been redeemed. That's what I thought the first few days I was at Tom's. After that, I forgot about it, I'd get so pissed off. But those first few days, it seemed like I had a second chance. Even when I was drinking the worst, I never forgot about Kate for a minute. I'd pass out seeing her at night and wake up seeing her first thing in the morning. So you might say I never lost her except in all the ways that count. Tom didn't know it, and I sure as hell wasn't fixing to tell him, but I wasn't leaving. Wild horses couldn't drag me away. I couldn't leave him any more than I could leave a child alone in the woods. It was like suddenly finding a baby that had been stolen all those years. All you can do is thank God for it and count your blessings. That was the state I was in the first few days I was there. I couldn't believe I was so lucky.

As soon as I let the dogs in that night, Tom wanted to know how I knew they were there. I didn't say anything. I was trying to watch TV, and the dogs kept getting in my lap, licking my face and pawing at my arms, and I said, "Tom, why don't you shoot them?"

He said, "Wait till you're drunk. Those dogs are going to love you to death."

I said, "I told you I quit drinking. I don't get drunk."

He said, "Yeah. And they don't eat rations."

After a while Tom fixed supper. He ate the same thing every night. Frozen Mexican dinners made out of chili peppers and some kind of meat like dog food, a Coca-Cola, and oatmeal cookies. The same thing every night. For breakfast he had dry cereal, the sugar kind, and black coffee. For lunch it was canned soup—mostly chicken noodle—and apples and oatmeal cookies. That's all he had, day in and day out, unless he went into town, in which case he brought home a sack of McDonald hamburgers and ate on them the next few days. He tried heating them in the oven, and the meat'd be warm, but the buns were soggy. I thought at first he put them in water, but it wasn't that. That's how they did.

That night we had Mexican dinners. The dogs sat around the table and watched. We might've had Jesus Christ sitting there with us, they were so worshipful. I never saw dogs looking so hard. I watched one of them, a blue tick, and she didn't even blink her eyes. One time I dropped a fork. I started to get it when all of a sudden all three of them were on my hand mouthing it before I even knew what had happened.

I said, "Did you see that?" I held up my hand. It was all wet. "They didn't even go for the fork."

Tom said, "They're smarter than you are. Can't eat a fork."

I said, "How come you don't feed them first? They look awful hungry."

He said, "They are."

Then he got up and turned on the TV. The TV was something he couldn't hear good, so he turned it up real loud. He got a fifty-pound sack of Jim Dandy Dog Rations from under the sink and poured a pile on the floor. The dogs scooped it up like a vacuum cleaner. I looked at it later, and there wasn't a thing left, not even a crumb. It was just wet from where they'd been licking. After they ate, they trotted down the hall to bed, and Tom started talking to the news. That's how he did. He'd turn on the news and talk back to it. I don't mean it was a regular thing. It was more like every so often. Walter Cronkite would say something, and all of a sudden Tom would say something back to him. It bothered me, the first time he did it. It's like he thought the TV was real. Then after that I got used to it. I even caught myself doing it once or twice and Tom looking at me like I was crazy.

After we got finished eating, there weren't any dishes. That's the best thing about Mexican dinners. You throw out the platters like a Coca-Cola can.

I said, "That was real good, Tom." I patted my stomach. "I like Mexican food."

He said, "It's the best."

Tom was laying in the recliner. He had his shoes off. His socks were white from the ankles up. From there down, where they'd been in his boots, they were kind of clay-colored. He had his eyes shut, and the stove was getting real hot. It must have been eighty degrees in there. I could see he wasn't paying attention. He was fixing to take a nap, so I started talking about Kate. That woke him up. He cocked one eye and looked at me. Then he pretended he was falling asleep. I kept on talking, asking about things before I knew her. That's what

I was interested in. She had this whole other life, and I didn't know a thing about it. I'd look at her pictures. Tom had a whole bunch of pictures his wife took before she died, and I used to like to look at them. In most of them Kate was a little girl, sitting on the steps trying to pull a dog's head around so they could take a picture of it. Tom loved dogs all his life, and most of the pictures had a dog in them somewhere, sitting beside Kate or just passing through or laying around like rugs on the floor or piles of burlap. I'd look at the pictures—black-and-white pictures so old they were almost yellow—and half the time I didn't even see the dogs. They blended right in. I can't even think of Kate as a baby without thinking of dogs or horses or goats. Every picture Tom had of her she was in a cowboy outfit riding a pony or sitting in the front seat of a goat cart holding the reins.

I said, "Tom, where are those pictures?"

Thinking about it made me want to see them again.

He said, "What pictures?"

I said, "The ones of Kate."

He said, "I don't have them."

I said, "How come?"

He didn't answer.

I said, "Where are they?" and stood up like I was going to go get them.

He cocked his eye open and said, "I burned them."

I sat down. I couldn't believe it. It was like burning the Bible or something. Burning a whole part of my life. The pictures were gone, my life was gone with them. I couldn't remember except by them. It was stealing my memories.

I said, "What do you mean, *burned them?*"

He said, "I didn't want them. It wasn't healthy. All them old days are gone. I got the rest of my life to get on with. I ain't like you, getting drunk and mooning around looking at pictures. 'The Lord giveth, the Lord taketh away.' That's what I figure. I'm too busy to be thinking about things."

I said, "You can't help but think about things."

He said, "I mean dead things. Times past. I'm too busy to think about that."

I said, "What do you think about, then?"

He said, "Business."

I said, "Business?"

I knew he didn't have any business. He'd been retired from the army eight years, and he didn't have much business then, except in a war.

It went on like that all through the news. Then it was a game show. They were giving away a million dollars in car radios and washers and dryers. You could outfit a whole town with it. I sat there and watched it and listened to Tom. They'd get the answer, he'd grunt at them.

After a while I said, "What about that old place behind here?"

He said, "What old place?"

I said, "That old home place."

He said, "What about it?"

I said, "Whose is it?"

He didn't answer. I found out the next day it was his. It was the house he was born and raised in. All the woods on either side of the branch were cleared, and his daddy farmed it until he fell on a harrow and cut himself up the middle. After that, they moved into town. His daddy worked in a cotton mill. It was the Depression by that time, and Tom joined the CCC and after that the army. But they kept the place. They couldn't sell that land up there, so it stayed in the family, and the family divided and subdivided and moved to Atlanta and Florida and South Carolina and Detroit and New York City, and finally ten or twelve of them owned it. By that time the house had fallen in. There was nothing left but white oak sills and a little siding and a part of the roof made from old wood shakes split with a froe. You could see the cellar hole and a couple of rock piers, and that was about it except for the trunk of a hollow gum tree stuck in the spring. It was still there. The water boiled up inside the section of tree like a barrel and spilled over down the sides. The wood stayed so wet from all that water, it never rotted. Tom said it was just like it was when he was a baby. The fields grew up in pines and poplars, the porch rotted, the walls fell in. The only thing that stayed the same was the hollow gum tree in the spring, the rock chimney, and the road. All the rest of it was gone.

Tom said it took him two years to buy it, there were so many that owned a piece. I asked him how come he bothered. It didn't seem worth it, but he said it was to him. It was his home. That's all he'd say. He never would talk about it again. He'd been everywhere in the world—Paris, France, Rome, Italy, the Philippine Islands, Germany, Korea, and I don't know where all—and the only place he knew to come back to was that old place where nobody lived and nobody even bothered to visit.

With Tom, it was a place. He walked around that land he bought, and he saw the house like it used to be and his momma shelling peas on the porch and his daddy riding an old cultivator or cutting the pasture weeds with a scythe, and all I saw was woods and dirt. Because with me, it wasn't a place. It was a person. Tom was the only one who knew Kate besides me and that book of old pictures, and the pictures were burned, so that left him. He didn't know it, but he was the only thing I had left.

All this time Tom was watching TV. They had on a comedy about two orphans from outer space. A mailman finds them and takes them home. They looked green, but Tom said no. That was the set. The color was off. He kept claiming they were just children. He didn't know they were from outer space. They'd do something funny you're supposed to laugh at, something funny from outer space, and he didn't know what they were doing. Everybody else'd be laughing on TV, and he'd look at me and grunt. After a while he cut it off and wanted to know when I was leaving.

And that's how it went the first few days, him talking about one thing and me talking about another. The only things we had in common were Mexican dinners and dogs.

7

We were going on like that when finally one day Tom said, "You ready?"

I said, "I reckon."

I'd been ready. I'd been ready for almost a week, but I didn't want to tell him that. I figured I'd better lay low and see what he was talking about. One thing I learned is you can't trust him. Just when you got him all figured out, he'll turn around and do something different.

Like then. I didn't know it at the time, but as soon as he heard me coming down that gravel road and ran out in the woods to see who it was, before I even turned around, before he even said hello and asked how long I was fixing to stay, he already had it all figured out.

There weren't but two ways he was going to get rid of me. One was for him to call the sheriff when I got drunk and burned down the trailer and the dogs ran off and he was sitting out under a tree and figured he had enough. That was the hard way. The other was easy. All he had to do was get me a job. Find somebody fool enough to give me a job when I was just fresh out of Reidsville so I could move out and get me a little place of my own till it caught up with me again and I got fired or put in jail or moved on and left him alone for a while. He didn't know I joined AA. He didn't know I quit drinking. He didn't know I got a special assignment from God. He didn't know any of that. He sat there and talked to me four whole days and didn't hear a word I said. He thought I was just like I was before. I don't blame him, but looking back at it, that's how come we lay around there four whole days talking about Kate and when I was leaving and what's on TV. Then we'd eat supper and go to bed and wait for the dogs to start creeping in, trying to get in bed with us. The same thing every day. He was trying to wear me down. He knew a man couldn't stand that for long. He was just waiting. And then one day he gave up and asked if I was ready.

I said, "Yeah."

He said, "Let's go."

He got up and put on his coat. It was an old one. I'd seen it before. He said it was from Canada. He got it in an Army-Navy store, and it was made out of canvas lined with green wool. There must have been a whole sheep in it. The coat was so stiff, it could stand up by itself. He called it his coon hunting coat. He had a hat and gloves in the pocket. He put them on. Then he went over to the dinette chair and picked up the car battery. He was already out the door with the dogs boiling and barking around him before I even got straightened up from where I was laying back in the recliner.

I got outside, Tom already had the hood up on his car, putting in the battery. I didn't think about it at the time, but later on I asked him about it, and he said somebody stole it one time, and he wasn't fixing to let them again. That was one thing. The other was, it was weak, and he took it in the house to warm it up.

I said, "Where are we going?"

I didn't much care. I was just making conversation.

Tom said, "Get in."

The car had seventy-eight thousand, two hundred and eighty-five miles and two-tenths on the odometer and no telling how many others. Tom said it got twelve miles to the gallon, but I paid for most of the gas, and I figure it was more like eight. After a while the engine caught, and Tom said, "You son of a bitch"—meaning the car. "This is one damn good car."

I said, "Where are we going?"

He put it in gear and turned around. The dogs were jumping and barking at us, and he said, "Benny. What day is it?"

I said, "Saturday."

He said, "That's right. What time is it?"

I looked at my watch.

I said, "Ten o'clock."

He said, "That's right. That's where he is."

I said, "Where's that?" But he didn't answer. I looked back, and the dogs were gone. There was nothing there but empty road. It looked just the same forwards as backwards. There wasn't much to it except trees and dirt. But that was all right with me. The heater was running. There was a gospel song on the radio and a woman singing through her nose. Tom was beating his fist on the wheel and singing along with her. The sun was zipping along in the trees, and every now and then it would flash in the window like an explosion. I didn't know where we were going, but I'd rather be there riding with Tom, hearing him sing and have a good time, than anywhere else I could think of. Besides, I knew what he meant. It wasn't ever a question of where. The question was who. Who was Benny, and how come we were going to see him?

It was kind of like destiny. Benny was waiting there like fate, but we didn't know it.

There are two passes over the Cohutta Mountains. The one to the north goes over the mountains. The one to the south skirts the edge and goes around them. We went south. Pretty soon we were out of town. We passed a place called a laundromat-nursery. There were cars parked outside with women going in and out with bundles of laundry and piles of bushes tied up with string. Tom was singing about unspeakable joy, the celestial railroad, fountains of blood, and so on and so forth. I looked at the scenery. Most of it was houses—what there was of it—and woods and fields with mountains rising up out of the trees like wild hogs. We passed a house trailer that said BAR-B-Q and another that said PETE'S EATS. A little after that we turned off at Pleasant Gap Church and went down a dirt road for a while. Then on another. And then we were there.

It was a knife-edge ridge with rocky pasture falling off on either side and a house or two in the hollow. The road went along the top of the ridge a couple of hundred feet. Then the cars started piling up. Tom drove as far as he could and stopped.

I said, "What's this? Some kind of fair?"

It looked like it might have been that. Or a rodeo. Tom's Ford and a brand-new red-and-black Mercury were the only passenger cars I saw. The rest were all trucks. The buildings looked like somebody who didn't know what he was doing made them in his spare time out of scrap lumber.

Tom didn't say one way or the other. He just got out and started walking. I followed along behind him. We got to the Mercury, Tom beat on the fender and said, "That's Benny. I told you he'd be here."

We were heading for a big old chicken house. I don't mean where they raised a few chickens. I mean a commercial broiler house except it was old and made out of slabs and rough-cut lumber from some jackleg sawmill set up in the woods nearby. The sides were covered in white see-through plastic nailed on instead of windows. Some of it tore loose and flapped in the wind and scratched against the dry weeds growing up alongside the wall. The roof was tin and rusted in streaks like somebody hacked at it with a knife. Around the side there was a door. Tom opened it and went on in. The door was on springs and slammed shut so fast it looked like it ate him. I pushed it open, and as soon as I did a fat man in bib overalls got right in front of me in the doorway and blocked it.

His stomach was a foot or two out from his chin, and I said, "Excuse me."

I pushed him a little, trying to ease past. It was like bumping a watermelon. But he didn't move. I could smell him breathing. It smelled a little like horse manure, but I knew that couldn't have been it. No matter how old a chicken house is or how much you clean it, it's still going to smell a little rich. Not like chicken shit exactly. More like wet dirt and horse manure. That's what I was probably smelling. That and tobacco.

The fat man said, "What do you want?" and I got a good whiff. He talked kind of breathy. Hoarse and breathy. All I could think of to say was "Benny," and that's all it took. The man started grinning. He shuffled aside and said, "Seven dollars."

He started stapling a ticket on the lapel of my coat when Tom came up and said, "Make that fourteen. He's paying for me."

The man grinned again and said, "Old Sarge. He's a cracker, ain't he, son? I hear he's been to the Philippine Islands."

I gave him the fourteen dollars and pushed on past.

As soon as I got in, I could taste it. The smell of old chickens, dry as feathers. The sunshine cut the dark into stripes, and the dust floated in it like pieces of fire. I came out, I was under a bleacher. I looked up, there was nothing but feet. Row after row of feet and an aisle in the middle just like a ball park except it was made out of two-by-eight oak, and the whole thing went straight up to the ceiling.

I looked around for Tom, but I didn't see him at first. I was too busy watching these two men inside a hog wire cage right in front of where I was standing. They both had chickens in their arms they were cuddling like babies, kind of swaying and rocking back and forth. I thought they were trying to put them to sleep. Then pretty soon they came dancing across the cage, sashaying and rocking back and forth, and when they got close enough to reach, the chickens stuck their necks out like snakes and struck at each other. The men kept swaying back and forth, and the chickens kept striking in time to the beat, biting their combs and pulling out pieces of feathers.

All this time I could hear somebody yelling behind me. I turned around, and there was Tom squeezed in between a quilt full of women and a white-haired man in a down jacket and business suit. Tom's pretty tall. Six-one or -two before he started shrinking a little. But the man beside him was at least half a foot taller than that. They were sitting down, of course, but Tom's head barely came to his shoulder.

Tom saw me and started waving. It looked like he was flagging a train. The other man quit yelling and said something to him, and Tom started climbing over the women. They couldn't stand up because of the quilt. I could see them trying to get out of the way, but they weren't fast enough, and Tom wasn't waiting. The seats didn't have a back to them, just the seat, and the women almost went over backwards all in one piece like three brass monkeys welded together before Tom pushed past them and came down to get me.

"Come on up here," Tom said. "I got somebody I want you to meet."

He turned around and started climbing back up the bleachers. He stepped over some boys and lost his balance and reached out and steadied himself on a man's head. The man looked up at him like he was praying and saw a vision, he was so surprised at what happened. Then Tom was at the women again, but they were ready for him this time. They jumped up and whipped off the quilt just as he went charging past. I was following in his wake, you might say, the women handing me from one to the other, passing me along. Tom was already sitting by then. The women were getting settled again, flapping like hens. They kept looking at me, cutting their eyes and mumbling something, but I couldn't hear them. The man beside Tom was yelling too loud. He was waving his hands around his head and shaking a whole fistful of money.

"Fifty dollars!" he was yelling. "Fifty dollars on the red!"

I never did understand the betting. The man beside Tom—it turned out to be Benny—was the only one yelling like that. The rest of them were just sitting there, watching the fights. Then whenever a chicken would die, they all started paying off. Sometimes Benny would pass out some money, and an old man with a face like a rock would nod at him and touch the brim of his hat and put the money in his pocket. But most of the time two or three of them would pitch in together and get up some money and pass it to Benny.

They were betting two or three dollars. Sometimes five or ten. No more than that. Some were even betting less. I saw some of them passing loose change. Quarters, fifty-cent pieces. Some were betting shotgun shells. One old man in bib overalls and a bush-hog cap had a couple of boxes of Western Upland sitting on the seat besides him, and he was passing them out like dollar bills. The only one with any real money was Benny. The rest of them had to pitch in together. That's why the women were there, I figured. They never bet. They just sat there, whispering together and laughing at something that probably didn't have a thing to do with the chicken fights. It was like a football game. Most of them probably didn't know the rules. But all of a sudden one of them would turn to a man in front of her and talk to him in earnest. The man would be nodding his head and smiling. The woman would be scowling and looking cross. Then they'd break off, and she'd go back to whispering and laughing. Some of the younger women might have enjoyed it, but the older ones seemed like they were there for one reason and one reason only. To keep their eye on the men. If it weren't for Benny, they wouldn't have had to. But then again, if it weren't for Benny making big bets it took two or three of them to match, where would all the excitement be? Shotgun shells were all right for old men. But young men need danger. They need the risk, else they might as well stay at home and watch TV. Lose thirty or forty dollars to Benny when all you get is a hundred a week, that's real gambling. That's where you put your life on the line. Do it enough, they foreclose on you or garnishee your wages or your children go hungry. The old women knew that, and the young ones were learning. Some of the women were out for excitement, but most of them just sat there with a worried look on their face too scared to say anything and too concerned to stay away.

Benny was where the chance came in. There was the glory of betting and the hope they felt then. That's all that sustained them. And then when they lost, it was still there. The hope never left them. They could still do it. Not that time maybe. But there'd be another.

Money gives a lot to a man, but it doesn't give what Benny had. I didn't know what to make of it then, and I still don't exactly, but Benny didn't do it for himself. It's like he was giving them a gift. That's what surprised me. Later on when I got to know him, I'd look at him, and his eyes would be as flat and transparent as ice cubes, they were so blue. It seemed like you could see right through them. No matter what he did to somebody or how bad it was, he never had a guilty thought in his life. He was as innocent as a child. That's how come he looked like a preacher. That or a banker. He wasn't down in the pit with the rest of us. He was up in the bleachers all his life, betting money and running the whole thing, keeping it going. He told me one time that he could look back on the rest of life, and it was a series of unselfish acts. That's what he called them. *Unselfish acts.* Benny was not only one of the people, he was the best they had to offer. He was what they might have been if they weren't ignorant and sick and poor and no count and downright sorry. He was like all their potential fulfilled.

As soon as there was a break in the fights, Tom kept trying to introduce me to Benny, but he was too busy. There were folks talking to him on all four sides at once, and Tom kept saying, "Benny, Benny," pulling his sleeve to get his attention.

Benny finally got pissed off and said, "What the hell you pulling at me for?"

Tom said, "This is the one I told you about."

Benny said, "How you doing?" and held out a hand for me to shake. "Old Sarge here says you're just out of Reidsville."

I said, "Shit! He told you that?"

Benny grinned and said, "Don't worry. Everybody's entitled to a little mistake. Sarge here says you want a job."

I said, "That's right," but I was surprised. I didn't believe it.

Benny said, "Listen. I'm busy right now. Why don't you go down to the pit and help out Roy. He's shorthanded. They're about to start a new derby."

I said, "Help? I don't know what the hell they're doing."

Benny looked at me. He quit smiling and said, "Listen. I told you I'm busy. I'm talking to Mrs. Walker."

I could see this woman behind him. She was leaning on his back, an elbow on one shoulder and a hand on the other, whispering something in his ear.

"She's got a problem I'm trying to help her with," Benny said, "and you're interrupting. Get on down there and come back later."

Then he turned and smiled at Mrs. Walker like I wasn't even there.

Tom said, "Come on."

He got up and started pushing at me, trying to get me past the women.

"He likes you," Tom said. "We're coming back later."

I said, "How can you tell?"

Tom said, "He wants to give you a job."

I said, "Doing what?"

He said, "Working with me."

8

Benny had about eighteen birds, which was more than twice as much as the others. I was mostly carrying out dead ones. That was my job. I took them out and threw them in this gully they showed me. The rest of the time I sat around and watched.

There was this doctor there helping us out. He said he was a doctor, but you couldn't prove it by me. He was drinking a pint bottle of whiskey and said he was there to shoot the birds. Benny hired him special to do it. He had a bag full of hypodermic needles, and I'd hold the birds, and he'd shoot them up before a derby. I asked what it was, and the doctor said, "Strychnine and vitamins."

I said, "Ain't that a poison?" But he didn't answer. He was too busy talking about cancer. That was his subject. Cancer and hemorrhoids. He just went to Pennsylvania and took a course on how to treat hemorrhoids without surgery. The way you did was shoot them with needles full of salt water, and that shrunk them up.

I said, "What about cancer? What do you do for it?"

He said, "Coffee enemas."

I said, "How about strychnine? What's that for?"

He said, "Hemorrhoids."

That was a joke. He was sober enough to know what he was do-ing and drunk enough not to care.

He said, "What's poison to us is like whiskey to them."

It turned out strychnine makes fighting cocks lively. It was like amphetamines. It made them high.

It was finally getting down to the end of the derby. Roy was fight-ing one of Benny's birds. It was supposed to be a Red, cross-matched with something or other. The doctor wasn't too clear about it, but he said it was special, the best bird Benny had, a three-time champion that already won thousands of dollars in prize money. Everybody was real excited about it. Betting was heavy, and there was a whole lot of shouting and yelling. A few minutes later it was all over. The three-time champion was laying in the corner like a pile of rags, and the other chicken was sitting on it, pecking its eyes out.

"That's it," the doctor said.

Tom said, "Benny ain't going to like it."

The doctor said, "He got to know."

Tom said, "You tell him." But the doctor just walked away. He went and leaned on the rail of the main pit and watched the proceedings. So Tom went and told Benny.

That's one thing I'll say about Tom. He's like one of those chick-ens. He might not want to do something, leave him to his own de-vices, but if he got to, he will. That's one of the things I like about him. He might not have a bit of sense, but he got a whole lot of grit.

I went over and picked up the three-time champion and took off the spurs. I wiped off the blood and put them in a special little box that looked like a briefcase. It was lined with blue velvet with grooves for the spurs just like a pistol case. Then I picked up the champion by the legs and carried it out to the gully.

After that, I got something to eat. There was like a food concession at one end of the chicken house, near the stove. The woman inside had hot dogs and barbecue sandwiches and coffee and Coca-Colas and candy. I asked her if she made the candy herself, and she said, "Yeah," so I didn't get any.

I said, "Give me a barbecue sandwich and a Coca-Cola, and leave off the sauce."

She stuck her head out. The food concession was behind a door. They sawed off the top and put a board across the middle, and that was the counter. Inside was an icebox and a stove and a sink and table piled up with bread wrappers and old pots and pans with something in them. There was a cat on the table eating out of one of the pans. As soon as I looked in and saw that, I knew I was right.

The woman said, "Leave off the sauce? That's the best part."

I said, "You make it from scratch?"

She said, "Of course I do."

She sounded offended.

I said, "In that case, I wish I could, but barbecue sauce makes me break out."

She nodded her head.

"It's the tomatoes."

I said, "Yes, ma'am. And the chili pepper."

She said, "We don't use chili pepper."

I said, "I know you don't. I mean if you did."

The sandwich was wrapped in a piece of wax paper so I could eat it without getting it dirty. I unwrapped it halfway and took a bite and went over to eat the rest by the stove. Tom was already over there, talking to Benny. So was everybody else. Benny was laughing and carrying on with them. Some of the women were there, too, wrapped up in quilts. Some of them even looked like they might have been smiling when something real funny came up. Their mouths slit a little, and their eyes narrowed.

I wasn't paying too much attention. I was mostly surprised at Tom. Usually he didn't give a shit for man nor beast, but there he was sucking up to Benny. It was a real puzzle to me. I stood there watching Tom and wondering about it, eating my sandwich and drinking my Coca-Cola and trying to ease up to the stove. A woman in a quilt turned around and give me a hard look. She must have thought I was getting too close. I lifted my hands and smiled and said, "It sure is cold," but she didn't say anything. She turned back the other way and gave all her attention to Benny.

The stove was a fifty-gallon oil drum set sideways on concrete blocks with a door cut in front and a hole in the top for the pipe to come out. I finally edged my way past the woman and got up to the heat. Benny was on the other side of the stove, warming his hands. Tom was right behind him, smiling. Benny looked at me and said, "How do you like the fights so far?"

I said, "There're more?"

He said, "Of course there're more. How do you like them?"

I said, "All right, considering it's chickens. I've been carrying out dead ones all morning."

I was just about to step aside and let the lady have the heat—she kept pushing and crowding my ass, so I knew she was cold, otherwise she wouldn't have done it—when Benny said, "You know what I like about a cock? A cock's steadfast. It's the only animal that is, except for a lion. It says that in the Bible."

I said, "What about dogs? They're man's best friend."

But that wasn't the kind of steadfast he meant. He wasn't talking about loving your master and being loyal.

He said, "You wouldn't expect to find that in a cock."

I said, "No, sir. Not the ones I saw."

He said he meant fight to the death. That kind of steadfast. Not backing off no matter what happened.

I said, "You ever been to a dog fight?"

He said, "No, sir. I never have, and I never will, and I'll tell you why. God made cocks to fight. He put it in them just like he put a brain in your head and made you a man. I figure it's like a moral lesson."

I said, "How do you figure that?"

I wasn't being a smart-ass. I didn't know what he was talking about. But he looked at me cautious again and said, "A lesson in courage. It teaches me how to be."

Everybody approved of that. They were nodding and carrying on, saying, "Yes, sir. That's right. You're right about that."

I said, "Where's it say that in the Bible? I'd like to read it."

He said, "In the Gospels. Jesus Christ said it. The cock crowed and denied Him three times."

But it wasn't in the Bible. I looked it up later and found that part about the cock and St. Peter denying Him three times, but it never said anything about cocks being steadfast. Benny just made it up.

About that time they announced the next derby, and the crowd started breaking up. Benny looked at me and said, "I can see how come you were in Reidsville."

He started to leave, I said, "How's that?"

He said, "I just hope you learned your lesson."

Then they carried him off to the bleachers.

* * *

The last bird was finally killed in the last derby, and the doctor started cleaning the spurs. He was rubbing them down with hydrogen peroxide and swabs of cotton. He said, "Benny's mighty particular about his birds. I got to be careful."

I said, "What about people? He particular about people, too?" I told him people were a damn sight more important than chickens, and a lot of them couldn't afford to go to the doctor. I couldn't myself.

I was getting all het up about it when Tom came and said, "What's going on?"

The doctor said, "Is this your friend?"

Tom said, "He's my son-in-law"—like that was a separate category.

The doctor said, "He's bad-mouthing Benny."

Tom wanted to know what I said, but the doctor just looked at him. You could see the doctor couldn't remember.

I told Tom, and he said, "That's a damn fool thing to say."

"That's what I mean," the doctor said. He shook a spur at me. It looked like a finger, except it was crooked. "Any man saves my life, I'm going to take care of his chickens every Saturday that comes around for free, and I don't give a damn who knows it."

I said, "Yeah," and took the spur out of his hand. I wiped off the blood and slipped it in a velvet groove in the case.

The doctor put his head down and started spitting between his knees. Some of it was on the ground, some of it was on his right shoe. Tom was leaning over talking to him.

Then Tom came over to me and said, "What the hell you think you're doing?"

I told him, "Nothing. I was just talking."

He said, "Lay off."

I said, "Lay off what?"

He said, "Smart-assing Benny."

I told him I didn't give a shit about Benny.

I was tired of the whole damn thing. But it showed me something. I was starting to get all the essential information about Benny just seeing how folks acted around him. What I didn't know yet was why.

W e were loading up at the end of the day when Roy came out and said, "Benny's waiting. He's out in the car."

I dropped what I had and went looking for him. The road to the pasture was just about empty. The only thing left were a few pickup trucks and the red-and-black Mercury. There was a crowd standing around it. Benny was in the driver's seat. He had the window beside him rolled down, and a couple of men were bent over, talking to him. The rest were just standing around, leaning on the fenders, waiting.

I was just about to the car when Tom caught up and said, "Don't say anything. Let me do the talking. I got it all fixed. Just get in the car."

We climbed in back and Benny said, "Where you from, boy?"— talking to me.

I told him I wasn't from nowhere in particular.

He said, "I hear you're from Reidsville. How did you like it?"

I told him I liked it all right. It was better than what I saw here so far, present company excepted, of course. I didn't much like chicken fights.

Benny laughed. He turned to Tom and slapped his knee and said, "I like him. I told you I would. You say you vouch for him, he's all right with me."

"I vouch for him," Tom said.

It was like making a promise to God.

Benny said, "He don't drink, does he? He don't take dope?"—talking about me like I wasn't there. I expected to see him roll up my lips and check my gums any minute.

I said, "You fixing to buy me, or what?"

Benny said, "He's a joker, though, ain't he?"

Tom said, "Yes, sir. That's a problem."

Benny said, "I know it is." He turned to me. "You work for me, boy, I tell the jokes. You hear me? I tell the jokes and you laugh, you hear?"

I was looking at him, trying to figure him out. I could hardly remember the joke, it was so mild, when Tom said, "Yes, sir. He hears you."

Benny said, "All right. What did they put you in Reidsville for? Sarge here says you killed a man."

I said, "No, sir."

Benny said, "What did you do, then?"

I said, "Beat up on him."

Tom said, "He *wished* he was dead. That's what I meant. He beat him up so bad he *wished* he was dead."

Benny said, "Assault and battery?"

Tom said, "Yes, sir. That and armed robbery. He's real mean."

"Sarge says you're real mean," Benny said. "Is that right?"

I said, "I reckon."

I didn't know what he was getting at, so I played the cards close to my vest. I didn't tell him I couldn't remember why I was in Reidsville. I knew what they told me, and it might have been assault and battery, and it might have been armed robbery. I did both at one time or another.

I told Benny it wasn't my fault I was in prison. I didn't know what I was doing. And besides, I wasn't mean. I just did what I had to.

Benny snorted in his nose and said, "Damn right. That's how it is, ain't it, boy? It ain't being mean. It's just doing what you got to, ain't it?"

Tom said that was right.

I didn't say anything. I was just waiting.

Benny said, "You ain't from around here. That's a drawback. But most folks around here ain't been in Reidsville, and that's a plus. Besides which, Sarge here says he vouches for you."

"Damn right," Tom said. "I vouch for him. You'll like him, Benny."

Benny said, "I know I will. I already do."

He was still smiling at me, and I was looking at him, still waiting. It was kind of like fishing except I couldn't figure out what he was using for bait. I didn't trust him. He smiled too much. I never knew anybody before eager to hire a man fresh out of prison except Bubba Jones, and he was a preacher and I figured he had to, not to mention the fact that it was his business.

"Besides which," Benny was saying, "old Sarge here's a combat veteran. He knows what I need. Ain't that right?"

Tom was nodding and saying, "That's right."

He was like one of those torture victims, agree to anything. That should have tipped me off right there. But I didn't pay any attention to him. I was still concentrating on Benny.

He was saying how old Sarge here was a cousin of his. Second or third, they couldn't agree on that maybe. But it was blood. There was the same blood running in one as ran in the other. So even if I didn't hardly know where I was from, I married in, and Tom vouched for me, and that was the next best thing to growing up there and being a native. That's what Benny figured.

Then he finally got around to it.

He said, "How would you like to work for me, boy?"

I told him I wouldn't.

Tom looked at me like I just blew the car to pieces. He had this last look on his face like he was taking one last look before he disappeared from the face of the earth.

Benny laughed and said, "How come?" He never had a man refuse him before, not when he made him a proposition. "Women . . . ," he said. "Women rarely. But never a man. How come?"

I told him I was through with the chicken business.

Benny looked at Tom and said, "Chicken business? What's he talking about? You didn't tell him?"

Tom said, "No, sir. I wasn't able."

Benny said, "I'm looking for a few good men ain't afraid to do what they got to. You take Sarge here. He's like you. He killed a man. Hell, he might have killed a dozen. Ain't no telling how many he killed."

Tom was nodding and saying, That's right. He didn't count them.

He was in the motor pool in Korea, and the only one he might have killed was his wife maybe from worrying her to death. But I didn't say anything. I just let him ramble.

Benny kept right on anyway. He said, "Listen. I'm fixing to hire you, boy."

I said, "What for?"

He said, "County police."

I said, "They wouldn't let me in. I got a record."

He said, "It ain't that kind of police."

I said, "What kind is it?"

He said, "Undercover. Sarge'll tell you all about it. I got to go." He stuck his fist over the seat and shook my hand. "It sure has been a pleasure," he said. "What did you used to do, by the way, when you weren't killing folks in Reidsville?"

I told him I was a house painter.

He said, "That's good. You start next week. You and Sarge. He's going to help you. You got any questions, ask him."

I said, "He don't know shit about painting."

But he didn't hear me. He was gone. I barely got my leg out of the car before he was gone in a cloud of dust and chicken feathers.

Going back home, Tom was so happy he sang all the way:

> My heavenly home is bright and fair.
> I feel like traveling on.
> No pain nor death can enter there.
> I feel like traveling on.

I wasn't paying him any attention. I was busy checking out the landscape and watching the sun move through the trees. If a person hadn't seen it before and didn't know what it was doing, he might think it was some kind of dog running through the woods beside him, chasing the car. I tried staring at it, but it was too bright. I concentrated on the trees. It was like looking through Venetian blinds, except they went sideways. The trees were bare at that time of year, and I could see the humps of the hills piling up on top of each other till they crashed against the side of the mountains and stopped dead. The mountains were like a wall, steely and blue as gates. They were darker blue than the sky, almost black, and they looked at the edges like they might have even been turning darker with night coming on.

Tom's voice would come drifting in and out of my thoughts like an old radio. "It's not easy, going to heaven," he sang. Thorns on the path, and I don't know what all. I was half asleep by then. I couldn't have told the singing from the landscape outside, the way it all ran together. Then I got to thinking about where we were going and what we were doing, and that woke me up. It was like the other side of the mountains.

I said, "Who is Benny, anyway, Tom? He looked like a banker the way he was dressed. He rich or what?"

Tom said, "You better believe it. He owns half the county."

I said, "That's what I figured. What's he do?"

He said, "County commissioner."

I said, "County commissioner?"

I couldn't believe it.

I said, "What's all that about undercover police? I thought that was some kind of joke."

Tom said, "It is."

He drove on a ways. We turned a curve and came out on a church and a paved road.

"It is and it isn't," Tom said.

I didn't know much about the law except the parts that applied to me personal at various times in my life, but I knew about county commissioners. They might tolerate chicken fights if there were enough votes to make it worthwhile, but they wouldn't ever go to one.

I told Tom it didn't make sense.

"It's like a public whorehouse," I said. "A county commissioner might tolerate one if it was a real going concern and contributed to the well-being of the community. But he isn't going to go there himself. He's a public servant."

I was fixing to go on about that, exposing how ignorant I was, when I could see Tom wasn't paying me any attention. He was humming and beating his hand on the steering wheel, keeping time to the music. I could see he was through with that subject.

I was drunk more than half my life, and the rest of it I was married or locked up in prison. I was like a child in that respect. And Tom was, too. He was in the army most of his life, and that's the next best thing to being in prison. We were still virgins. That's what they call the young boys at Reidsville, come down there acting tough. They might have raped ten or twelve women or killed their own daddies, but they're still virgins. And we were, too. We didn't know what was fixing to happen to us any more than they did. That's how innocent we were.

I watched the trees slipping away, gliding past. The bark was silver on the hardwoods. We came to some pines, and the trunks turned black, and the needles were silver. They looked splintered and cracked in the light. Then they were gone. There was a frame house and a man in the yard splitting wood. He looked up and waved at us. Then he slid past, and it was just a wall of woods. The next thing I knew the door was open, and there was a pile of dogs coming at me, boiling over the steering wheel, trying to lick my face.

I was back to where I came from, but I hadn't gotten to where I was going.

9

Benny owned most of the houses in east Etowah, and what he didn't own belonged to his daddy. Most of them had six-inch clapboard siding painted white with no sealer in the walls and no insulation. The moisture got in and lifted the paint inside of a year. They looked like mushrooms the way they were peeling. The outsides were all flaking and rotten. I'd have to work for the rest of my life going around from one to the other just to keep up. Painting's a hopeless job anyway, but this was more hopeless than most. Still it was good to be out in the morning. It was getting on to spring, and I'd drive down to Spiker's and get my paint. Spiker's Supply, south of town. Benny set me up an account. I got all my tools there, and if I needed paint, that's where I got it. Benny owned the place himself. Bought it from Spiker and kept the name, so he was just shifting the money from one pocket to the other. That's how he did. That's how he did with paint. That's how he did with people.

After I got my supplies, I drove back over the river to Etowah and started work if it wasn't too cold. There was something about painting I truly loved. I liked to see it flow off the brush and shine in the sun like a fresh coat of pudding. It was so bright I could hardly look at it in the light. I'd get through with a wall and step back to get a good look, and one of Benny's aunts or cousins would come out of the house and stand there beside me shading their eyes and telling me what a good job I did. It was like a new beginning. No matter how old those people were or what happened to them or how hopeless they might have got, there was still something about it that reminded them of better times.

I'd stand on the ladder and look at the sun shining on the raw wood where I scraped it and on the fresh coat of paint, seeing the shadows and light move across it, and the whole thing seemed different. I don't know why. I felt like I was doing something worthwhile, and I'd get to thinking about what made it different. How come I didn't mind doing it so much? How come I wasn't sick of it and wanting to get drunk? How come I wasn't hopeless about it? How come when I opened a can of paint, I didn't want to drink the whole thing, it smelled so good?

The only thing I could figure out was that I had a new place to live and a new job and Tom and the dogs, and that was enough for me right then. And all of a sudden the painting made sense. If the sun made sense shining each day, warming the wood and making it shine and fading it both, then painting it made sense, too. I'd stand on the ladder and think crazy things like that. And worse than that sometimes. I got to where I was figuring out the whole world and everything in it. It was the first time since I got out of Reidsville that

I felt free, and the reason I did was I knew what to do. I had a plan, and it was working. I was starting a whole new life.

Sometimes Tom came along with me, and I'd put him to scraping or rolling on paint. I wouldn't let him work with a brush. His hands shook too bad, and half the time he'd forget what he was doing. Mostly he just sat on his haunches and mixed the paint and talked to me or got a chair from the porch and sat in it and sang songs or told jokes and made up stories. And that was all right with me. I didn't mind him. It was somebody else besides me, and that's what I needed. He wasn't Kate, but he was the next best thing I had, and sometimes I got him to talk about her, and that made it worthwhile. They were good times. I used to ask him what he was thinking, and he'd say, Nothing, and I believed him. That's how he did. That's why I liked him. He was real comfortable.

The fact is, Tom didn't have to work. He had a pension from the army and Social Security and Medicare payments for emphysema. What he did for Benny was more in the line of having something to do with his time besides sit and listen to dogs. It was mostly odd jobs, this and that. Running and fetching.

I asked Tom what it was exactly, and he said, "Personal contact. There's a lot of personal contact in being county commissioner. Benny can't do it all, so I help him out."

I said, "Like what?"

He said, "Like carrying out welfare checks and talking to people, see they're all right. Benny says, 'Go out there and check on the Stovers, see how they're getting along. They're so old, I don't see how they're getting their groceries. Make sure somebody's doing it for them.' And I'll go out there and sit on the porch and talk, ask them how they're getting along and who's getting their groceries. Things like that."

He carried out papers for people to sign and set them up for food stamps and Medicare payments and Meals on Wheels and checked if they ate it. He went down to the County Health and set people up for flu shots and pneumonia. He got them typhoid and DPT and signed them up for Literacy Action and GEDs.

"You see that house?" Tom said. He pointed down the road to a house with trash all over the porch, spilling out in the yard. The door was open, and there wasn't a screen, and it looked like it was running out from inside.

I said, "Yeah."

He said, "That's it. That's where he was born."

It was like a shrine to Abraham Lincoln.

Tom said Benny was raised real poor just like everybody else around there. His daddy was a farmer, and when Benny was little, he used to help him haul produce to the Farmers' Market and sell it for gas money, if he sold it at all, and it didn't take Benny long to figure out that he didn't have to go to the trouble of raising the produce. All he had to do was find somebody just like his daddy and buy it off him and sell it himself. And that's what he did. Pretty soon he was hauling produce all over the state and making a whole lot of money, so he opened up a produce store and got his daddy to drive the truck, and he stayed there selling produce and bringing in business. Tom said folks liked to be with Benny even then, when he was just tending store. They used to come in there and listen to him laughing and talking and carrying on. Folks just liked being around him.

And he helped them out. If they didn't have money at the end of the
month, Benny just let it ride. He took a real pleasure in helping folks
out and never took a bit of credit for it. All he did was follow the
Bible. Tom said he could quote it chapter and verse, just like a
preacher. He memorized all four of the Gospels when he was just a
little boy, and he could still remember most of it. After that, it was
just the next step to public office.

He ran for the City Council and won. He ran for the School
Board. He ran for tax commissioner. He ran for the mayor of
Etowah. And he won every one of them. There wasn't an office in
the county worth having that he wasn't elected to before he was
thirty. Then he ran for the State Legislature, representing Beaufort
and part of Sims, and went down to Atlanta and did what he could.
But he didn't like it. He said it was a waste of time. All he did was
shuffle papers and pass legislation. What he liked was the laying on
of hands. That's what he called it. People came to him needing his
help, and he reached out and laid his hands on them. Personal politics. That's what he liked. He had what you call the common touch.

So he came back from the State Legislature and ran for county
commissioner on the Republican ticket. He was the first Republican ever to run for public office in that part of the county, and Tom
said it was like he went off to the city and came back a Jew or a Ro-
man Catholic. Folks didn't know what to make of it. There wasn't
a Republican in the county and hadn't been since the Civil War. Of
course, there's a whole lot of them now, ever since Benny brought
it in and folks started making a little money. The richer they get, the
more Republican they are. But at that time they were mostly all
poor, and everybody running for office was still a Democrat and always had been. But people liked Benny, and they elected him

anyway and kept on doing it every chance they got. Tom said Benny made a whole career out of running the county and lending a helping hand when he could. There were people around there so young by now they couldn't even remember when he wasn't in office. He was like the courthouse, he'd been there so long. Tom said he was a real American and not only that, a damn good man.

After work, I went down the road to look at the house where Benny was born. I was standing there in the yard trying to see in the dark of the door when a woman came out with some trash in her hand. It was a plastic sack full of apple peels. She went to the edge of the porch and dumped them out, and the chickens came running from under the house and started pecking and scratching and gobbling and scratching.

I saw her looking at me and said, "Good evening. I hear this was the county commissioner's house when he was a boy."

She said "It is," like I was some kind of fool living in hedges, never saw a house before. "It is and it was and it still will be if he ever comes around to claim it."

She was his mother.

I was sitting on Tom's patio one Saturday morning not too long after that, throwing Cheerios at the dogs. I had a box of them in my lap, and I'd reach in and get one and throw it, and one of the dogs would jump up and grab it before it even hit the ground. And the funny thing was they took turns at it just like it was batting practice. They'd get one and then go around to the end of the line. I was

just sitting there, working my way through the box, when Tom came
out and said, "All right. Let's go."

I looked up and said, "Where?"

He said, "Benny."

I said, "What about him?"

But he didn't answer. He was already calling the dogs. They ran
over thinking he was going to play with them, but he rounded them
up and pushed them inside the trailer and slammed the door on
them. I used to feel sort of sorry for them when Tom put them in
the trailer like that. All they wanted to do was chase the car down
the road a ways, then make their way back to the patio and sleep in
the sun. But they were purebred coon dogs, Tom said, treed with all
four feet, and he didn't want somebody running off with them.

We got to town, I parked the car, and we went to the courthouse.
There were four or five white columns in front with pigeon nests on
top of them and a couple of benches with signs advertising the Tip
Top Hardware and Blue Ridge Auto Parts. The benches were usually full of old men from the nursing home, those who could make
it that far. The parts of the courthouse that weren't wood were made
out of brick. The brick was white or had been when it was painted
fifty or sixty years ago. Since then the paint wore off, and the whole
thing got kind of mingledy-looking. It was hard to say what color
it was. Underneath it was red. Different shades and colors of red.
The edges and bottom looked darker than that, like they might have
been burned one time or another.

We opened the door and went in, and it was like going down in
a mine. Outside, it was light and sunny. The wind blew, and the rain
fell. Inside, it was still and dark. I could hardly see where I was going. The walls were made out of beaded board stained brown or

covered with soot. It was hard to tell. The ceiling was pressed tin, and it might have been white originally. It must have been fifteen or eighteen feet high and so dark and full of shadows I could hardly make out the design on the tin let alone tell what color it was. The floor was squares of linoleum tile with white streaks in it. I could see where the floorboards were curled at the edge and wore through the tile. It looked like grooves of silver knives, the way the light was falling on it.

After a while, my eyes got adjusted, and I could see there was nothing there but an empty hall that ran the whole length of the building. There were benches pushed up against the walls and a couple of people sitting on them like they might have been waiting on a train. They were that kind of benches. Here and there among the benches there were doors, but they were all closed and had little green-and-white signs with clock faces on them saying what time they were going to be back. They all said nine o'clock, like time stopped then or it was a sign of the end of the world.

A little ways down, there was a door standing open and light spilling out like at the end of a tunnel. Inside was an empty office. A little ways in front was a counter like at a laundry and behind the counter some desks with papers all over them heaped up so high it looked like it might have built up in layers like rocks at a road cut. One of the desks had a Coca-Cola bottle sitting on top of the pile. The bottle had branches of wild plum blossoms stuck in it, but they were mostly all gone. The petals dropped, and the pollen scattered around in a circle like bug droppings or grains of dirt. The other desk had a calendar from Etowah Auto Parts on top, like somebody was sitting there counting the days. There was a typewriter drawn up to one side of a desk covered with a plastic sheet and sitting on a little old scrawny table that looked like a spider. On the back wall was a fireplace with a space heater in it and in the corner a wash-stand and mirror from when it used to be a hotel. Beside the wash-stand was another door, but it was closed.

Tom and I went in and stood there for a while. I didn't know what we were supposed to be doing, and Tom didn't tell me. There was a fly batting at one of the windows. It sounded like somebody tapping on the glass with the end of his finger trying to get me to look over there and let him in. That was the only sound in the room.

Then I heard somebody say, "Come on in."

We ducked under the hole in the counter and went on in, and Benny said, "Sit down."

He pointed at a couple of oak chairs on the other side of the desk from where he was sitting. He was lolling around in a big leather chair and had his feet stuck up on the desk. From where I sat I was looking right at them. It was like sitting behind somebody wearing a hat in the picture show. I couldn't see Benny for the feet. All I saw was a hole in one shoe and a smear of dried mud or dog shit packed up against the heel of the other.

I said, "You mind if I move?"

He said, "Go ahead," and waved his hand like he was giving me a million dollars and it didn't mean a thing to him.

I slid the chair over a couple of feet.

Benny said, "That better?"

I said, "Yes, sir."

He said, "All right. I got a little job I want you to do."

I said, "What kind of job?"

He said, "A favor."

I said, "What kind of favor?"

He took his feet down and leaned forward. I thought he was fixing to jump on me in a minute. Then he eased off. He leaned back and looked at Tom and smiled and said, "I got a little something I want you to do as a special favor. You know what that means?"

I said, "No, sir."

Tom said, "Shit. You know what he means."

But I couldn't help it. I didn't like Benny. I didn't know him, but as soon as I saw him, I didn't like him. It's like I was born with it already in me. I was one thing, and he was another. I'd get around Benny, and it felt like something was sucking the soul out of my body. The first time I saw him, I knew what he was, and I don't mean what he was as a person. I mean what he *was*.

Tom said, "Shit. A favor's a favor. Quit being an asshole."

Benny said, "That's all right," holding his hand up. "Let him talk."

I said, "I'm finished."

He said, "In that case listen to me. I'm a politician. That's what I do. I run this county the best way I know how, and I like to think I've done some good. I helped out folks that needed helping and ran a good government here so they could raise their families in peace, each one according to his own nature, so they can grow and flourish like it says in the Bible"—and I almost fell out of my seat. He said, "'Blessed is the man that walketh not in the counsel of the ungodly, nor standeth in the way of sinners, nor sitteth in the seat of the scornful. He shall be like a tree planted by the rivers of water, that bringeth forth his fruit in his season,'" and I saw him look at Tom and wink. "I've done lots of favors for folks in my time," he said, "and they've done a lot of favors for me. That's the way we do around here. Like you"—talking to me. "Take your own case. You probably wouldn't even be sitting here if it wasn't for Tom. Who's going to hire you fresh out of Reidsville?"

I said, "Nobody."

He said, "That's right. Not unless somebody does you a favor. That's what I mean. Tom did you one, and now you're going to do him one. That's how it works. You owe him, and he owes me, and pretty soon we're going to end up owing each other."

That's what I figured. Benny was right. Do a man a favor one time, you're in his debt the rest of your life, and I didn't want Benny owing me a thing. I was afraid he might pay me back.

"You're going to be my own right hand," Benny said, "like it says in the Bible: 'The right hand of the Lord reached out and smote his enemies.' Listen now. We got us a problem."

There was this man and woman, Benny said, finally getting around to it. The first thing anybody knew about them, they showed up at Blue Ridge Lake. They had a van and were living in it. They were there a couple of months, and the camping permit expired. They kept on renewing it till finally the park ranger said they had to leave, and they kept saying, "Where can we go?"

The ranger asked them where they were from, and they said, "Arizona."

The ranger said, "Go back to Arizona, then."

The woman said, "There ain't nothing there."

Anyway, it went on like that, Benny said, and the upshot was they got in the van and drove across the line into Beaufort County, and the man got a job with Ike Waters. Ike makes what he calls vacation homes. Log cabins with Styrofoam chinking and box houses sitting on poles all up and down the Cartecay River. All he pays is minimum wage for trained carpenters and skilled electricians and plumbers, so nobody'll work for him except a bunch of Mexicans left over from picking apples, and drifters who stay for a month or two and move on to better things.

The man told Ike they'd been on vacation, spending their savings. That's how they did. They worked a while and went on vacation, but they liked it here, and now that winter was coming on, they figured they might as well stay a while. So Ike gave them a job and rented them a house he had. Or his uncle had. Or a cousin of his. It wasn't clear whose house it was, and it didn't matter, Benny said. The main thing was Ike wanted them out.

The man was all right. He was an electrician by trade, and Ike said he liked him. He came to work and did like he was supposed to most of the time. It was the woman he couldn't stand. She came to work with the man and flopped around in the weeds all day. Benny said he went out to see them and tried to talk some sense to them, and all of a sudden the woman was laying down. Benny said he couldn't keep his eyes off her, it was so unusual.

I asked him if she had a fit, and he said, No. She was like a child. She'd get tired, she'd lay down. Talk to her, she'd walk away right in the middle of what you were saying. It's like she didn't have any sense. Ike figured she was crazy or on drugs, one or the other, and he didn't want a drug-crazed woman flopping around in the weeds at the work site. He said his insurance wouldn't allow it, not to mention how it looked. He was in business. He wasn't running an insane asylum. Besides, he just hired a Mexican, a brother of one he already had, said he knew how to do electrical work, so he wasn't hurting. He didn't need the man anyway, so what he did, he fired him.

And the long and short of it was, Benny said, the man wouldn't go. He kept on living in the house. He stayed off the job site after a while, but Benny said he kept on coming back every few days wanting Ike to change his mind. He just sat in the cab of the van and looked out the window, watching them work. Then he'd drive off and come back later. He did that a while, and every so often the man would go talk to Ike, and the woman would get out and walk around. Anybody else would wait in the van, but Ike said she was real restless. She walked around like she was jerked and talked fast and scratched at herself.

After a while they quit coming to work, but Ike couldn't get them out of the house. They signed a year's lease, and they told him as long as they were paying their rent, he didn't have any way to evict them. Just because they weren't working for him didn't matter. The house didn't go with the job.

Benny said he went out there to reason with them. Ike's a good friend of his. They grew up together, and besides, the houses he's building down at the river bring in a lot of money in taxes. Not only that, Benny said, it's a bad example. He didn't want any drugs in the county. He had trouble enough with whiskey. Get in drugs, ain't no telling what they might do. And who's going to supply them? Drugs don't just grow on trees.

I told him I thought they did. He wanted to know what I meant by that, and I told him they just grew on trees, that's all. Every drug I ever heard of.

He said, "Bullshit."

Tom did, too.

I said, "I mean to begin with."

Benny said, "We ain't talking about to begin with. We're talking about heroin. We're talking about cocaine. You ever hear of a cocaine bush?"

I started to say, Yeah. But I let it go. It wasn't worth it.

Benny said he went out there and tried to tell them Ike made a mistake signing a lease on that house for a year.

"Hell," Benny said, "it wasn't even Ike's house to begin with. He sold it to his brother six months ago," and showed them the deed. "See that date?" he said, flashing it at them. "That date's signed six months ago."

The man said he didn't care about that. All he knew is he had a lease, and if Ike wasn't supposed to sign it, that was his lookout. He could straighten that out with his brother.

"There're laws against signing false documents," he said.

Benny asked him who he'd been talking to, and the man said, "Legal Aid. They got laws about what you're doing."

Benny said, "That Legal Aid got to go." He didn't tell that to the man. He told it to Tom.

Benny said, "That's something else you might want to work on."

Tom nodded his head like he already knew it.

The Legal Aid lawyer told the man that all he had to do was pay his rent and do like the lease said, and he could stay there till it ran out, which in this case was nine more months. It wasn't his fault if Ike lied to him. That was between him and his brother. You can't go around signing false documents. That's a clear case of fraud. And Benny said he was right. He checked it out with the county attorney.

"Besides which," Benny said, "it wasn't his brother's house, anyway." The county attorney just drew up a false deed and told Benny to take it out there and see if he could bluff the man with it.

"Just wave it at him," the county attorney said. "Show him the date, but don't let him hold it."

Benny said he told the man he could fix it where nobody in the three-county area would give him a job. No job, no rent. No rent, no lease. He told the man, "It's just a matter of time. Why don't you go somewhere else?"

But the man said he liked it here. Where else was he going to find a house for thirty-five dollars a month? He had enough money for that.

Benny said, "How?"

And the man said, "Unemployment."

He got to draw unemployment for every month he worked for Ike. It was just like money in the bank. And Benny couldn't do a thing about it. That was the federal government. If it was the county, he'd know what to do. But with the poverty grant for the golf course still in the works and the Appalachian Development funds, it wouldn't be worth it. That's how come he called us in on it. He wanted us to fix it for him.

"Yes, sir," Tom said.

I said, "How? What did you have in mind?"

Benny said he didn't even want to know. He looked at his watch. "This is the eighth. I want them out of there in a week."

I said, "How come? They're paying rent."

Benny didn't say anything at first. He just looked at Tom, and Tom looked at him. Then he leaned forward and looked at me and said, "Listen to me. We're good folks here. We're poor, but we're decent. We don't want the scum of the earth living among us. And on top of that, they're on drugs."

"Or crazy," I said. "You don't know if she's on drugs or not."

"Same damn thing," Benny said. "I don't care if it happened to her or she did it all by herself. The fact is her wires are fused, and I ain't fixing to have her here. I got my own people to think of."

"Damn right," Tom said and stood up. I don't know how he knew it was over, but he did.

"Sarge knows what to do," Benny said and started rooting around his desk like he didn't even know we were there.

I looked at Tom, and he was nodding.

He knew what to do.

10

wo or three days later I was eating a frozen Mexican dinner and drinking a Coca-Cola. Tom was already through
with his. He finished off the sugar cookies, wadded up the
package, threw it in the sink, and said, "Let's go."

I said, "I'm not finished yet." But he was already out the door. I took
the plate with me and got in the car and said, "Where are we going?"

He didn't answer, so I ate the rest of the dinner and threw the
platter out the window. I licked the spoon and stuck it in my coat
pocket and laid back and relaxed. I shut my eyes and let it happen.
When I was in Reidsville that last time, I figured I was just wasting
my time trying to plan things. So I quit doing it. And then when I
started living with Tom, there wasn't any use anyway. He never
thought about what he was fixing to do till he already did it, and it
wouldn't have been any use in me pulling one way and him the
other. So I let it pass. There was always another house to paint. Besides, I knew where we were going. What I didn't know was what
we were going to do when we got there.

It was a real nice night anyway. Tom was singing and carrying on. I could see the sun set over the mountains. The air was mild. We kept on passing through pockets of cold where the night chill had already settled. It was like meeting a ghost. Every time we did it, I'd think about Kate. Then it would pass, and we'd go on through to warm again. I was thinking how it couldn't be better, considering the circumstances.

I said, "Hey, Tom."

He quit singing.

I said, "This is all right, isn't it?"

He said, "What?"

I said, "All this."

He said, "All what?"

I waved my hand to show what I meant. I didn't know what I was talking about, so I couldn't tell him. It wasn't something I could say. It was more like a feeling of being at home. I wasn't alone. That was the difference. But I didn't know that then. All I knew was that it was all right, driving along with Tom in the evening watching the sky catch on fire and the forest getting dark. I was thankful I was alive. It was like a great gift, and that's all I needed. The rest of it was like the woods. I was just passing through. When I was alone, it didn't make sense. I didn't know the way, and now all of a sudden I did.

We must have gone six or eight miles when we turned off on a dirt road past a brick church and a couple of houses. Then the road dropped to the river, cutting back along the ridge and angling down. The road followed the river a ways, then crossed an old metal bridge. It was getting on toward dark, and I could hear the boards slapping and rattling under the tires. It sounded like a stick on a fence. Then we were on the dirt again, pulling up the hill on the other side of the river. We got to the top, Tom turned to the right and drove straight at the woods. A hole opened up, but it wasn't wide enough for the car. We went through the bushes. They were slapping and snatching at the sides of the car. Tom couldn't see where he was going. It wasn't a road. It was more like a couple of tire tracks heading off through the trees. Most of it was overgrown, and where it wasn't, it was rutted. Tom eased over the worst of the ruts, but the shocks weren't too good, and we were rocking back and forth, rolling sideways and scraping the bottom. It was a low-slung car anyway, and I figured he was going to knock off the muffler when all of a sudden the road widened out and we were there.

It was almost dark when the road turned, and all of a sudden the headlights picked up an old two-story, gabled house. It was painted white and had a tin roof with streaks of rust showing through the aluminum paint. All I could see at first were the gables sticking up through the roof and the whole thing floating over a field of young pines. The road cut back in the woods again, and we lost it. Then I saw the roof again through the trees with the moon shining on it. It looked like a field of ice breaking up. It was all angles. Then we came out in the moonlight ourselves, and I could see the blank white side of the house and the dark windows and the black porch running across the front.

Tom drove up to the steps and stopped. He went up on the porch and tried the door. It wasn't open, so he broke one of the little windows on the side and reached in and turned the knob.

I said, "Tom, that's breaking and entering."

He said, "Where's the light switch?"

I felt on the wall beside the door and turned it on. All of a sudden it was like a flash of lightning that stayed there and froze. It was so bright I could hardly see for a while. Then my eyes got used to it, and I could see all that was there, which wasn't much.

There were a couple of mule ear chairs and a sofa sitting in front of the fireplace. The rest of it was mostly old clothes and trash. The fireplace was so full of garbage it spilled out on the floor, and one of the walls was smeared with what might have been mud. The only thing in the room that looked different from what you might have expected were a couple of stereo speakers along one wall with a chair in the middle and a turntable and a stack of records sitting on it. All that equipment was brand-new. There was a rope across the wall in one corner with washing on it. Socks mostly and women's panties with rust stains in the crotch. The whole place looked empty and lived in at once. It was like rooting around in somebody's closet. It made me uneasy. The whole thing was too bright. There was too much of other people in there to suit me.

I said, "Tom, let's go. What if they're here?"

But he didn't pay me any attention. He said, "Get that chair over there." He pointed at a mule ear chair. "Pull down those curtains."

Then he went out in the other room, and I followed him. I wasn't about to be left alone in there all by myself. The other room was the kitchen. Tom turned on the stove and laid a wood chair with a cane seat on the burner. Then he got a can of grease and poured it all over the chair. He saw me and said, "Go get some papers." I got him the papers, and he stuffed them around the chair. They caught on fire, and it ran up the wall. I could see the paint blister. Then it turned black. Pretty soon the wood in the wall was burning.

Tom went back in the living room and said, "Get up those papers." I started to pick up some of the trash when I saw a camera. I put it aside and picked up some more trash, and there was another.

I rooted around and came up with two others. That made four. I took them over to Tom and showed him. We looked around and found some jewelry in a box. In one of the closets there was a fur coat and a whole set of silverware wrapped in special pieces of cloth with ribbons around them and a pile of plates and serving bowls that looked like they'd been burned in a fire, they were so black. Tom said they were silver, too. Another room was full of equipment. Lawn mowers and chain saws, mostly. We never did find the drugs. Tom said they were probably stuffed up the chimney, so he lit the garbage, and pretty soon the fire was spilling out on the floor, setting some of the trash out there on fire. Tom checked in the kitchen, and it was still burning, so he got the lawn mowers and ran them out in the living room and turned them upside down and poured out the gasoline from the tanks. Then he dumped out the gas in the chain saws. Some were empty, and some were full. The chain saws he poured all over the sofa and pushed it up against the wall. Then he poured out the chain oil till the sofa was real dark and greasy. He threw a burning bread wrapper on it. The wrapper just sat there a minute, and then it exploded. The whole thing went up in flames. I could see the light from the kitchen eating through the wall. I figured the fire had already run upstairs by then, so I said, "Let's go." But Tom wouldn't stop. He was setting fires everywhere.

I said, "Tom, come on. We're going to get burned up in here. This house is old. It's going to go up like a match." But he didn't pay me any attention till I said, "What about the equipment?"

He said, "What equipment?"

I went and got the fur coat and said, "This equipment. What about the cameras? What about the chain saws? There are thousands of dollars in here."

That sobered him up. But it was too late. The fire was too hot to stand. It was burning up the walls and creeping across the ceiling. If we didn't get out of there soon, the whole thing was going to fall in on us. I looked around, and all I could see were the lawn mowers. The handles were sticking up out of the flames, and most of the paint was already gone. The chain saws were sitting there like some kind of slugs that came out of the fire. Then I thought of the cameras. I started to get them, but I couldn't make it. I grabbed Tom and pushed him out the door.

"Come on!" I said. "Run!"

I just thought of the stove in the kitchen. If it was gas, it was propane, and if it was propane, where was the tank?

I said, "Propane! It's going to blow!"

We got in the car and just about made it to the edge of the woods when one whole wall of the house blew out. It shook the car like a great wind. Tom pulled over and got out and stood there staring at the fire like it was something he knew before from some other time. It looked like he was hypnotized by it.

I got out and stood there with him. Fire was coming out from under the roof by then, curling up on the tin from the fascia boards. The wall that blew out seemed to be back in place again except for the fact that it was just fire. Pretty soon the whole thing was fire, all the outside walls and the porch. I was amazed at how fast it went and how long it burned. Sparks were floating up in the sky. The breeze came up, and it was like a river of sparks rising in the dark night sky. There were so many it looked like the stars. The wind died down, and I could see a pine tree burning, and the woods around it, they were on fire. I showed it to Tom and said, "Let's go. The woods are on fire." But I couldn't get him to move. It was like in the house. He wasn't going till it burned him out or the last tree fell on his head.

He told me later it was like something he made. He didn't know how to describe it. Something real beautiful. He kept saying, "That's fine, ain't it? That's real fine?" I kept telling him to get out of there. Somebody was going to see it and come. I hardly got through saying that when all of a sudden there were the headlights. I could see them in the woods, coming toward us, flipping on and off through the trees.

I said, "Come on. They're coming now, Tom." I grabbed him by the arm, but he wouldn't move. I said, "Look there," and showed him the headlights just about the same time they broke out of the woods into the clearing and lit up the house. The fire turned pale and white in the glare. Then they were back in the woods again, and the fire rose up and burned in the dark.

Tom said, "It's too late. They're already here."

I said, "What are we going to tell them?"

He said, "Tell them we saw it and came to help."

They came bearing down at us going fifty or sixty miles an hour, skidding and sliding. I knew who they were as soon as they passed. The man was driving. The woman was sitting there beside him. She had both hands covering her mouth. Then they were gone like a face in a train. They were heading straight for the house when all of a sudden they stopped and backed up. They must have finally realized they saw us.

The man got out and said, "What happened?" but the woman didn't stop. It's like she was fired out of a rifle. She was headed straight for the house, running and screaming and holding her hands out in front of her like she was in a horror movie and there was the horror right in her face.

Tom said to the man, "What's she saying?"

The man said, "Same thing she *been* saying ever since we turned in and saw it."

Tom said, "What's that?"

The man said he didn't know. What happened?

Tom said he didn't know. "We were just passing and came to see if we could help."

He could hardly keep his eyes off the fire long enough to talk to the man, he was so fascinated. He told me later it was like something he thought up all by himself, and there it was, just like he imagined it.

The woman was just about at the house by then, and I said, "What's she fixing to do?"

It looked like she was going to run in it.

The man said he didn't know. It didn't look like there was much she *could* do.

I said, "I mean to herself. Is she all right?"

The man said, "I reckon. She always has been."

I could hear her crying and wailing.

I said, "She doesn't sound all right."

The man said, "She misses her things. They're all in there. Everything she ever owned."

And some she didn't, I thought to myself. But I didn't say anything. I didn't need to. They lost it all anyway.

Just then the back of the house gave way, and the woman came running back to the van, screaming and yelling. The rest of the house settled down after that like a dog on its haunches.

The woman pulled up and said, "Do something!"

I said, "Do what?"

She said, "Something! Do something!"

Then it's like she gave up. She fell back against the side of the van and put her face in her hands and cried. It wasn't like a human being. It was more like a ghost in a horror movie, mourning the dead. I never heard anything like it before. She didn't seem to be crying because of what she lost in the house or because she was having to go somewhere and start out all over with nothing but the clothes she had on her back and a couple of sacks of groceries and what was left of an unemployment check. It was like everything she never had and thought she would when she was a girl and young enough to believe she'd marry a good man who loved her, and they'd get them a house and a garden and lots of children and live there together till they got old and died in each other's arms. I listened to her weeping and wailing, and it sounded like everybody who ever lived mourning for every dream they lost—all the missed chances and things gone wrong. It was like hearing the grief of the world and the pain and sorrow of being alive all rolled up in one. I didn't know what to do. I looked at Tom, and he looked at me, and I looked at the man, and he cut his eyes at me, then looked away and studied the house a while like he was fixing to do something about it as soon as he figured out what it was.

Finally Tom said, "What's the matter with her?"

The man looked at him. It didn't seem like he had any eyes, the way the shadows fell on his face.

The man said, "She's upset."

Tom said, "I can see she that. What are you fixing to do about it?"

The woman quit howling and looked at them. It's like she was stunned or forgot where she was, and all of a sudden she heard human voices and stopped what she was doing to listen.

The man said, "There's nothing *to* do."

As soon as he said it, there was this loud creaking and rending like something tearing loose, and the whole house slid sideways. One wall went out, and the other went in. Sparks were flying everywhere. It was like a great explosion. The fire lifted up in the air for a minute. Then the roof came down and started buckling. The sheets of tin twisted like paper. The gables on the roof collapsed and sat there looking out of the fire like two eyes in a skull.

Tom put his hand out, reaching for it like he was fixing to say something to it. His mouth was working, and he took a couple of steps and stopped. I couldn't tell what he was thinking, but it's like he saw something and started to call it or say something to it. Then the roof came down, and he never did say it. The moment was lost. There was nothing there but the skull looking at him with the fire burning behind its eyes.

And then even that was gone.

The woman quit crying after that and got in the van. She left the door open, and the man went over and shut it for her like that was the least he could do. He stood there looking at her, and she put her hand on the inside of the window. The fingers were spread out like a foot. I didn't know what she was doing, and the man didn't either. He just looked at her like she'd gone off somewhere in some other life, and there wasn't a thing he could do about it.

"Well," Tom said, "that's about it."

The fire was still raging around the house, and there were some trees in the woods on fire.

Tom said, "We better report it."

The man said, "Report what?"

Tom said, "Report the fire. The woods are burning. It might take this whole section around here. We got to report it."

"Okay," the man said.

I looked at the van. The woman was sitting there with one hand at her mouth like she was trying to hold her teeth in. She saw me look at her and put her hand on the window again. I looked away. I didn't want to see it. It was like she was trying to say something I didn't want to hear.

The man said, "What do you think we ought to do? Where can we go?"

"Anywhere you want to," Tom said.

He turned to me and said, "Let's go."

The man said, "Wait a minute. Let me stay with you. We don't have a place to stay."

"Stay at a motel," Tom said.

He got in the car, and I said to the man, "We don't have room."

I started to leave, and the man followed me. "Just till we get on our feet," he said. "Just till we get us another place."

Tom stuck his head out of the window and said, "Where are you from?"

The man said, "Arizona."

"Better go back," Tom said. "You got a truck. You got a good woman. You're still a young man. You got your whole life in front of you."

I heard him say that, but I wasn't paying him any attention. I was looking at the woman in the van. Her hair was frizzed and sticking out all around her head in a glory. I could see the fire through it, guttering and flickering, and the flames in the trees burning like torches lighting the dark woods, and it was like her hair was on fire. It was all dark with the flames shooting through it, and I thought to myself, Tom's right. They still got their whole life together.

The man walked over to the van and got in. The woman said something, but he didn't answer. He turned around and drove off. They passed us, and the woman put her hand up on the window again. It was like seeing a fish in a bowl. I looked at it and looked away. It was too pitiful.

Then they were gone. All the way back home, I kept thinking about that woman and seeing her hand pressed on the window.

That night I had a dream. I was standing beside the highway. Traffic was passing in both directions, but no one was driving. The cars were empty except for people sitting in front in the passenger's seat. They were all women. The cars would pass, and the women would look out and see me and put their hands on the window just like that woman when she was leaving. The hands were stuck to the side of the glass, and the women kept turning around as they passed as though they were pleading for me to come get them and set them free or release them from whatever they were caught up in. The car, the trip, the dream itself, maybe. I must have seen ten or twenty women pass by like that before I knew it was Kate. They were all different or else I would have known who it was as soon as I saw her. But it was her, too. They were all her, and she was asking me to release her. But I couldn't do it. She was going too fast. I'd just see her, and she'd put her hand up, and I'd cry out, and she was gone, turning back to look at me as long as she could, her hand fixed on the side of the glass, pleading for me to help her.

She wanted me to set her free.

* * *

The next day, I was working in back of a house in Etowah, mixing some paint, when Benny came by and touched me on the shoulder and said, "Come on over here a minute."

He walked over to the shade of a big black walnut tree and sat right down in the grass. That's one thing I liked about Benny. He had on a blue business suit, a white shirt starched so much it could have stood up by itself, a bright red tie, and wing-tip shoes with little rows of holes on the top, and he sat right down on the ground like a regular person. He might have had on an old pair of khaki trousers with paint all over them like me and jogging shoes with the toes coming out he got from Sky City and an old white T-shirt with Budweiser on it, the way he was acting. Except it wasn't exactly an act. He knew about people. He knew how to be with them just like he was with me, sitting on that thin scurf of grass down the street from where he was born and raised, acting like he never left the place. He might have been a millionaire ten times over, and probably was, but it didn't show in the way he acted. He still had the common touch.

As soon as we got settled, Benny said, "All right. What happened?"

I told him Tom ran them off.

He said, "I know that. I mean how come you burned the house down?"

I said, "That's how he did it."

Benny said, "That's kind of extreme, ain't it? You could have talked to them."

I said, "They weren't home." I didn't mention the way Tom acted about the fire. If Benny didn't know, I wasn't about to tell him. Besides, it was news to me. I hadn't had time to sort it out yet.

Benny said, "Well, Ike's pissed off."

I said, "Yeah? Why's that?"

Benny said,"He didn't have any insurance."

I didn't know that. Fact is, I didn't even think about it.

I said, "That's too bad. Old house like that. It must have been over a hundred years old. They don't make houses like that anymore."

"Not only that," Benny said, "he blames me for it. He says if it wasn't for me, the house would still be there."

I said, "Well, he's got a point there."

"Law and order," Benny said. "I'm a good Republican. Law and order's important to me. And right now that son-of-a-bitch father-in-law of yours is a wild card, you know that?"

I told him I did.

He said, "You can't count on him."

I nodded my head. He was right about that.

He said, "You don't know what he's fixing to do."

I said, "That's right."

He couldn't be more right than that.

He said, "I don't want to turn him in."

All of a sudden I quit nodding. I just sat there looking at him, thinking two or three different things at once. Then I said, "What about you? You fixing to turn yourself in, too?"

He said, "I didn't light the match. I didn't even tell him to do it. Besides which I'd deny the whole thing."

"And they'd believe you?"

He said, "That's right. People around here believe what I say. That's how come they elect me to office. I got their own best interests at heart. They know that. But that son-of-a-bitch father-in-law of yours, he's been away in the army too long. Nobody knows who he is."

And he was right. That's just what would happen. I looked at Benny, and he looked at me, and I figured I had one more card.

I said, "Why don't you let me handle it, Benny?"

He said, "You've been handling it."

I said, "I mean better. We'll just lay low and wait till it's over."

He said, "If he don't burn you out first."

I said, "He's not going to burn me out. I'm going to talk to him. He just got this one wild hair, that's all. Other than that he's all right."

"I know he is," Benny said. "I don't want to turn him in, but I ain't having him burn down the county. You hear that? I'd just as soon run him off to Atlanta. There're a lot of good folks in this county, and all I'm trying to do is protect them."

I said, "I know you are. And Tom's one of them, except for this one time."

I was still thinking of it as some kind of disease. Give it time, let it run its course, Tom was going to be all right. One day he'd wake up, and the fever would be gone just like a dream, and he'd be his old self again. But it wasn't like that. You never wake up. You never become your old self again. And the reason you don't is you change. You aren't the same person you were. Tom wasn't what he used to be and never would be again. But I didn't know that and neither did Benny.

Benny said, "All right. Those houses have been waiting fifty years. They can wait another week for you to get around to painting them. Stay there with him, you hear? Talk to him, try to see why he did it. It ain't natural. Son of a bitch is out of control, is all I can see. Old Sarge is a good man. I don't want to lose him. But I got to know I can trust him. Meanwhile, tell him I got something else for him if he ever gets himself together."

I said, "What do you mean?"

He said, "I'll talk to Sarge about it later, you ever get him straightened out."

That seemed to put it all out in the open. Tom was the one working for Benny. I more or less worked for Tom, if you can say the baby-sitter works for the baby.

"Well," Benny said, "that's about it." He stood up and dusted himself off. "Tell him to check with me before he does something like burn down a house with no insurance. Ike Waters is a tax-paying citizen and as such deserving of respect, even if he is a measly-ass son of a bitch."

I walked him back to the car and said, "That's right. Tell him he shouldn't have rented it to them and signed a year's lease if he didn't want them staying that long."

Benny laughed and said, "I'll tell him. I'll tell him you said so." He looked at the house I'd been painting and nodded his head. "I like what you're doing. I wouldn't want anything to happen to you, so watch him, you hear? Old Sarge is getting to be an old man now, and old men need watching. They ain't like young ones. They get strange ways."

He got in the car, and I stuck my head in the window and said, "Young ones get strange ways, too."

I didn't exactly know what I meant.

When Benny was gone, I went back to painting. I stood on the ladder all afternoon and cut in the trim on the second story of that big old house and let my mind drift with the clouds. I thought about Benny and what he said and what else he was trying to tell me, which isn't always exactly the same. He knew there was something wrong with Tom. He didn't know how he carried on about that fire because I didn't tell him. It was like seeing a vision of glory. Benny didn't know that, though. So what was he talking about? What was he trying to tell me? If he thought Tom was getting too old, why didn't he just fire his ass?

Then it came to me. What else Benny was trying to tell me was that Tom and I were in it together. We were like Siamese twins. That's how come he was talking to me. I was the one responsible for him. And in a way, of course, I was.

I couldn't even hear Tom cuss and beat on the dogs or see him trying to talk with his mouth full, dribbling and drooling down his shirt, without thinking about Kate and how lovely she was and how it was some kind of miracle that she could have come out of that. And then he'd look at me sometimes, and my heart would stop, and my head would start pounding, and I couldn't breathe. My hair would stand up on top of my head, I'd get goose pimples all over my body, he looked so much like her. It was like seeing a ghost appear in the daylight. It wasn't a trick. It was a real part of my life.

But what about Benny? What's that to him? Then I remembered he told me one time—we were running somebody off, I forget who, the Mexicans or the newspaper editor, one—and he said it was like he had some kind of mission. The good Lord showered him with blessings. His whole life was blessing on blessing. He didn't know what he did to deserve it. But he figured he had to pay it back or suffer for it in another life, one or the other. There were lots of folks, Benny said, the whole county was full of them, and he didn't mean just women and children, he meant grown men, old as I was, who had been born with some kind of weakness. The Good Lord saw fit to send them afflictions and sorrow, and they got sick and lost their jobs or had their house burn down on them or their wives just up and died for no reason, and there they were just like Job in the Bible cast out of the wheel of life through no real fault of their own, and it was his job to comfort them just like it would be any good Christian.

Hearing him go on like that made me kind of sick to my stomach, especially when I figured out that what he meant by *his people* were the good, clean, decent folks of Beaufort County who worked hard and had loving families and went to church on a regular basis and got along with their neighbors and didn't cause any trouble. And didn't need anybody helping them either, as far as I could see. I thought at first he was going to say that it was his job to comfort the ones that really needed it. I mean the real sick of heart, the poor, weak, pitiful sinners like me who hunger and thirst after righteousness. But they weren't his people. They were *my people,* but they weren't his. Benny and I lived in two different worlds.

That's how come I was surprised. Hearing Benny worried about Tom was like seeing a dog and all of a sudden it started talking. I thought of Tom as one of my people. He looked like a poor, weak, pitiful sinner to me. But he was born and raised in that county and was some kind of kin to half of them there, including Benny. He might have left and joined the army, but he came back there to die, and Benny was going to take care of him till he did it. That's what it was. Tom qualified. He was one of Benny's people. And besides, Benny figured he might come in handy.

Benny didn't know it yet, of course, but he didn't have to tell me to take care of Tom. I'd have done it anyway. That's how come I was there. That and the fact that I didn't know what else to do with myself. Tom was the only hope I had. Benny was a good man in some ways. That's what I've been trying to say. He wasn't all bad. But he didn't have the experience I did. He never loved somebody so much that he was desperate and almost driven out of his mind with longing and desire. Benny was a lot of things, some of them good, like I said. But he wasn't desperate. He wasn't ever a man of passion. And I was. Sometimes I think that's all I was. And that made a difference.

It turned out, that's what made all the difference.

11

The next few weeks I stayed home with Tom, and he seemed real pleased and happy to have me. The first few days he was up early, singing and humming before I even got out of bed. He'd have breakfast going and the dogs mostly fed except for what he gave them after I ate. I mean the bacon grease and pieces of toast and scraps from the table. Then he'd take them out and play with them, which consisted mostly of wrestling with them while they were trying to bite his ears off. Then he let them out of the pen to run around the trailer and bark. Then he'd try to catch them again, after which it was time to sit on the patio and look at the flies. I read the paper and listened to the morning news or worked in the garden to try to catch the cool of the day. In the afternoon Tom watched a couple of soap operas on TV. He knew the names of all the stars and what they were up to just like they were part of his family. I tried watching it with him sometimes just to be friendly, but my mind would get to wandering, and I'd start thinking about my own troubles, and the only thing that got my attention was when they switched to a commercial. I ended up knowing all about laundry detergent and feminine hygiene, but I never could tell one of the soap opera stars from another. They all looked alike, for one thing. They were all about the same age, and they all had the same problem as far as I could tell, which was mostly sex. They were either doing it to each other and getting pissed off or not doing it to each other, in which case they were pissed off, too, and getting divorces. I'd sit there and try to watch it with Tom and think, If I had a problem like that, I'd be happy. I wouldn't put it on TV. I'd just sit back and enjoy it because my problem was the opposite of that. I wasn't doing it to anybody, and it wasn't because I was turned on by men like some of the ones on TV. Put it another way, my problem was having to sit there and listen to them piss and moan about it.

It was making me real depressed, but I didn't know what was wrong. I just knew something was troubling me. It got so bad one afternoon I went out in the woods and beat on a tree till my arms got so tired I couldn't even put the stick back down on the ground, they were trembling so bad. I sat down and leaned back against the trunk of the tree and smelled where Tom was burning the garbage. I looked at my shoes, and they didn't seem like they were mine. They were like the shoes on a dead man, and I wondered what I was doing there.

That night I was laying in bed on top of the sheet listening to the heat bugs sing and seeing the moon shine in the window. The moon was so clean, it reminded me of Kate. I was so dirty. I smelled of sweat and garbage smoke, and I don't know what all. I smelled of myself. My arms were like pieces of wood somebody set in the bed beside me. I could hardly move, they were so heavy. All I wanted to do was die or get drunk so I could forget it. The only thing I saw worth a shit was that moon in the window. I kept looking at it and thinking about how calm and beautiful it was. It was still shining when I went to sleep.

The next morning I woke up, it was like something had left me. I wasn't exactly back to myself, but I wasn't as restless. I laid there a while and looked at the ceiling and thought about coming back from the dead. Then I thought about being alive and what that was like. And all of a sudden I knew what to do.

I got up and started frying some eggs and banana peppers. Tom wouldn't grow Mexican chilies. He said it was like eating fire. I told him a man with his kind of interests shouldn't mind that. And he said it was one thing to set a fire. It was another thing to eat it. I told him an old man like him ought to eat chilies. They say they get your gonads going. But he said they were going enough. He could take a piss when he wanted, and that was gonads enough for him.

I said, "Listen. I know what's the matter. I woke up this morning, I knew what it was."

He said, "What's that?"

I said, "A woman."

He said, "What kind of woman?"

I said, "Shit, Tom. What kind they got?"

He said, "Well, shit," and started smiling. "You ain't been out of jail but six months. What you need a woman for? It must be all them chilies you're eating." He was still grinning and carrying on when he went over to the telephone book and started rooting around in it. He said, "When do you want me to set it up?"

I said, "Whenever. Right now."

I was real horny. But it wasn't just that. The only woman I wanted was Kate, and I wasn't even horny for her. The trouble was, I couldn't breathe. I knew I couldn't hold out much longer. I was just about to drown, I was wanting to breathe so bad.

Tom said, "All right. Go take a shower. You smell like a bear."

I took a shower and put on a new Levi's shirt with pointy pockets and a clean pair of jeans and new black shoes I hadn't even had on my feet. I could still see myself in the toes, they were so shiny.

I walked out, and Tom looked at me and whistled.

He said, "You look like you're going to church."

I said, "Lay off."

He said, "I like your hair."

I had it slicked down with water and combed straight back without a part.

He said, "It makes you look like Rudolph Valentino."

I said, "You get me a date or what?"

He said, "Damn right. She said, 'Come on.' She's waiting right now."

As soon as he said that, I started getting cold feet. I hadn't had a woman in so long, I was afraid I'd knock on the door and just stand there. What would I say? How would I even know it was her? I hadn't ever seen her before. It might be her sister. Then I thought, How old is she? I was thinking about Tom. He's the one called her. She might be a hundred years old.

I asked him about it, and he said, "Hell, I don't know. They all look alike to me."

I said, "What's her name? How am I going to know who it is?"

We were in the bathroom by then. Tom pulled the lid down on the toilet and was sitting on it, talking to me. I was standing at the mirror, shaving. I just got through and was slapping on the Aqua

Velva when Tom got up and walked out. I dried my hands under my armpits to get some of the smell in there and followed him out.

The dogs were already howling and running around, flinging themselves at the sides of the pen and trying to paw through the wire. Tom came up and said something to me, but the dogs were so loud, I couldn't hear him.

He shouted in my ear and said, "We'll go in my car."

I said, "Okay."

I wasn't thinking. I was too nervous. The dogs were acting just like I was feeling. Otherwise I wouldn't have done it.

Tom's car smelled of dog. The seat cushions were worn out, and there were little bits and pieces of stuffing, looked like toast crumbs, scattered all over. I got in the passenger's seat. Tom cranked it up and as soon as he hit the paved road, he started humming. I tried not to listen, but I couldn't help it. I was getting nervous again. He'd hum a few bars. Then he'd start to sing a few lines and run out of words and start in to humming again. Most of the words he was singing weren't right. He made them up as he went along, and even then he ran out in a minute.

I closed my eyes and tried not to think. I tried looking down a deep well. But that didn't work. Then I tried counting sheep. By the time I got to a hundred and thirty-seven, I could feel the car slow down. I opened my eyes, and Tom was pulling off the pavement into a clearing on the side of the road. At the far end, near the woods, was a yellow house trailer set up on concrete blocks. The rest of it was mostly just raw dirt and gravel.

Tom drove up to the first big mud hole and stopped. It was about twenty-five feet from the trailer. He cut off the engine and said, "Let's go."

I said, "Let's go? What the hell are you talking about?"

He said, "I'll watch TV."

I said, "You mean in there?"

He nodded his head.

I said, "I don't want you in there with me."

He said, "Okay. I'll wait in the car."

I said, "Shit, I don't want you in the car."

It was bad enough going in there without thinking about him sitting out in the car, waiting.

I said, "Come back and get me."

He said, "How am I going to know when to do it?"

I hadn't even thought about that. We sat there a while looking at each other. My mind went blank, and I didn't even know why I was there.

Tom said, "I tell you what. Call me. You get through, give me a call, and I'll come and get you."

I said, "You mean on the telephone?"

He said, "That's right. She got a phone. Give me a call."

I got out and Tom backed the car around. Then he stopped and stuck his head out the window. I thought he was going to say something funny, but all he did was grin. Then he was gone.

It was like a dream. I couldn't believe it.

There I was.

I looked around, but I couldn't have told you where I was or even how to get there. It was just a clearing on the edge of the woods with a road at one end and a trailer set sideways to the road at the other. The trailer seemed brand-new. Right beside it was an old swing set. One of the swings was broken and hanging down on one chain. The other was missing. The swing set was so old and rusty-looking it didn't seem to go with the trailer. It was twenty or thirty years old at least. The slide was so rusted it didn't even have galvanize on it. Along the back side of the clearing where the bulldozer cut into the side of the hill, I could see bits and pieces of something shining real bright. The wind would blow, and the branches in the trees would shift, and the sunlight would move across the bare, red clay of the bank, and something would gleam and flash in the sun like it had veins of gold or pieces of diamond. I started to go over and check it out, but I was afraid she might see me doing it. I didn't want to stand there either, so I started walking.

There were a couple of prefab concrete steps in front of the trailer and a flowerpot with some dead flowers in it and toys scattered all over the ground. They were mostly just bits and pieces—a pink and yellow plastic duck, a couple of stuffed animals that had been out there so long I couldn't tell what they were. They might have been lambs, they might have been owls, they were so wet and swole up from the weather. The fur was all muddy. There was a doll with the hair all gone, and a doghouse beside the steps with the dog gone. I stooped down and looked in, and there was nothing there except a muddy piece of blue carpet laying half in and half out the door.

I went up the steps and knocked. The screen was loose and rattled around, banging back and forth. Nothing happened. I was just about to hit it again when the door opened and a woman said, "You the one that called up, or you come to repossess the trailer? You tell that son of a bitch he already got it all. He ain't getting the trailer, too."

I said, "No, ma'am."

She said, "'No, ma'am,' what?"

I said, "No, ma'am. Neither one."

She said, "Well, shit," and started to close the door, but I reached out and grabbed it.

She said, "What do you want?"

I said, "You."

It just popped out. I was so surprised I almost looked around to see who it was. I never said anything like that in my life.

The woman looked at me for a minute. Then she started laughing and opened the door and said, "Of course you do, honey. Come on in. He tell you it'd be thirty dollars?"

I was so ashamed of myself I didn't say anything for fear of what else might pop out. I was looking at her ass going across the room, and I might end up saying something about that, so I just went in and sat down on a dinette chair beside the TV. The whole place was pretty much like Tom's except the furniture was mostly all yellow Naugahyde—a sofa and a couple of Easy Boy recliners. The carpet was blue like in the doghouse and covered with pieces of lint and stuff.

I was sitting there looking around when the woman said, "You want to sit over here by me?"

She meant the sofa.

I said, "No, ma'am."

Then it was quiet. I didn't say anything, and she didn't either. She was about twenty-six or twenty-seven years old, but she was rough. They were hard years. She looked like she already lived long enough and did everything there was to do and then some. I don't exactly know how I knew that except I was a little that way myself. It took me longer to get there maybe, but I wasn't a woman. I kept looking around for the beer cans and whiskey bottles, but I didn't see any. I found out later she didn't drink. She just had a hard time living.

We were just sitting there like that, checking each other out. She arranged herself on the sofa like they do in the movies, sitting sideways on one leg so I could see the other one sticking out from under her bathrobe. She didn't have on regular clothes. She had on a red bathrobe that looked like it might have belonged to her husband. Except for the fact that her hair was fixed up and she had on lipstick and some kind of stuff on top of her eyelids that made them look black, I might have thought she just got out of bed, and it was eleven o'clock in the morning by then. I checked my watch.

She saw me look at it and said, "What time is it?"

I told her, and she said, "Time enough"—whatever that meant— and went back to smiling.

She had this smile glued on her face. It looked like it might have been put there by the undertaker except for the eyes, which didn't match up to the way she was smiling. The smile was saying one thing, but the eyes were trying to size me up. I didn't like her eyes too much. They were too black and dismal-looking. Her skin was good except for a bump or a mole on one cheek. Her teeth were good, too. I could see that from how she was smiling. The rest of her was ordinary. I couldn't see in her eyes till later, after she took off all that stuff, and they turned out to be the best thing about her. They were real black. Looking at them was like looking out at the dark. They just kept on going. She wasn't one of the prettiest women I ever saw, but I'll say this. It wasn't her looks. When I got to know her, I figured that out. Her breasts were little, and I like them big. Her skin was too white. Her nipples were too red. Not only that, she was too boney. I like women soft and round, but it all stood out on her. It was real definite. Looking at her naked in bed, you knew what it was. You wanted a woman, you had you a woman. There was no mistaking her for a man. She was like the thing itself. It was real powerful. It almost took my breath away.

After a while she quit smiling and got up and knelt down in front of me and started trying to unzip my fly, but I had on jeans, and it was too tight. She couldn't get the zipper started. She looked up at me and grinned like she was doing something real amusing.

I said, "Why don't we go in the bedroom?"

She said, "I thought you'd never ask." Then she said, "You want to do it here?"

I said, "Where?"

I looked around. All I could see was the sofa.

She said, "Here. On the floor. On the table. In the sink." She started laughing. "You ever do it in the sink?"

I said, "No."

She said, "Me neither."

I said, "I wouldn't want to."

She said, "Why not?"

I couldn't think of why not.

She started laughing again and said, "I could run the water on you."

I said, "Hell, no! Besides, it's full of dirty dishes."

She didn't pay any attention to that. She said, "How about the bathtub?"

I said, "How about the bed? You ever do it in the bed?"

She laughed and said, "Once or twice with my husband. I didn't know you were my husband."

I said, "I ain't."

She quit laughing at that and stood there a minute, looking at me. She pulled her robe around her and said, "All right. Let's go to bed."

I followed her down the hall to the bedroom. The bed was messed up. The covers were twisted up in a knot. She leaned over to throw them on the floor. Her robe fell open, and I reached inside and cupped her breast. It felt like a fruit hanging down in my hand, and I started getting hard again. She rolled over and fell on the bed, and I fell on top and started to kiss her, but she turned her head sideways and sat up and said, "What are you doing with all those clothes on?" and started trying to pull them off.

I had my shirt off by then and was working on my shoes. She kept messing around with my chest, rubbing the nipples. I was finally able to get my socks off and was just beginning to get out of my jeans when she started in on my Jockey shorts. We were both pulling and tugging. I was rolling back and forth trying to help her, and she was laughing and flashing those big white teeth at me.

She bit my stomach and said, "What do you want? You're paying for it. You get to say."

I said, "Get on your back."

She rolled over on her back.

I said, "Now spread your legs."

I started to get on, but she didn't bend her knees. Her legs were still flat on the bed. I said, "Bend your knees. You know what I want."

She said, "You want some pussy."

She arched her back and lifted it right in my face. "You want to suck it?"

I said, "Hell, no! What the hell's the matter with you?"

She still kept it arched. I could see the dew on it, running out between the lips. The hairs were wet and stuck together.

She said, "You want to touch it?" and started moving it back and forth.

I fell back on my heels and watched. It was like seeing a snake coiling and uncoiling. I was fascinated by what she was doing and breathing hard, I was so excited. But there was something that made me uneasy, like some kind of danger. I never knew a woman like that. Kate would get up under the covers, and we'd turn the light out, and I hardly knew what we were doing till it was over and I was holding her in my arms smelling her hair and all the lotion she had on her skin and hearing her say how much she loved me, and I almost cried every time, I was so grateful. With Kate it wasn't just doing it. Holding her after and hearing her talk and knowing how much we loved each other, that was the main thing about it for me. Sometimes we'd lay there half the night, talking and sharing our secrets together till there wasn't a thing I didn't end up knowing about her.

That's how come seeing Laurie coiling and uncoiling made me uneasy. I never did know a whole lot of women. I mean after Kate. They don't have much use for you if you're drinking, and that was all right with me. I did what I wanted and stayed like I was. But I couldn't figure this one out. She was a real whore, all right. I could see that from the way she was acting. A decent woman wouldn't do like that. And neither would most whores, for that matter. That's what I couldn't figure out. Most whores, you did your business and left. They didn't want you messing around. In and out, that's how they liked it. And that's how I liked it, too. But this one, hell, she was acting almost as horny as I was. Hornier, maybe.

I said, "Get your ass down on the bed," and pushed her knee. I started to climb on when all of a sudden I looked at her. She had her eyes closed. I said, "Open your eyes."

She opened her eyes and looked at me, and it's like I never saw her before.

I said, "What's your name?"

I was still kneeling over her. Our eyes were locked, and she was so wet I went right in. She started moaning and closed her eyes.

I said, "Open your eyes."

She opened her eyes.

I said, "What's your name?"

She said, "Annie Laurie." Then she started laughing and said, "This is a hell of a time to be asking my name."

I moved on her faster, and she started groaning. I said, "You know what mine is?"

She closed her eyes.

I said, "Open your eyes. Look at me." I told her my name, and she was moaning and closing her eyes, and I said, "Don't close your eyes. Keep them open. Look at me. I want you to see me."

She said something. I didn't know if it was just groaning or she was agreeing with me or what, but she kept her eyes open. Even when she reached it and kept on reaching it over and over, she was still looking at me. Our eyes were like the part where we met. They were the thing that hooked us together. Our bodies and the other part down below were flailing around, shouting and moaning. I couldn't have told you what we were saying, me or her, either one, if it was words. But it wasn't words. And all the while our eyes were still looking. Our eyes didn't move. They stayed locked and fixed on each other. I felt like I went deeper inside her looking at her like that than I was in her body down below, where I was in her.

I was just about to reach it myself when all of a sudden, I thought about Kate. I tried to put it out of my mind, but it wouldn't go away. It kept rising up. The more I tried, the more I couldn't help myself. I just couldn't shake it till I finally reached it anyway.

It was Kate's face. I kept seeing Kate's face in a photograph I had. That was the last thing I saw when I reached it. It was Kate's face, but it was Annie Laurie's eyes.

I rolled over and looked at the ceiling. Laurie put her head on my shoulder, but I didn't pay any attention to her. I was thinking about when I looked at her face, and it was like a mask she was wearing, and I could see her eyes up in there looking out like a whole other person.

She reached up and touched my face. I looked at her, and she dug her head in my neck and said, "How was it?"

I didn't want to talk about it. I said it was all right.

She pulled away and said, "All right? You crazy or what?"

Then she went back to nuzzling my neck.

We laid there awhile, and I could hear the birds singing outside the window. They were all around the trailer, making a racket. Now and then there was a car, but mostly it was just real quiet, the way it is out in the country.

Being on the edge of the woods like that was like being on the edge of the ocean. There wasn't anybody there but us. It went on for hundreds and thousands of miles, and all of a sudden I felt like talking.

I said, "Tell me about your husband."

Tom said they were separated or something.

She said, "He's a son of a bitch," and that's all she'd say.

I figured she didn't want to talk about it, so I tried a few other subjects, like what were all those toys doing out there and what happened to the dog, but I didn't get very far with them either. But I felt like talking, so I kept on going.

It felt real sweet to lay there with her. I didn't know how much I missed it. We might have been the only ones in the world. It was like being half awake and half asleep, in the woods and out of the woods, drifting back and forth from one to the other, sunlight to shadow. I could hardly keep my eyes open. Then all of a sudden she started crying.

That woke me up fast. I tried to console her, but I didn't know what to say. I didn't even know what was the matter. I put my arm around her and touched her breast and kissed her cheek, and little by little she quieted down and started talking.

12

We laid there most of the afternoon. Laurie told me the story of her life, and I told her mine except about Kate and being in prison. I figured she wouldn't be interested in that, and I didn't want her to know anyway. She probably did the same thing herself, left out a few things or changed them around. We might have been laying there naked, touching each other, but that didn't mean we told the truth. We didn't even know each other. It was a while before I found out the truth about Laurie, and then when I did, I couldn't believe it. It wasn't anything I could have even imagined.

What she told me that first day was that her daddy was a fisherman. He had his own boat. I thought that meant he was rich, but Laurie said it was a little old boat, about as big as a rowboat. He wore himself out scooping oysters in the bay and never did make any money. It was a little old piss-ant operation.

They lived in a trailer just like the one we were in except it was older. Her daddy got it repossessed. She and her momma sanded the rust and painted it pink, and her daddy built a shed over it to keep it from being too hot. They had it sitting on the water. You could stand in the door and spit in the river.

She told me all about going to school. She liked it all right, but after a while, she got too busy. I thought to myself, I guess you were. The boys must have swarmed around you like flies. She said she wanted some pretty clothes and a place of her own. She had a friend, and they were going to rent an apartment together. So she dropped out of school as soon as she could in the tenth grade and started working in a wholesale fish house at East Point, and that's where she met her future husband.

"The son of a bitch," I said.

She looked up at me and started grinning.

"The no-good son of a bitch," she said.

He was real handsome, she said. I figured he would be. I figured that'd be the first requirement. But she said he didn't have any sense.

I told her, "Hell, they hang everybody that ain't got good sense, they'd hang half the human race."

She said, "Yeah. All the men, anyway. He took my baby."

I didn't see how that proved a thing. It wasn't till later that I knew what she meant. Anybody with any sense never would have taken her baby.

I said, "Where's your baby now, anyway?"

I was thinking about all those toys. They looked like they might have been out there for months.

She said, "His momma's, last I heard." She was quiet after that till finally she said, "I met him, he was hauling shrimp. He had his own business. F and N Sea Food. I saw it painted on the side of the truck and asked what it meant. His name was Newton. I figured that explained the N. But what about the F? I thought at first he might have a partner. But he said, 'Fig.' That's what they called him. He - didn't want that on the side of the truck. He said *Fig Newton* didn't sound like a business."

I said, "It sounds like a cookie to me."

She said, "That's what he thought. All you men think alike. I kind of liked it. *Fig Newton Sea Food.* Sounds pretty good to me."

Besides how he looked and the way he acted—full of high spirits, always joking and carrying on—what she liked about him the best was that he wasn't from Florida and seemed to have a whole lot of money. She already had to move back in with her family when her girlfriend got pregnant, and she was getting tired of working all day and going home at night and helping her momma take care of the babies. Her momma had a new one every year. Some of them died, some of the older ones ran off, mostly the boys as soon as they went to work for their daddy and saw what it was going to be like. The ones that stayed were the ones that had asthma. It ran in the family. She said she'd go to the bathroom at night, and there'd be one of the children sitting at the window, trying to breathe. She said she knew just how they felt. She couldn't breathe either. The walls were coming in on her. But it wasn't asthma. All she could see for herself in the future was marrying somebody just like her daddy and living in a trailer the rest of her life and not ever getting out, just sitting at the window trying to breathe when all she had to do was open the door and walk out. The whole world was full of air.

A woman who thinks like that is real trouble. But I didn't care. I didn't even think about it. I just closed my eyes and let the words flow over me like a stream of cool water. I was like a man in a desert who came to a river and took off his clothes and laid down and let it run through him till after a while he couldn't tell where he started and it left off. I couldn't have got out of bed if I wanted.

Most of what she said, of course, I already knew or could have guessed at. She was just a poor young girl who hadn't had much happen to her yet. It was all about her momma and daddy and girl-friends at school. She didn't talk about boyfriends too much. She said she was wild, and boys kept coming up in the story. She said they were mostly just like her daddy. They'd go in the bay and scrape oysters and come back and get drunk and want to beat up on some-body. They didn't have wives or children yet, so they beat up each other. She said she couldn't count the times when she had a date and ended up sitting on the fender of a truck with the lights on at night watching her date fight somebody in a palmetto clearing on the edge of town. Most of the time they didn't even know what they were fighting about except their life and what it was doing to them. Then when they finally grew up to be as old as her daddy, they were all burned out. All they had to beat up on then were their wives and children and the ones that loved them.

I said, "What's a young girl to do? It's that way all over. If it ain't oys-tering, it's something else. Life's going to beat you down somehow."

She said, "Not me."

She drooled on my chest, and wiped it up and said, "I'm sorry."

Then she told about getting married and how she figured he was different. He liked the company of a woman, for one thing. He said he'd rather talk to a woman than talk to a man, and that was some-thing new to her. Compared to all the boys she'd been dating, he might have been a space alien and dropped down from Mars. He didn't even talk like them. He talked like someplace far away. Someplace better than swamps and palmettos, sun and salt water burning your eyes out and ruining your complexion.

It took her a month. That was four visits. He'd come down at the end of the week to haul shrimp back to the mountains, and by the time he'd come four times, she was riding back with him already pregnant. They hadn't been married but two or three years, and it didn't take her but eight months of that to find out he was no good and North Georgia wasn't much different from South Alabama or North Florida. She might have just as well stayed home.

I said, "That's right," and patted her shoulder.

She told it like a prize story, but the fact is, I heard it before, or something just like it. She was just a poor young girl who married the wrong man. The rest of it hadn't started yet. I mean the real pain and sorrow. Or maybe it was just beginning. I asked about the baby, but she didn't want to talk about that.

She said, "Good God! Look at me! I've been talking all day!"

I said, "No. No really."

By that time I was getting horny again. I rubbed my hand across her breast real slow, and the nipples got hard. They looked like she might have put lipstick on them, they were so red. I rolled her over and got on top, and it was the same as before, only better. I knew her better, and that made it different. She kept on going as long as I did.

Then I held her again after that, and I started telling her a little about Kate. It was like something broke loose, and it all started coming out. I surprised myself at what I was saying. Some of it I didn't know I remembered.

I finally got to the end of it, and we laid there a while staring at the ceiling till I said, "You mind if I use the phone?"

I got out of bed and put on my trousers and buttoned up my shirt. Laurie was still laying there naked, and it looked like we were in two different places. I was already gone somewhere else, and she was still back where we started.

She said, "The phone's in the kitchen," and got up and put on her husband's robe. "You want a Coca-Cola?"

I said, "No, ma'am."

She said, "What?"

"I said, 'No, ma'am.'"

I was too busy dialing the number to wonder what she was laughing about. I just looked at her.

Tom picked it up at the first ring and said, "That you?"

I said, "Yeah."

He said, "Well, they get there yet?"

I said, "Who?"

He said, "Nine-one-one," and started laughing.

I said, "Tom, cut the crap. Come on and get me."

That just got him going again. He must have been sitting there all day making up jokes and telling the dogs, practicing what to say. Then when I called, it all came pouring out at once.

I held the phone away from my ear, and I could still hear him squawking. His voice was kind of high and squeaky, squawking in the air like that. I put it up to my ear again. He was still in the middle of it, and I said, "Tom, listen. I'm ready. Come on and get me, you hear?"

Then I hung up.

Laurie said, "He sounds real frisky. How old is he?"

I said, "Old enough to know better and too old to be able to do it. All he wants to do is talk."

She said, "That's right, they get off on that the older they are. I've known them to lay in bed all day and talk about nothing."

I cut my eyes at her, but she was just drinking her Coca-Cola. She might not have been talking about me. But then again she might. I couldn't tell. I caught her eyes looking at me over the rim of the can, but there was nothing there that I could see. They were about as dark and deep as a well.

I said, "I reckon he'll be here in a minute. How much do I owe you?"

She put down the can of Coke on the table and said, "Thirty dollars."

I got out my wallet and thumbed through it. Then I said, "You take credit cards?"

She said, "You get that joking from him?"—meaning Tom. "He tell you to say that?"

I said, "No, ma'am."

She said, "I'm sorry to charge you for it, but I don't have a choice. I got to buy groceries."

I said, "I know. Everybody's got to eat."

Just about then I heard a car horn honking outside and a door slamming, and Tom was already stomping up the steps, beating on the side of the trailer.

I said, "That's him."

She said, "When are you coming to see me again?"

"I don't know. Real soon."

I was just trying to get out of there.

She said, "What about tomorrow?"

I said, "Tomorrow?"

I hadn't even thought about tomorrow.

She said, "Yeah. Tomorrow morning. I need some groceries."

She pulled her robe open, and the whole front of her bosom came out. She came over and put her arms around me and hung on like she wasn't ever going to turn me loose. Then she lifted her head and kissed me. It was the first time she kissed me all day, and I was amazed. It seemed almost sweeter than what we'd been doing. I thought for a minute it came from the heart.

She pulled away and looked at me sideways like she was wondering what I thought. I could still taste her tongue in my mouth and said, "What's that for?" That shows how surprised I was. I was so stupid I had to ask.

She didn't say a word. She just stepped back and drew her robe around her waist and ducked her head and touched her hair like you see little girls do sometimes when somebody says something to them and they're too shy to know what to say. It almost broke my heart to see her do that. I wished I knew her when she was a child. It was like finding part of a treasure that fell and got broken a long time ago and all the pieces were scattered and lost except for that one piece.

Later on, driving home, Tom kept wanting me to tell him what happened, and I'd tell him something, he'd whoop and holler and carry on like that was the best thing he ever heard. I never saw a happier man. He might have been twelve years old again and heard stories about people fucking but never thought he'd ever know somebody that actually did it. He acted like I was a traveler come back from some far, distant land. He couldn't get enough of it. Then it started playing out. I already told him most of it, and he ran through all of the jokes he made up. Then he got quiet, and we were just driving along watching the landscape rip itself loose and go tearing past us.

That night I was laying in bed thinking about Laurie. I could hear Tom coughing and the dogs rattling a tin bowl. One of them barked. Then the others started up, leaping and howling and flinging themselves at the side of the pen. Something was passing in the night. Then it was gone, and they got quiet, whining and growling in their throats, settling down to sleep for an hour till one of them smelled something else, and they all started up again. It went on like that all night long. Most nights I didn't even hear it. I could sleep through it as good as Tom. But this night I was laying awake and wondering how I ever stood it.

I finally went to the window and yelled, "Shut up, you goddamn sons of bitches!"

As soon as they heard me, they got all excited again. A human voice was like fire to them. They were just waiting. They heard me yell, they all went crazy. Even Tom woke up and wanted to know what happened.

I went back to bed, and after a while the dogs got quiet except for one rattling the bowl. Then Tom started snoring, and I heard a night bird sing. Then an owl, mourning a death. I kept trying to see the ceiling, but it was too dark. It was like I crawled up inside my own head. All I could think about was Laurie. If I could just go to sleep, I'd wake up, and it would be morning, and I wouldn't have to think anymore. But there in the dark, in the middle of the night like that, all I could do was think, and none of it made any sense.

How come Laurie enjoyed it so much? That's one thing I wondered. Whores aren't supposed to enjoy it like that. Or if they do, they're just putting on, unless there's something the matter with them, in which case they're crazy. But Laurie wasn't crazy. She was *unusual,* but she wasn't crazy. She probably hadn't had a man in a while, not since her husband left. But I knew that wasn't true. That's how she'd been making a living. She probably just liked it. That's how she acted. There wasn't anything she wouldn't do. Then I thought maybe she was just lonely. That's why she talked to me like that. But I knew that wasn't true either. She wouldn't have done it unless I got her started. And why did she kiss me? What did that mean? And what did she want me to come back there for? Then I thought maybe she liked me. But that was probably just an act. I finally decided she was a natural. She loved making love so much she didn't even have to pretend. She purely enjoyed it. Then I thought that didn't matter. She liked me anyway or else she wouldn't have wanted to see me. But that wasn't it. Not all of it, anyway. I knew in my heart there was something else, but I just couldn't put my finger on it. She wanted something. That's as far as I could get. I didn't know if it was me or something I didn't even know about yet. Or maybe both. Maybe it was a little of both.

I kept going around and around like that, wearing myself out like a rag in the ocean, sloshing back and forth, rotting with motion, till I finally fell asleep.

I dreamed that I was back in bed with Laurie. We were twisted up together making love like a couple of snakes when all of sudden the bed started filling up with blood. I didn't know where it was coming from. I thought for a minute I might have killed her, or she might have killed me, or we might have been eating on each other instead of making love, and that's where all the blood came from.

Except it wasn't me exactly. It was, and it wasn't. I was in the bed with Laurie, but it wasn't me. It was somebody else, and it wasn't her bleeding to death, it was him. The whole bed filled up with his blood, and I liked to gag on it, but I didn't stop. I kept on making love to her. I didn't ever want to stop. I loved her too much.

The next morning I woke up and couldn't get it off my mind. It was just getting light, and Tom wasn't up yet. I went down the hall and crept in his room and looked at him sleeping. The moon hadn't set, and the light came in a strip across the bed. It was as flat and bright as the light in an icebox. There wasn't any depth to it at all. It fell on his face and made him look old. If I couldn't see he was still breathing, I would have probably thought he was dead. He didn't seem to have any blood in him, and I couldn't stand it. It was like waking and seeing my dream except I knew it wasn't a dream. It was real.

It was really happening.

13

L ater on, Tom and I were having breakfast. I was eating oatmeal. He was eating sugar cookies, and I told him I was leaving.

He quit chewing and looked at me like he didn't know what I was talking about.

I said, "I'm going over to Laurie's."

He said, "Where?"

I said, "That woman's."

He said, "You just been. What the hell's the matter with you?"

I said, "I promised."

He said, "Promised what?"

I said, "Promised to take her to the store."

He stood up and said, "Shit!" He went over to the sink and ran his cookie under the water. Then he ate it. He said, "That woman's got a husband. He catch you taking her to the store, he's going to shoot your ass off."

I said, "How come?"

He said, "He don't want you messing with her."

I said, "He ran off. She told me he left her."

He said, "That don't matter. He still don't want you messing with her."

I said, "What about what I already did?"

He said, "That's private. He doesn't even know about that. But taking her to the store—that's putting a claim on her. He's going to pay attention to that. Besides, Benny told you to stay here with me. He don't want me getting in trouble."

I said, "You won't."

He said, "How do you know? I don't even know it myself."

I almost felt sorry for him for a minute, sitting there with that look on his face, old and forgetful, not being able to trust himself. I must have sat there a thousand times myself looking just like that, wondering if I was going to stay sober. It's like I had two minds about it, one telling me what I ought to do and the other one wanting to do something different. And that was the strongest. It was like a dark tide swelling up in me. I couldn't resist it. Before I even took the first drink, I knew I wasn't going to get what I wanted, but I went ahead anyway because it seemed like it came so close. There was always an hour or two before I got too drunk to know what I was doing when I thought I had it. I almost had it. All it would take would be a few more drinks. But I never could get drunk enough. I'd wake up the next morning sick at heart, yearning for Kate, and nothing was different. She was still dead, and I didn't want to live without her.

I finally went out and got in the car. Tom came running out like he was fixing to get in with me, but I was too quick. I drove off before he got there. I looked back in the rearview mirror and saw him take a few steps and stop. Then he shaded his eyes with his hand like he was looking straight at the sun. But it wasn't there. It was in another direction. He looked like I was the only one left in the world, and when I was gone, there wouldn't be anyone else but him.

I couldn't stand it. I stopped the car. Tom came running up, but I already locked the door. He ran around to the driver's side, and I said, "Tom, I'll see you later. You fix supper. I'm going to be back real soon."

He said, "I'll fix you a bowl of shit."

I said, "That'll be fine."

He said, "I ain't staying."

But I didn't care. I was already gone. I looked back in the rearview mirror, and he was still standing in the middle of the road, yelling something. That was the last thing I heard. That and the dogs circling back over the ridge behind the old home place. It must have been a rabbit they were chasing, and it was leading them in circles as usual.

I got over to Laurie's, it was real quiet. I cut off the engine and listened, but all I heard was a squadron of blue jays crossing the clearing, fussing and squawking, arguing about which way they were going.

I got out of the car and started walking toward the trailer when all of a sudden she came barreling out the door and threw herself on me like she'd been standing behind it all morning, just waiting for me to show up. I was real happy to see her.

The first thing we did, we went to town and got her some groceries. Then we came back, and she fixed us some dinner. We went to bed after that and made love all afternoon, and when we weren't making love, we were resting and talking. I might have been lying there all by myself sleeping and dreaming. There wasn't any strain

at all being with her. It was real easy. I told her whatever I thought
about. I didn't hold anything back, and neither did she. That's the
way it seemed, anyway. Sometimes she pushed me a little too far in
the lovemaking department, wanting to do something I hadn't done
and hadn't even thought about.

What Kate and I did is nobody's business, so I'll just say this. We
were so young, and making love seemed so new and amazing, we
didn't bother to branch out much. We were pretty happy doing the
same thing over and over. I heard about doing other things, and I
didn't think Kate would be interested in them, so I didn't push her.
What would I want to push her for? I figured there couldn't have
been anything better than what we already did. If she lived longer,
it might have been different. And after she died, I didn't much want
to. The women I was mostly with then, I just wanted to get in and
get out the fastest way I knew how. I didn't want to hang around or
do anything that wasn't natural. But Laurie was different. She
wanted to try everything in the book and then some.

The next few days after that, I'd go over there first thing in the
morning and spend the day with her. We were in and out of bed
mostly, talking and messing around, getting to know each other, you
might say.

I remember one day toward the end of the week, around five o'clock
in the afternoon, I got up and told Laurie I better go. It was getting
late. But she wouldn't let me. She pulled me back on her. I told her
Tom was waiting all day, and I was getting worried about him. As
soon as I started thinking about Tom, my mind wasn't on it anyway.
I wanted to get out of there real fast. I had to put my clothes on with

her sitting on my back, and I could hardly do it, I was laughing so much. If she wasn't naked, we could be in the circus, I told her. Folks would pay money to see me do that.

"Folks would pay a whole lot more to see this," Laurie said, cupping her hands under her breasts.

I said, "I don't doubt it, but I got to go."

I was halfway down the steps when she came flying out the door and landed on top of me again. I tripped on one of the toys in the yard and almost fell. When I finally got her off my back, I saw she was naked and said, "Good God! Get in the house!"

She didn't even bother to answer. She took me by the arm and walked me to the car just like she thought she had on a dress. I was afraid somebody would see her. Then I was afraid she was going to go with me. That's how she was. I never knew what she was fixing to do. It was like dealing with a wild animal. She'd be all right for a while and then all of a sudden do something crazy.

I opened the door of the car and got in. Laurie just stood there. Then she leaned in the window and kissed me. And that was it. I turned the car around and left. The last thing I saw in the rearview mirror, Laurie was still standing there naked, waving good-bye. I almost wrecked two or three times just thinking about it.

Ghosts aren't always like in the movies. Sometimes they aren't even dead. Your mind gets haunted, and you see them at noon in the broad light of day. Seeing Laurie standing there naked was like seeing a vision or staring at the sun too long. You keep on seeing it a long time after except it isn't bright anymore. It's dark and round as a black disk of darkness everywhere you look.

I kept thinking about the story of Lot in the Bible. I couldn't remember too much about it, but his wife died, and he was just leaving Hell after going in to rescue her. He was leading her back out of the darkness. He was in front. She was following close behind. He wasn't supposed to turn around and look at her or else she'd turn into a pillar of salt. But it had been so long, and he missed her so much. He kept remembering how beautiful she was and how much he loved her, and he turned around to see her again, and she was gone. He lost her forever.

I was still on the pavement a mile or two from home taking a curve when all of a sudden I saw something come out of the woods and run at the car like a shadow fleeing back into the light. I put on the brakes and skidded to keep from hitting it. Then I heard it bark and looked out the window and saw Tom's red bone hound. I opened the door and flung it in the backseat just as the other two came up, barking and howling. I threw them in with it and drove home.

After I got the dogs penned up, the first thing I noticed was that Tom wasn't there. I don't exactly know how I knew that. He would have already been there for one thing, especially considering I had a car full of dogs that ran off and got themselves lost. I went in the trailer, but all I saw was a can of spaghetti opened on the kitchen table and an empty box of saltine crackers. The spoon was still in the can where he ate it. I went down the hall and checked in his room. Then I checked mine, but he wasn't there.

It was quieter than I ever knew it around there. Then it came to me. Tom's car was gone. I was so busy with the dogs, it didn't register at first. The fuel pump had been going bad for a while. I'd tried to fix it, but I finally gave up. The car wouldn't move. That's how come I trusted him with it. The only way he'd get it to move would be to call up the wrecker.

I went in and called Nixon's Garage, and Nixon said, Yeah. He hauled it in that morning. I asked him what time, and he said, "Early. About eight or nine o'clock."

I hung up and sat there listening, but all I heard were the dogs in the distance and layers of silence like quilts on a bed. Then I thought about calling up Benny. There weren't but two people in the world who cared about Tom. One was me, and the other was Benny.

Mary Phalen answered the phone. She said Benny was awful busy. She kept wanting me to state my business. I didn't want to tell her about Tom, so I said, "Tell him it's of a personal nature."

She said, "All business is of a personal nature. Benny got to work on the budget." Then she just sat there, waiting me out.

Mary Phalen's a stout, heavyset girl, and her breathing's hard as a hog. I knew she was fixing to hang up in a minute, so I said, "Tell him it's a threat."

That got her attention. She wasn't surprised, I'll say that for her. Mary Phalen wasn't ever surprised in her life. She just said, "In that case, wait a minute."

Threats were what passed for politics up there. It was the element Benny lived in. After a minute he got on the phone and said, "Who is this, you son of a bitch?"

I was nervous about having to call him, so I just sat there trying to get my thoughts together. I could hear Benny breathing. It sounded like slats or Venetian blinds with the wind blowing through them. Then I heard a click, and there were two breaths on the line. One would breathe and then the other.

I said, "Miss Phalen?"

Benny said, "Is that you, Mary? I got the phone."

She said, "I'm sorry, Benny," and hung up.

I said, "Listen. We got us a problem."

I didn't want to tell him about Laurie. I just said I had to go to the store to get some groceries, and Tom wouldn't go. He said he wasn't feeling good. He got in bed and laid there looking blue at the mouth, so I went by myself.

"I wasn't gone more than an hour," I said, "and I got back, he wasn't there."

Benny said, "You know where he went?"

I said, "No, sir. That's why I'm calling."

He said, "He went here, that's where he went. He's been in and out of my office bothering me and Miss Phalen all day."

I said, "Yes, sir." I was relieved to hear it. Tom could talk to Benny all day as far as I was concerned. But then I thought if Tom was there, Benny might think I was lying to him.

Benny said, "What did you lie to me for?"

I couldn't believe it. It was like he heard me thinking.

I said, "Lie? What you mean, 'lie'?"

Benny said he knew about me and that woman I'd been hanging out with.

I said, "Hanging out? I just knew her a few days."

Benny said, "I'm not going to argue about it. You lay off her, you hear? I don't want you messing with her. She's no damn good. She came here from Florida"—like that was the reason.

I said, "Lots of folks come from Florida. What's she done?"

He said, "She's a whore. I don't tolerate whores in this county."

I told him he was wrong about that. She was just lonely. I said, "Run off all the lonely housewives you got sitting in trailers looking for a good time, you're going to run off half the county. All the women, anyway."

He said, "I had to go out with the sheriff and take her baby. You call that a good time?"

I said, "What's that got to do with it?"

He said, "Don't smart-ass me, son. I already told you. Lay off her. That's my advice. You're already neck deep in trouble. She's just going to drag you down with her. Besides, you got enough to look after."

Then he got going on about what a good husband she had and how she was no goddamn good or else she'd be grateful. A house and a family, a lot of women would be grateful for that.

I said, "A trailer."

He said, "What?"

I said, "It isn't a house, it's a trailer."

He said, "A trailer? What's the matter with you, anyway? You know what's the matter with you?"

I said, "Yes, sir. I wasn't smart-assing you."

He didn't believe me, but that was the truth.

Benny said, "Listen. I'm fixing to tell you something. As far as I'm concerned, you're a shit. If it wasn't for Tom, you wouldn't be here."

That was the truth.

I said, "Yes, sir. And not only that, I wouldn't want to."

He said, "The trouble with you is you don't have enough to do. Come by tomorrow. I got something I want you to do. You rested enough."

I said, "What is it?"

He said, "I'll tell you tomorrow," and hung up.

I was just about ready to shoot myself, it seemed so hopeless, when all of a sudden I saw this flash in the trees. Then it was gone. It did that a couple of times, turning off and on like a mirror flashing in the sun. The dogs knew what it was before I did. They had the pen almost tore up when Tom pulled across what he called the lawn right up to the front of the trailer. I stood in the door and looked at him. The way I was feeling, if we were married, I'd get a divorce.

I said, "Where have you been?"

I didn't tell him I knew already.

He smiled and said, "It seems like you're in a peck of trouble. I wouldn't want to be in your shoes." He acted like that was real good news. He might have been telling me I just won a million dollars.

I said, "How come?"

He said, "For going off and leaving me. Benny said I might have done something."

I said, "Bullshit!"

He said, "That's the truth. Benny said you're not worth shit, going off and leaving me like that."

I said, "Tom, I'm real tired. You want to burn down the woods, go ahead. Go ahead and burn down the trailer. Burn down the whole damn county, why don't you?"

I went in my room and closed the door. A few minutes later I could hear him rooting around in the fifty-pound sack of Jim Dandy Dog Rations. He called out and said, "Where's the scoop?"

He had a scoop he made out of a gallon milk jug.

I said, "I think you left it in the pen. I saw that black and tan chewing on something, but I didn't know what it was. If it was the scoop, it's gone now. You're going to have to go get their bowl. What do you want for supper?"

But he didn't answer. He went and turned on the TV set. I came out, he was sitting on the sofa watching it.

A woman on the news was talking about a man who robbed a bank in a ski mask. It was in Tucson. The temperature was a hundred and ten degrees in the shade, and he wore a ski mask. That was the unusual part of the robbery. I looked at Tom, and I could see he wasn't listening. He was worried about the scoop.

I said, "Listen. I'll feed the dogs."

He said, "You will?"

I could see he didn't want to. The older he got the harder it was for him to figure things out, especially if it was something new. It's like it depressed him. He'd rather go sit somewhere and stare. He didn't want to make the effort.

I said, "You know he wants us tomorrow?"—trying to cheer him up.

He said, "Benny?"

I said, "That's right."

He said, "I know it."

Then he got up and came over to where I was fooling around with the dog rations, pouring them into a saucepan I found. I could see he was smiling already.

"He tell you what it was?" I asked.

He said, "Not yet. He's fixing to. He said it's real big. Give me that."

I gave him the saucepan, and he went out and fed the dogs. I could hear them going crazy. Then they got quiet. A few minutes later Tom came back in. I could see he forgot the saucepan, but I didn't say anything. The worst they could do was eat up the handle, and that wasn't worth getting him upset about. I could go get it after supper. Meanwhile, Tom seemed to be happy. The dogs were fed, I was fixing something for supper, and he was sitting on the sofa singing softly to himself, listening to the news. Working for Benny was all right, I figured. There were worse things we could be doing.

I was saving my money each month and making Tom put up some of his. Pretty soon we'd have enough to get rid of that trailer and rebuild the house.

I'd say, "Tom, how'd you like to live in the old home place again?"—just to try to cheer him up.

He'd say, "What home place?"

I'd say, "The one you were raised in. The one in the woods in back of the trailer."

He'd say, "It's gone. There ain't nothing there but the chimney."

But I could see it made him real happy. It was like a dream we had, a reason for living, something we were working on, doing together.

Benny was right about that, I figured. All Tom needed was something to do. It made me happy just hearing him sometimes, carrying on with the TV set. He couldn't listen. The news was too boring. But he could sit there and sing to himself and get the comfort of thinking there was somebody else in the room with him. I knew how he felt because I was the same way myself except it wasn't the TV, it was Tom. At least I wasn't alone anymore, going over the same old things in my head, over and over.

The same old memories and regrets.

14

The next day Tom got dressed up in his best suit of clothes. We got to Benny's office, but he wasn't there. Mary Phalen said he hadn't come in yet. Did we want to wait?

I told her no. I'd just as soon not do it.

It was a joke, but she didn't get it, or else she didn't think it was funny. She looked right through me like I wasn't even there. I'd seen animals do that before. I remember a bird in a zoo, a hawk or an eagle. I must have stood there two or three minutes staring at it, trying to catch its eye. I even got down on eye level with it and looked square at it, but it didn't see me. That's how Mary Phalen did.

She finally said, "In that case, suit yourself."

I said, "I will if I can. I just wish he was here when he said."

Tom already went and sat down. I stood there a minute looking at Mary Phalen. Then I went over and sat down beside Tom. I looked around for something to do, but there wasn't a thing in the room except some pictures on the wall. I just got up to look at them when Benny came in, hustling and bustling, apologizing for being late.

He said, "I got tied up at the jail. They got a prisoner trying to hang himself. Brought him in drunk last night, and he tried to hang himself two times."

I said, "What did he try to do it with?"

Benny said the first time it was a belt. They took all his clothes, but an hour later he almost killed himself with the bedsheets. They finally got him in a bare cell. Moved out all the furniture. Now the only way he can do it is brain himself against the wall.

"That wouldn't hang him," I said. "Sounds to me like he's bent on hanging."

"He's bent on killing himself," Benny said. "If he don't get sober, he might do it. I finally got a deputy in there to restrain him. Come on in. That son of a bitch Bobby woke me up at four forty-five in the morning."

I knew Bobby—Bobby Pace. He was the sheriff. I met him one time in Benny's office.

Benny was walking by Mary Phalen and touched her shoulder.

She looked up and said, "He already did it."

Benny said, "Who?"

She said, "That prisoner. Bobby called."

He said, "How did he do it?"

She said, "The deputy shot him. He tried to get his gun away."

Benny said, "I told that son of a bitch Bobby what he needed to do was tie him up. Thank you, Miss Phalen. Come on in, boys. I want to talk to you about running for sheriff."

He turned back to Mary Phalen. "I'm going to be busy for a while, Mrs. Phalen. Tell them I'm down at the jail attending to matters. And tell Bobby don't say a word to McCormick. Don't make a statement. Don't answer any questions. I want to talk to Mc-Cormick myself."

McCormick was the editor of the local paper, and that's what Benny wanted to talk to us about.

"Timothy J. McCormick," Benny said. "Came down here and bought the paper, and the first thing he did was start looking for graft and corruption, except it wasn't Washington, D.C., where he'd have enough to go on for a year. It was just Beaufort County, and there wasn't enough to suit him, so he started making it up.

"Besides that," Benny said, "McCormick got political ambitions himself. You ever hear of David Rockefeller?"

I said, "No, sir."

Tom said, "I did."

That surprised me. It was like a cat in a chair woke up and started talking.

Tom said, "He's the one that ran for president, ain't he?"

Benny said, "No. That's one of the others. You know what David did? He bought a whole state."

Tom said, "A whole state of what?"

"A whole state of the United States," Benny said.

I could see Tom didn't believe him.

He said, "What state is that?"—looking suspicious.

Benny said, "West Virginia."

"West Virginia," Tom said, turning it over. "How much did it cost?"

"That's besides the point," Benny said. "The point is he had the money and moved in just like McCormick. He got the power. He got the money. He got an expensive education, and he comes down here and buys a paper and starts trying to stir things up. What's it seem to add up to you?"

I said, "The same thing it does to you."

"Damn right," Benny said. "You can't come in with a lot of money and expect to buy people's opinion. Folks know that, and they don't like it."

"I don't blame them," I said. "We got too many rich men in this country, think they can buy whatever they want to."

"That ain't the trouble," Benny said. "There's nothing wrong with being rich. It's how you feel in your heart about people, and that's where McCormick's lacking. Folks know that. You can't fool the people. They look at him, and they look at me, and they know the difference. The whole town's getting riled up about it. We got a chance to get rid of him now. But I don't want you hurting him, hear?"

Tom looked a little puzzled at that. He trusted Benny more than he trusted General Patton, but he couldn't figure that one out.

Benny said, "There are a lot of boys around here just itching for something to do. All it takes is somebody to show them."

I said, "Show them what?"

I wanted him to spell it out.

He said, "You know. It don't take me to tell you that. I'd rather not know."

Tom said, "He got a family?"

Benny said, "I don't want you hurting his family. Him *or* his family."

But Tom didn't hear. He couldn't hear. He wasn't trained to hear. He was like a guard dog. Whatever came over the fence was his. If he told me once, he must have told me a thousand times that what you want is maximum force. You don't want to see how little it takes. You want to give it everything you got and overwhelm the sons of bitches. That's the main thing he learned in the army.

I said, "Let me think about it."

"Think about what?" Benny said.

"What we're fixing to do."

"We already know what we're fixing to do," Tom said.

"Listen," Benny said. "Feelings are running real high at the moment. There're lots of folks sitting around waiting, wishing they knew what to do. All we got to do is show them the way. Choose your own time, but don't make it too long. He's ripe for the picking."

I said, "Show them the way like what?"

I was still trying to pin him down.

Benny waved his hand and smiled. "I said I was going to leave that to you. Now if you'll just excuse me, boys, I better go call in Miss Phalen and see what's happening about that prisoner. "

Tom got up and started to leave. I just sat there looking at Benny. I was studying a wart on his forehead. It looked like something coming out from inside his head, working its way to the surface. One cheek had a piece of something on it. I couldn't tell if it was toothpaste or not. It might have been egg, but it was too light for that.

I said, "You got something on your face."

Benny just looked at me. He didn't ask where. He didn't try to wipe it off. He didn't say what it was or nothing. He just sat there and looked at me.

"What about dogs?" Tom said.

"I don't know about dogs," Benny said, still looking at me. "You want the dogs?"

Tom said, "I don't know. I might."

Benny said, "All right, you got them."

I didn't know what he was talking about till later on, and then when I did, I wished I didn't.

I wished I wasn't even there.

I quit staying home after that and went back to painting. Ike wasn't complaining about his house anymore—not all the time, anyway— and Tom was back to doing his usual stuff for Benny, setting up child support for women they figured deserved it, getting vaccinations for children, carrying out food to the sick and the shut-ins, arranging for Meals on Wheels and visiting nurses and preachers to come in and comfort the dying and see they weren't lonely, and I don't know what all. I was spending most of my time with Laurie. I almost forgot all about McCormick till one day Tom said it was time.

Benny was right about the house. It set back from the road a half a mile or more. Tom turned in the driveway, and I didn't even know what it was at first. It looked just like a paved road. The only thing different was, it didn't have a center line. After a little, Tom cut off the lights and everything disappeared. There was nothing but a hole in the sky where the moon was shining and a wall of trees on either side solid as concrete. I couldn't see a thing in between them. Not only that, Tom was still driving. I couldn't see where we were going, but I could feel the car under us hurtling forward into the darkness. I started to grab the wheel, but I was afraid I might wreck us.

Then I thought about the ignition. I fumbled around on the dash and turned off the key. The car started slowing down and Tom said, "What happened? It quit running."

I said, "I cut it off."

He said, "What for?"

Then I thought of the emergency brake. I pulled it on, and we jerked to a stop. I opened the door and got out. I looked at the moon and took some deep breaths. It was like drinking a cool glass of water. The moon was bright enough to see by. Inside the car it was dark. Outside, I could make out the trees. They were mostly all pines with thick underbrush. They must have been forty or fifty years old. I thought at first it was an old field. Then I saw they had been planted. The rows were straight and orderly. They went out in the dark like streets as far as I could see. It was real peaceful there. I thought of somebody setting them out, marking the rows and planting them, and then getting to see them grow, and I wished I was orderly like that. I wished I was clear and bright as the moon without all this mess of needing people and getting all mixed up with them.

"What the hell you doing?" Tom said. "Taking a piss?"

I said, "No, I'm thinking."

He said, "Get in the car. We'll ease on down there."

I went over to the driver's side, opened the door, and said, "Get out."

Tom climbed out and said, "What for?"

I said, "I'm driving."

He said, "All right. Don't turn on the lights."

I started the car and stuck my head out the side window. By that time my eyes had adjusted a little, and I could see the edge of the road. The asphalt was smooth and shining with moonlight. The woods be-

yond that were dark, and I could make out the trees. It wasn't just a
wall anymore. As long as the moon didn't set, we were all right.

We must have gone a quarter of a mile or more when the trees fell
away like a curtain went up, and the whole world filled with light. We
were in an open field. But I didn't know that at first. I thought it
might have been a lake, it was so bright with the moon shining on
it. Then I saw a cow. It was standing beside a fence. Then there were
horses. Three of them. They came running over to check us out.

"There it is," Tom said. "Pull over here."

I looked at where he was pointing, and I could see a house on a
hill with a steep flight of steps leading up to it. The house was bright
and gay in the moonlight, and the steps looked like a waterfall. It
was just like Benny described it except he didn't mention the moon
and how the steps seemed to fill the pasture with bright running
water. He didn't say how beautiful it was.

I pulled off the road and stared at it.

"Now what?" I said.

Tom said, "Ease on down."

I said, "They'll hear us."

He said, "Go to the left."

Just before it got to the house, the driveway forked. One part
went to the left, behind the house. The other turned toward the
front. I let the car roll in neutral all the way to the fork. Then I put
it in gear and crept up the hill toward the woods in back.

We were just about at the line of trees, where the road seemed to
disappear into the shadows. I pulled over and Tom got out. There
was a screech owl screeching nearby, and Tom said that meant
death. I told him somebody's always dying. He slammed the door,
and I almost jumped out of my skin.

I said, "What the hell do you think you're doing? You want them to hear us?"

"They won't hear us," Tom said.

I got out and looked around. We were right beside a lawn with tables and chairs scattered around and garden terraces made out of rock. On one side were tennis courts. On the other was some kind of garden, and in the middle of that was McCormick's house. I couldn't make out much about it except for the windows, and they were shining in the dark and reflecting the light in the sky like ice. They looked all rippledy from where we were standing.

"Look at this," Tom said. "This is a rich son of a bitch. Look at those flowers."

I said, "That's right. What's the plan?"

He said, "What plan?"

That's what I figured. I should have known.

Tom went around to the back of the car and started rooting around in the trunk. He straightened up and slammed it shut. I started to say something about it. Then I saw what he had in his hand.

I said, "What's the gun for?"

Then I saw the bag. He had the gun in one hand and a bag in another. Except for the gun and the way he was dressed, he might have been a doctor. That's the kind of bag it was.

I said, "What the hell are you doing, Tom? What's all that for?"

He said, "The dog."

I said, "What dog?"

He said, "McCormick's dog."

I said, "What the hell are you going to do to it?"

He said, "Castrate it."

I couldn't believe what I was hearing.

I said, "Castrate it? How are you going to castrate it?"

He said, "The same way you castrate a bull."

I said, "You ever do it?"

He said, "Yeah. I helped my daddy."

I said, "Hell, Tom. That was sixty years ago. You ever do it by yourself?"

He shook his head, no.

I said, "How do you know how to do it, then?"

I wasn't fixing to castrate a dog. The more I thought about it, the more I thought he must be crazy. We were still standing by the car, and all of a sudden I thought, What dog? There's no dog. If there was a dog, it'd already be here.

I said, "Tom, there's no dog."

He said, "That's what you think. Look there."

I turned around to where he was pointing, and there was a dog standing on the edge of the woods no more than twenty yards away. I couldn't tell what kind it was, but it had short hair. The moonlight was shining across it like water. Its head was pointy, and its ears were cropped. They were sticking up on top of its head like horns. It was hard to tell how big it was, but it was big. It stood about as high as my waist.

I said, "Tom, that's a Doberman."

He said, "It might be."

The dog just stood there looking at us. It seemed real strange it wasn't barking.

I said, "How come it isn't barking?"

Tom didn't say anything at first. He just started moving toward the car.

"Get in the car," he said. "Don't move fast. Just ease on over."

That got me alarmed. Tom knew more about dogs than I did, and if he said get in the car, I was fixing to get in the car. The only problem was I couldn't do it, not without having to move. If I tried to move, the dog might not like it. As long as I was standing still, I figured I was safe.

"Get in the car," Tom said.

He was already in the driver's seat. I started running, and as soon as I did, the dog started coming. Tom slammed the door just about the same time the dog hit the window right by his head. By that time I was around the side of the car, getting in the other door. I just got it shut when the dog came at Tom again. It bounced off the window and came at it and bounced off again.

"He's trying to get me," Tom said. "He's like a fly. He don't seem to know too much about windows."

The dog bounced off again. Each time he hit it, I felt the car shake. I looked up and all I saw were teeth. It was trying to bite at the glass. Then it stood up on its hind legs and started pawing at it and snarling and snapping.

"How come it isn't barking?" I said.

"Some of them don't," Tom said. "Some of them just do like that."

I said, "What are we going to do?"

"I don't know," Tom said. "Run over it."

He started to crank up the car, but I still had the keys.

He said, "Give me the keys."

Just then the dog ran around the car and started jumping at the window beside me. He must have just seen I was there. Every time he hit the window, there was this thud, and the car shook. It was like a whirlwind of teeth and paws coming at you and then all of a sudden stopping a few inches away from your head.

Tom started laughing.

"Good thing the glass is there," he said, "else it'd already eat off your face."

"Face, hell. It'd eat off my head."

"That's what I mean," Tom said. "That dog is vicious."

It was standing up at the window, pawing. I could hear the toenails hitting the glass and sliding down. It wasn't scratching. It was more like bugs hitting the window. I looked out, and it wasn't trying to bite at my head. It was looking in the window at me just like a person except it had this puzzled look on its face. It was so tall on its hind legs it was almost as big as a man. It had to bend down its head a little just to be able to look in the window. Then I saw what it was.

I said, "Well, I tell you one thing."

Tom said, "What's that?"

I said, "You aren't going to be able to castrate it."

He said, "How come?"

I said, "It ain't a he."

"Well, shit," Tom said.

I didn't even know what had happened then, it happened so fast. The first thing I knew the door was open, and the next minute Tom was out and the dog was gone, and there was this loud explosion, and the dog howled, and I got out, and at first I couldn't see anything but smoke. It caught in the moonlight and hung there frozen. Then I saw Tom with the gun in his hand and the dog laying dead at his feet.

It was real quiet for a minute. Then the whole place lit up. There were lights everywhere. Then I heard running. It wasn't coming down the road. It was coming through the woods. I could hear the bushes crashing and the scuffling and scurrying in the dry leaves.

I heard a man yell, "There they are! I see them! Down there!"

Then a woman said, "Don't go down there, Mack. You hear me?"

The man said, "Where's my gun? Go get my gun. I'll get it my-self. "

Then the yelling faded away.

We were in the woods by then. Tom stopped and said, "I'm too old. You go on."

I said, "Wait here. Give me the keys."

He gave me the keys, and I said, "Don't move. No matter what happens, stay where you are. I'll be right back."

Then I started running. I got to the car, and I couldn't believe it was just sitting there. I kept the lights off and drove the road blind. I could see the flashlights going like crazy sticks, beating on something.

I got to where I left him, and Tom wasn't there. I waited a minute, then set the hand brake and went in to get him.

He was crouched behind a bush. I helped him up the side of the bank, but he kept slipping on the leaves.

I said, "You're too old for this kind of work."

He said, "It ain't that. I got leather soles on my shoes."

I finally got him out of the woods and into the car. Before I could stop him, he slammed the door. It sounded like another explosion, and somebody yelled, "What's that?" And somebody else said, "There they are!"

I turned around in the middle of the road, hit the ditch on the far side, and kept on going just about the same time I heard the first shot.

"Sons of bitches are shooting at us," Tom said.

I looked back in the rearview mirror and saw the flashes.

I said, "How many were there?"

He said, "Two or three. That dog's going to slow them down."

I said, "If they see it."

He said, "They're going to see it. Why you reckon they're shooting at us?"

I said, "Hell, Tom. Why do you think?"

He said, "I don't know. That's what I wonder. They didn't know what we were doing."

I said, "They heard a shot."

He said, "That's all."

I said, "That's enough."

He said, "Not for them to be doing like that. They didn't know who they were shooting at or what they were shooting for. They were just shooting. That takes a real son of a bitch."

The more he thought about it, the madder he got. He kept saying they could have killed us. I kept trying to explain it to him.

I said, "You were trespassing, Tom. That's one thing. Coming there in the middle of the night. And not only that, you were trying to castrate their dog."

He said, "I didn't do it."

I said, "That doesn't matter. Look what you did."

There was nothing I could say. According to him, that dog needed killing. It could have been anybody that did it. Killing that dog was just killing that dog. Hell, it could have eaten a child. But it didn't give McCormick the message, and that bothered him. That bothered him a lot.

15

The next day Tom talked about it to Benny. He called him up on the telephone, but Benny wouldn't talk to him. He said, Phones have ears, come and see him. So I drove Tom into town. I didn't want him going in his car for fear somebody might recognize it.

I dropped him off at the courthouse and went to see Laurie. I told him I'd be back in an hour, but I hadn't seen her in a while, and there was a lot we had to catch up on. I tried to go two or three times, but seeing her naked got me all excited again. She'd start laughing, knowing the power she had over me. It made her real sexy, and the wilder she got, the more I didn't want to leave. The only reason I didn't move in with her was because of Tom. And Kate. Mostly Kate, I guess. I didn't want to let her go. I loved her too much. I loved Laurie, too, in a way. But I loved Kate more. Laurie was all right, but I didn't trust her.

* * *

By the time I got back to the courthouse, Tom was already sitting out front with the old men, spitting and lying and telling stories most of them heard all their lives.

He saw me coming, he didn't even wave good-bye. He got in the car and said, "It's okay. Benny said we did great."

I said, "You mention castrating it?"

He looked at me with those big blue eyes of his and said, "Why should I? Benny's happy. He said we did great. 'Just what the occasion called for,' he said"—whatever that meant. "Not only that, it gave him the message."

I didn't believe it. It didn't seem reasonable to me. But Tom was so happy, I didn't want to argue with him. It turned out, though, I didn't need to. Benny was right.

Word got out that somebody killed McCormick's dog, and it was just like giving them permission. The high school boys started in on him first. They dumped his garbage and tore up his mailbox. Then they started in on his daughters. Somebody tailgated them one day. Then they ran them off the road. McCormick reported it to the sheriff and wrote an article in the paper about it. But that just made it worse. The sheriff came out to investigate, but he already knew how people were feeling, and he didn't want to stick his neck out. Besides, Benny said, even if there was evidence, which there wasn't, the sheriff wouldn't have been able to find it. He was like some dogs. He didn't have a nose for it. But that didn't mean he wasn't a good man. The county was run real tight, and there wasn't much lawlessness in it. People didn't tolerate lawlessness there except when it served a useful purpose, and then it wasn't lawlessness, Benny said. It was an expression of public opinion.

After two or three months of people expressing their opinion like that, McCormick got the idea and left. He did one final edition of the paper, accusing the town and everybody in it. I read the article he wrote, and the more I read, the more sense it seemed to make, and I started feeling sorry for him. There wasn't any reason to do him like that. I was sorry I got mixed up in it.

I didn't mind killing that dog. It deserved killing. If Tom hadn't killed it, it might have eaten a child. What I didn't like was the way the whole town started in on McCormick. I told Tom about it, and he agreed with me on that. He didn't stay agreeing, of course, because he already agreed with the rest of them, mostly.

"They didn't mind McCormick," I said. "Half of them didn't even know who he was. They didn't even know he owned the paper. Hell," I said, "half of them can't even read."

"So what?" Tom said. "They don't have to know how to read."

I said, "It wasn't McCormick. That isn't who they were getting at."

He said, "Who was it, then?"

I said, "I don't know. Benny maybe."

He said, "Benny? That's bullshit!"

I said, "Maybe so." I couldn't say what I meant exactly because I wasn't certain about it myself. But most of them were like a gun. They'd go off wherever you pointed it at. It didn't have to be McCormick. It could have been Benny, it could have been anybody in town because they were real pissed off about something, and they didn't even know what it was. McCormick was just some kind of excuse. They had all that meanness building up in them, that and the memory of something else, some kind of wildness they used to have they thought maybe they could get back to.

* * *

All the while I was living with Tom, I'd go over to Laurie's whenever I could and take her shopping or out to eat at the Burger King
or the White Columns for fried chicken. Sometimes we'd go to the
movies in Blue Ridge or even over to Dalton. We'd come back and
listen to the radio, and she'd take off her clothes and dance, or we'd
talk about things and have something to eat and then go to bed and
make love. She'd change a lot from day to day. It all depended on
how she was feeling and what kind of dreams she had last night and
how much she was worrying. She missed her baby. That was one
thing. She didn't talk about it much, but I could see it worried her.
She told me it was like part of her was missing. I don't know what
the rest of it was. Men, maybe. Every now and then the phone
would ring, and I'd answer it, and there would be a man on the line
wanting to talk to her. I'd tell them to fuck off, but they kept on doing it every so often.

One time I went over to see her, there was a truck in front of
the trailer. I went over to it and looked in the window. There was
nothing there but a Burger King bag and a new set of socket
wrenches. I went up the steps and opened the door, and there was
a man sitting on one of the dinette chairs, drinking a Coca-Cola.
Laurie was sitting across the room in a recliner. As soon as she
saw me, she popped the handle and laid back and looked up at the
ceiling.

I said, "What the hell's going on here?"

Neither one of them said anything.

The man was young, younger than I was. He couldn't have been
more than twenty-five, twenty-six years old. It was hard to tell. He
was probably older than he looked. He had that kind of face. It was
real regular. Some folks look sort of raw and unfinished. But he was

as smooth and neat as glass. His hair was blond with streaks of ash in it, and he had it pulled back in a ponytail. There was something real still and quiet about him. I mean inside.

I'd known folks like that before, and most of them made me uneasy. The ones I knew were mostly all roofers. I didn't like being around them, and they didn't much like being around me or anybody else except other roofers. Every construction job I'd ever been on, the roofers were different. They did the work nobody wanted, the hottest, dirtiest, most dangerous kind of work they could get and didn't seem to give a shit. They'd work all day stripping shingles and nailing down felt, putting in square after square of tiles with the hot sun beating down on them and never get tired, never quit, never rest, never even notice what they were doing because they didn't care. Nothing they did ever got to them. The only thing important to them they already had. They carried it around like a flame in a lantern.

That's what made me uneasy about him. He didn't need me. He didn't need Laurie. He didn't need a thing in the world except what he already had. I mean inside, behind the glass. That's what made the light in the lantern. And that's what put me at a big disadvantage because I didn't have a thing I needed. Everything I wanted was over where Laurie was laying back in the recliner. That's what made him dangerous. It was like looking at the blade of a knife. I couldn't take my eyes off him.

The man put his Coke down on the table and said, "What's this, Laurie? This the one?"

Then he looked at me and said, "I hear you've been in Reidsville?"

I said, "Yeah."

He said, "What for?"

I said, "Killing this woman's husband."

I already figured it was him.

Laurie popped the chair down and put her elbows on her knees, holding her head on, and looked at me. Then she looked at him. He started laughing, and she said, "This is Bobby. You know, my husband?—Bobby Newton."

He waved his hand and said, "How long you been knowing her?"

I told him a couple of months.

He said, "Well, you know all about her, or think you do. But you don't know a damn thing yet."

I said, "Is that right?"

He said, "That's right. It's going to take a couple of years yet."

I said, "What for?"

He said, "To get through the lies. It did me. It might take you longer."

He grinned at Laurie and said, "You sure got a good one this time, Laurie. It might take him ten or twelve years. He might never figure it out."

Laurie said, "Shut up."

Then she said to me, "Don't listen to him."

But I couldn't help it. He was like a snake. I couldn't keep my eyes off him.

Laurie and I were still at the stage where we were both lying a little. She was too old when I got to know her. Too many things had already happened, and she wasn't going to tell me about them. Not without lying. I knew all that, but it didn't matter till he brought it up. Then it did.

He said, "You ever tie her up, buddy? Try it sometimes. She's going to love it."

Laurie said, "I told you to shut up. Where's my baby?"

He said, "You know damn well where it is, Laurie. My momma's taking care of that baby. You ain't fit."

He turned to me and said, "She ain't a fit mother. You know that? Declared it in court. She ain't fit."

"No, they didn't," Laurie said.

She looked at me and shook her head.

"The court didn't say that."

He said, "The court order did. But that isn't why I came here, Laurie. I don't give a shit anymore about who's to blame and who did what unto who and wherefore and whereas and all that shit. That's all past and gone now, Laurie. We made a mistake, that's all. You made one, and I made one. We just weren't suited. I admit it. I ain't going to fight you on that anymore. I just want you out of here."

She turned to me. "He liked to kill me. He wanted to stick an ice pick in me."

He held up his hand and said, "We ain't talking about that now, are we? This is my home. I was born and raised right here. This is where I live."

He turned to me. "You know what she's doing? Fucking everybody in the county. I got to stay here. She can go back to Florida, Atlanta, get her a job, start all over. But she won't do it. You know why?"

Laurie said, "I got unfinished business, that's why. Give me my baby."

He said, "They ain't ever going to give you that baby. You know that, Laurie. Not the way you've been doing."

She said, "I didn't do it till they took my baby."

I said, "What did you expect her to do? She had to eat. You wouldn't help her. Nobody'd give her a job."

He said, "I offered her money. I told her I'd send her wherever she wanted. And not only that, the offer's still open."

He got up and went over to Laurie and stuck his face in hers and said, "You're finished here, Laurie. You shamed me enough. I ain't having it, you hear?"

I said, "She heard. Now lay off."

He turned around and grinned at me and said, "I'm just trying to do you a favor. Get rid of her, you're going to thank me. It ain't you, if that's what you're thinking. How old are you, forty-five?'

I wasn't but thirty-eight, but I didn't want to have to say.

He said, "And how old is she? Twenty-three? What the hell's she want you for? You're too damn old."

He was right about that. The more he talked, the more I knew how right he was. Laurie didn't want me. She couldn't love me. I didn't have anything I could give her. I already gave it all to Kate. It was too late for me to start over. I didn't even know if I wanted her, anyway. I couldn't trust her. She was too bold for me. She was too wild. Not to mention the fact that he was right. She already screwed half the men in the country. How could I trust her?

Laurie got up and shook the room coming over to kiss me, and as soon as she did, I forgot all about it.

She turned and said, "Bobby, just one thing."

He said, "What's that?"

She said, "Give me my baby, I'll leave in a minute."

He said, "I already told you, it ain't going to happen. I didn't come here to fight with you, Laurie. I'm asking you nice. Just don't shit with me, you hear?"

Then he left.

Talking about it later on, Laurie said it was a warning.

He told her he came to give her a warning.

Another time a couple of men came by. One was a young, hot-headed boy who didn't want to leave when I told him to. His buddy already got in the car, but he was still standing there, arguing with me, when Laurie came out. She didn't have on all her clothes. I just had on a pair of jeans, myself. They came up, we were in bed, messing around, and neither one of us had time to dress before they were already beating on the door.

The one on the steps kept looking at Laurie, trying to talk her into it with me standing right there beside him. He kept saying what did she care? His money was as good as mine, and so on and so forth. I thought I was going to have to fight him for sure.

His buddy finally got out of the car and said, "Come on, Jimmy. Let's go. You ain't doing no good here."

I said, "Damn right, Jimmy. Do like he says."

The one kept saying, "No hard feelings. Just an honest mistake, that's all."

The other one didn't say a word. He was like a dog that won't bark and won't back off, either. He was just standing there, holding his ground. The other one finally got him back in the car, and they drove off.

That was the only time her past came floating up to the surface. The rest of the time it was still down in there. I just didn't see it. I didn't know what to do with it, so I just let it be.

* * *

Those were the only bad times we had. The rest of it was pretty good. I got to liking Laurie a lot. I'd just as soon be there with her as anywhere else in the world I could think of. She taught me things about myself I never even knew were there. She drew them out of me like feathers. I might have been stuffed with them inside, packed in around my organs, and didn't even know it till she started pulling them out of my skin. That's how surprised I was. I learned something new every day. Some of it I wanted to know, and some I didn't.

Kate wasn't like that. She lifted me up. The more I loved her, the more I felt myself changing into her little by little. I was always better with Kate, better than I would have been by myself. I was like a different person. But Laurie made me more like myself. When I was with her, I was just me. I wasn't any better, but I might have been worse. I might have spent the rest of my life not knowing half the stuff that was in me if I hadn't met her. It was like a nest of snakes under the house. They could have been up there in the darkness, coming and going the rest of my life, and I wouldn't have known it except for her. I had a lot of good times with Laurie. Sometimes I thought we were born for each other. Being with her was just like being with yourself, only better. You weren't ever lonely.

Loving Laurie wasn't peaceful and didn't make me happy exactly. But one thing it was, it was real exciting. I never knew what was coming next. I'd been dead for a long time, ever since I buried Kate, and it was like feeling the blood coming back. I could hardly stand it sometimes. I was used to walking on stumps, and all of a sudden there I was tingling, needles sticking in me all over. I picked the worms off me and went out in the light and looked around and wondered where I'd been all that time. That's what loving Laurie was like. I couldn't tell a whole lot of difference between that and being alive.

A round that time—I don't remember exactly when—I was having breakfast with Tom. He was eating oatmeal cookies and drinking milk and talking to me with his mouth full as usual, and I was trying not to look.

I said, "Tom, why don't you lay off those cookies?"

I was eating fried eggs and bacon and mopping it up with bread and syrup.

I said, "Why don't you eat something healthy like me?"

He said, "Syrup ain't healthy."

We went around with that for a while. He kept saying eight oatmeal cookies was the same as eating a bowlful of oatmeal except for the milk. Then he told me he was working for Benny again.

It was like being hit with a brick. I was so busy with Laurie, I didn't know what Tom was doing. I thought he was staying home with the dogs and running errands as usual, keeping busy the way he did. I didn't know he was working for Benny.

I said, "Shit!" and got up and went out in the other room and watched TV. They were carrying somebody out in a stretcher and loading them in an ambulance. The announcer was saying something about a black male named Otis shot in a robbery after putting a man's eye out with a wire, but I wasn't able to pay any attention. I kept thinking about all that Benny didn't know about Tom because I didn't tell him. That had me worried.

Tom came out after a minute and stood in front of the TV and said, "You know what it is?"

I said, "No."

He said, "It's these Mexicans."

I said, "I ain't messing with Mexicans."

He said, "How come?"

I said, "I feel sorry for them, all them children, picking apples."

Tom said, "That's it. Benny got Panorama Orchards. . . ."

I said, "Panorama Orchards? What's he doing with Panorama Orchards?"

Tom said, "He just bought it. He's building houses all up the mountain. All the way on that road to the cross."

Panorama Orchards was on the highway south of town. Most of it went up the side of Blood Mountain, and the old man who used to own it built a big concrete cross thirty or forty feet high right on top of the mountain. Tom said it was Benny's idea to go up that old road to the cross and build houses all along it.

I said, "What about the apple trees?"

It didn't seem reasonable to me that Benny would sell the land and the trees both. I figured the trees were going to cost extra.

Tom said, "That's it. Benny hired these Mexicans to work in the orchard, and now they won't leave."

I said, "Where are they staying?"

He said, "The model house."

I thought that was pretty funny.

I said, "How did they get in the model home?"

Knowing Benny, the only way I could figure out was they crawled in the window when he wasn't looking.

Tom said, "He put them in. They just started building it. They already had up the frame and some of the wonderboard on the walls, and he told the Mexicans they could stay there till they got through picking the apples. He figured they could build around them, and the Mexicans could kind of look after the place, see nobody stole the building supplies. That way he'd kill two birds with one stone. Give them a place to stay and charge rent at the same time he got them to watch it for free. By the time they got to plumbing and wiring, Benny figured apple season'd be over, and the Mexicans'd be packed up and gone. But they wouldn't leave."

I said, "You mean they stayed?"

He said, "That's right. Legal Aid over in Dalton said they could do it. Benny can initiate proceedings, they said, but he can't evict them in less than three months."

I said, "How many are there?"

He said, "You can't hardly tell. It started off with five or six, but Benny says he doesn't know. They keep coming up from Texas."

I said, "They know how to talk?"

Tom said, "That's the problem. Benny talked to them, and I talked to them, and you can't get them to make any sense."

I said, "What's the lawyer say about it?"

Tom said, "You know. Civil rights. He said they don't own it. The lawyer said he explained that to them. They thought they bought it picking apples. Renting means owning. That's what they thought. They're all settled in. The contractor put in a brand-new stove before Benny could stop him, and you know what they use it for?"

I shrugged my shoulders.

"The children get in it."

I said, "What for?"

He said, "I don't know what for. We were standing there in the kitchen talking, me and Benny and Bobby"—he meant the sheriff,

Bobby Pace—"when all of sudden four or five children came in. The first children I saw in that house. They didn't even say a word. The oldest one went right to the stove like he was cooking dinner that evening. He opened the door to the oven, and the littlest one climbed in. Then the other one shut it, and they left. Benny said he thought they stored them in there."

I said, "What for?"

He said, "I don't know what for. How come they cook in the fireplace? Benny said they ruined it on him. He's going to have to tear it down and put a whole new facing on it."

I said, "Why doesn't he wait a few months and get them out legal?"

Tom said, "He doesn't have time, that's why. He's losing money paying interest every day they're in there. He got to sell it."

I said, "I can't do it, Tom. I'm too busy seeing Laurie. That husband of hers is a real asshole."

Tom said, "Yeah. So's his whole family. Benny likes them, though. I don't know why."

I said, "He's an asshole himself, that's why."

Tom said, "No. Benny's all right. You know that." He wasn't going to have me bad-mouthing Benny. "It's the Baptist Church. They're some kind of deacons. Go around building these houses."

I said, "What houses?"

He said, "I don't know. Jimmy Carter houses. They give them to people. The Baptist Church is big on that."

I said, "For free?"

He said, "Yeah. It's common knowledge."

It was news to me. The only thing ever I heard the Baptist Church being real big on were women and whiskey and dancing and playing cards. I didn't know they gave away houses.

185

Then it came to me.

I said, "That's it! Get them to give one to the Mexicans!"

Tom almost fell off the sofa, he was so surprised.

He said, "Son of a bitch! That's it! Let's go."

I said, "I don't like this, Tom. I don't like talking to Mexicans."

He said, "Don't worry about it. Look at it this way. You're doing them a favor."

16

We got over there, I was surprised. It was a fancy house with redwood siding and redwood decks and porches all over and a Tennessee rock foundation. It was real expensive. I couldn't have lived in a house like that, and neither could anybody I knew. I kept looking for signs of Mexicans, but Tom said they were inside. After they picked the apples last year, they holed up in there and wouldn't come out.

We went up on the porch and rang the bell. Nothing happened. I rang it again, but Tom said, "It doesn't work." So I beat on the door with the side of my fist. Tom said, "They might not hear you" at the same time an old woman opened the door and jabbered something and slammed it shut.

Tom said, "That's how they do. They've been doing like that."

I beat on the door again, but nothing happened.

Tom said, "You aren't going to get her now. They already know you're here."

I walked down the porch and looked in the window. I had to cup my hands to do it, the sun was so bright. It was like looking down a dark tunnel. At the other end was somebody's face looking at me. I didn't get a chance to see what it was, I jumped back so quick.

Tom laughed and said, "That's how they do. There's one at every window by now, front and back, looking out."

Just about that time the door opened, and one of them came out, a man about fifty or sixty years old. He was smiling this great big smile full of gold teeth and making motions for us to come in.

I said, "I thought you said they couldn't speak English."

Tom said, "They can't."

I said, "How come he heard me, then?"

Tom said, "He didn't. The old lady got him."

We went in, and the old man closed the door behind us. It was like being locked up in a cage with a bunch of wild animals. They came out of all the rooms at once, nosing and smelling and checking us out. I don't know how many there were. They kept coming and going.

I said, "What the hell are they doing?"

The old man was still standing there smiling and jabbering at the rest. The old lady that answered the door was the main one talking to him. The others were younger. One of the women was nursing a baby. She'd quit nursing, and it would start crying. There were a couple of men and large-size boys I kept my eye on. The children would come and stare a while. Then they'd start chasing each other or wander off and come back and suck their thumbs and stare some more. Every now and then one of the women would say something, but the old folks kept right on talking. They didn't pay a bit of attention, and the woman who said it would look at me and shrug her shoulders.

I looked around to see where I was, but I couldn't see much. Most of the furniture was building supplies—tables made out of sheets of plywood set up on concrete blocks. I could see they'd been cooking in the fireplace. That whole wall was black from the smoke. The mantel was scorched, and the floor was stained with food and grease.

Tom said, "Look. See all that crap?" He pointed at a bunch of pots and pans and tin cans and grocery sacks and buckets of water and piles of paper and garbage. "That's where they've been cooking.

"All right!" he shouted. "Gather around here and listen to me!"

Some of them looked at him. Some of them didn't. The ones that were talking kept right on talking. A couple of men walked out of the room.

"Go get them," Tom said and pointed at the door they went out. There was a woman right beside it. She pointed to herself and smiled.

"Not you," Tom said. "I mean them."

She was still smiling and nodding her head.

"Go get them," Tom said. "I got something I want them to hear."

I noticed he was talking louder. It was like driving in nails. Each word was separate. By the time he got finished with one and moved on to the next, you already forgot what he said. If I didn't already know what he wanted, I wouldn't have been able to understand him myself.

The woman just kept smiling at him. He turned to another, and she smiled and shrugged her shoulders. Pretty soon they were all standing there, smiling at us. The old man picked up a baby with its little peter sticking out. It didn't have on a diaper or anything, just a shirt. The old man held the baby out to Tom like he wanted to give it to him. The old man was grinning and nodding his head. Then he said something, and they all laughed. The baby was looking at Tom real serious. It was the only one that wasn't smiling.

"What the hell do they want?" Tom said.

I said, "They want you to take the baby."

He said, "What for? I don't want no goddamn baby."

I said, "Maybe he wants to give it to you. Looks like a pretty good baby to me."

The old man was still holding it out like a watermelon.

Tom said, "Shit."

The old man was still grinning at him, flashing his gold teeth, when the old woman went over to the fireplace and rooted around and got something and came back and gave it to me. It looked like a little dish of white Jell-O. That was in one hand. In the other was a red plastic spoon.

I said, "No, thank you. I'm not hungry. You might want to give it to him," meaning Tom.

She went over and gave it to Tom, and he took it and offered it to the baby. The baby grabbed it and was already eating it when the old woman screamed. But it was too late. The baby already ate most of it. The old lady grabbed what was left, and the baby started crying.

I said, "It must have been poisoned. She didn't mind you having it, but she didn't want that baby to eat it."

Tom said, "Who gives a shit?"

Then he turned to the rest of them and said, "Listen up. Anybody around here speak English?"

They just stood there and smiled like that was the best thing they heard all day. One or two of the men came back and leaned up against the wall with their arms folded across their chests, looking serious.

Tom made a kind of speech about how they were going to have to get out of the house right now. That house didn't belong to them.

It was private property. He had another house lined up the Baptist Church was going to give them for free.

They didn't understand a word he was saying.

I said, "Tom, they can't understand you."

He said, "To hell with that!" I could see he was getting excited. "They knew enough to work, didn't they? They knew enough to know how to pick apples."

I said, "That's nothing. All you got to do is point at a tree and give them a sack, they know what to do."

Tom said, "All right! Watch this!"

He went over and grabbed the old man by the arm and shoved him out the door. The old man started to come back in, and Tom shoved him out again.

"See that?" Tom yelled. "That's what I mean. *Get out!* That's what I've been trying to tell you."

That got them going. They started running around, acting excited. I could see they were all upset. Some of them came up to me and tried to say something. I told them they were going to have to talk English, but that didn't stop them. I looked over at the door, and the old man was still trying to push back in. Then all of a sudden he turned and ran off the porch.

I said, "Tom, where's he going?"

"Damn if I know. I think he went around the house."

Tom was halfway out the door looking to see where the old man went when the old lady came up behind him.

I said, "Tom, watch out!"

But it was too late. She already pushed him out the door and locked it behind him. I could hear Tom outside yelling something, but I couldn't make it out. I looked at the Mexicans, and they looked at me. I started to go open the door, and three of the men jumped me. All the women started screaming, and the children started running around, acting crazy. When Tom heard all the commotion, he began yelling louder, calling for me. I was yelling myself by then when all of a sudden the old man came running back in the room. He must have gone around the house and come in the back door. He said something to one of the men, and the man ran out. Then he said something else, and the ones who were holding me let me go. The old man came up and said something to me, and a couple of men grabbed me by the arms and took me upstairs and opened a window and pushed me out on the roof of the porch. Then they slammed the window shut. I could hear Tom under me, banging on the door and shouting, calling them Mexican sons of bitches and so on and so forth.

I went over to the edge of the porch and called Tom, but he couldn't hear me. He was shouting too loud. I waited for him to quiet down. Then I called again, and he said, "What? Where the hell are you?"

I said, "Up here. On the roof."

He said, "How the hell did you get up there?"

He walked down the steps so he could see me.

I said, "They put me out a window."

He said, "Go back in and open the door."

I said, "They won't let me. They got it locked."

He said, "Break the son of a bitch."

I said, "What with?"

He said, "Here," and threw me a piece of two-by-four.

I said, "Tom, there's going to be trouble."

He said, "There already is."

I went back to the window and looked in. There were a couple of men standing there. I showed them the two-by-four and shook it at them. They opened the window, and I stepped in it. I don't know if they understood me or not. Sometimes they seemed to know what you meant, and sometimes they didn't.

I went down the steps, and the women were all standing around crying and carrying on except for the old one. She and the old man and a couple of young men were talking together. I went to the door and opened it, and Tom came in and went right to the fireplace. The old lady saw what he was doing and started screaming. She ran over, and he'd pick up something, and she'd try to take it away from him, and he'd give it to her and pick up something else.

I said, "Tom, what are you doing?"

He didn't say anything. Then he picked up a quart can of lighter fluid they must have been using to start the fire.

I said, "Tom, put that back!"

But he wasn't listening. I might as well have been talking to the back of a train. He poured the lighter fluid on a pile of papers, and the Mexicans didn't even bother trying to stop him. They just started picking up things and carrying them out the door. Even the old lady. She was picking up pots and pans and stuffing them in paper sacks, and the old man would carry them out the door, or one of the children.

I said, "Tom, it's like burning a house to get rid of the roaches!"

But he already lit the match, and the papers blew up and exploded. The fire spread real fast. It was real strange at first, seeing the fire loose in the room. That was the most surprising part, seeing something as wild as that running around in the living room. It was like seeing a vision. The air was on fire. Pretty soon it would explode, and the whole world would disappear.

I couldn't keep my eyes off it. Neither could Tom.

Every now and then the old man would come up and say something to me. I could see there were tears in his eyes. I'd say to him, *"No comprende."* That's all the Mexican I had. Then he'd go over to Tom and do the same thing. The rest of them were running around like ants with the nest on fire, carrying off things. All of them except for the children. They'd creep up to the edge of the fire and stand there watching it with us. It was like standing at the edge of the ocean staring out, wondering what it meant.

Every now and then there'd be an explosion. Then it got too hot to stay. Most of the Mexicans were gone by then except for a couple of little ones standing behind me. I took them by the hand to lead them out when a woman came up and started yelling something at them.

The whole place was full of smoke. I went outside and looked for Tom, but I couldn't see him. I started to go back in the house, but the fire was too hot. I opened the door, and it was like hitting a wall. I couldn't have gone past the flames if I tried. I slammed the door shut again. There was nothing to do with the fire now except let it burn. I started looking for Tom again and found him halfway around the house.

I said, "Where have you been? The whole front of the house is gone."

He said, "So is the back. Look here."

He took me around to the back of the house and opened the door, and it was like opening a door to a furnace. The whole thing was full of fire. The flames had come out from inside the walls and burned right through them. It was like I could see for a minute out of this world into another. Everything in this one was gone.

Just about that time all the Mexicans came up at once, screaming and yelling, even the children.

Tom said, "What the hell's the matter?"

I said, "Well, Tom, you burned their house down. That got them upset."

Every now and then one of them would yell something at us and wave at the house, and Tom would say, "Yeah, I know." I never saw people so upset, especially the women. One of them tried to run in the house, and the others grabbed her to keep her from flinging herself in the flames.

I said, "Tom, we better go. These people are getting all upset."

By that time we were back around in front. There was nothing there but a pile of stuff the Mexicans hauled out of the house. Seeing it sitting out there in the sun, on the bare dirt, you wondered why anyone would go to the trouble of trying to save it. It was just a pile of trash. A few mattresses, old clothes, some bottles, pots and pans, grocery sacks full of groceries, hair combs and old shoes, a broken doll with a hole in its head, a bicycle without a seat and most of the spokes out of one wheel. That's all they had.

I said, "Tom, this is a bunch of shit. Look at that trash." I pointed at their pile of stuff. "That's pitiful, ain't it? That's all they got."

But he wasn't listening. He was looking at the fire. It was coming out the windows and creeping through the cracks in the siding like vines and tendrils growing up the sides of the wall. The outside of the house was hairy with fire.

The Mexicans were still running around, acting crazy. They'd look at us and rush at the house and stop and point. I didn't know what they were doing. I kept shrugging my shoulders and saying, *"No comprende."* Every now and then a woman would scream and run at the house and try to throw herself in the fire, and the others would catch her and drag her back. Just about then the old man came up and lifted both hands like he was holding a watermelon. He stood there and shook it up and down. Tears were running down his cheeks. Then he pointed at the house.

I said, "Good God, Tom! It's the baby!"

He said, "What baby?"

I said, "That one he was giving to you! It's inside the stove!"

Tom started running as soon as I said it. He was already inside the door before I was halfway up the steps. I hit the wall of fire and stopped. Tom had already gone on through. The fire was breathing in and out, opening and closing. After he got through, it closed after him. The whole door was full of fire. The frame and the walls around it were burning.

I remembered the kitchen was in back of the house, so I ran around there. The window was shut. It was about six feet high. I picked up a piece of scantling and beat at it till I knocked out the glass. Then I pulled myself up on the sill and looked in.

The room was so full of smoke I could hardly see at first. It was like trying to see through fog. The air was so thick, it was almost solid. Then it breathed, and the smoke drew back and lifted a little, and I could see Tom. He was laying on the floor. That whole side of the room was burning, and his clothes looked like they were on fire.

I started yelling something. I don't know what. I thought he was dead. I didn't know what I was doing till all of a sudden I got in the room and felt the fire and started breathing the smoke myself. The floor wasn't too bad. Most of the smoke was a little above it. I crawled on all fours till I got to Tom. By that time his clothes were still smoldering. His belt, his shoes, a few scraps of trousers around his waist. And the pockets. I remember thinking it didn't burn the pockets. They looked like pouches of skin hanging off him, he was so white except where he was burned, and that was all red and black.

I grabbed him by the arms and got him to the window. There were a bunch of Mexicans looking in. I figured they must have got something to stand on. I picked Tom up and gave him to them, and they pulled him out over the sill, and I turned around and looked for the stove. I couldn't see it standing up, so I got down on the floor again, and there it was along one wall ten or twelve feet away. The oven was closed, but at least the fire hadn't got to it. Of course, the baby still could have been cooked, especially with the oven closed. It must been two hundred degrees in there. Even when I got down on the floor and put my mouth against the tile, it still hurt to breathe. It was like poking a stick down my throat. I tried not to do it. I held my breath and got to the stove and opened the oven, and it was empty. I couldn't believe it. I even reached in and felt. It was so hot it burned my fingers. Then I turned around and left.

The Mexicans pulled me out of the window. They tried to catch me, but I slipped and fell and laid there gasping like a fish. I thought of Tom and looked around, but he wasn't there. They must have dragged him off somewhere. Then I looked at my clothes. I expected to see them burned off my body, but they were still on me. The only trouble I had was breathing. The Mexicans kept trying to tell me something, but I waved them off. I was too busy breathing. I finally figured they were trying to tell me about Tom, so I rolled over and tried to get up. One of them helped me, and the others kept holding their hands out and smiling. Every one of them had what looked like a watermelon they were trying to give me. Then the old man came up and held out the baby. It was just as serious as it ever was, looking at me like a little old man.

The Mexicans were all crowding around smiling and checking to see if I was all right. I didn't seem burned except for my fingers where I touched the oven. The only problem I had was breathing. It still hurt to do it. The most I could do was breath real shallow, and that seemed to help.

Then I got up and looked around and said, "Where's Tom?"— pointing at myself so they'd know what I meant. "The other *gringo*, where is he?"

They nodded their heads at that and looked happy. "Tom!" they kept saying. "Tom! Tom!"

They led me around to the front of the house, and they had him laying in the shade of a tree on one of the mattresses they saved from the fire. Somebody put a blanket on him. The old lady was sitting beside him praying with some beads in her hand.

I went over to check him out, and the old lady reached over and kissed my hand. I pulled it away as fast as I could, but she kept trying to grab it again, and I finally had to stand up.

I said, "Lay off, lady! Is he dead?"

The old lady looked at me like I just saved her whole family from death instead of burning down her house, and I felt real ashamed of myself. Just then a wall of the house gave way, and it settled down on one side like it was tired out all of a sudden.

I sat down beside Tom and pulled back the blanket. He was still breathing, but it was shallow like panting, and every now and then he shuddered all over. It was like an engine with bad sparks. It was real irregular and sounded like he might cut off any minute. I looked at his skin. It was worse than I thought. He was burned all over. What looked white inside the house was red in the light and blistered like sunburn. The red was like blood, and the rest was black like charred wood.

I covered him up and went for a doctor. The Mexicans saw me and started running after me, trying to get me to stay there with them. I don't know what they had in mind. I'd go a few steps and wave them off, and they'd try to pull me back. Finally they stopped. They stood in the road and looked at me, and the old man started waving, then the old woman, then the rest of them, one by one. They were all waving good-bye. The old lady ran up and grabbed my hand and kissed it again before I knew what she was doing. Then she stood there and waved.

I couldn't wait to get out of there. I didn't know what the hell they were doing. We just burned down their house, and they acted like I was Jesus Christ come back to save them. I turned around and looked, and they were still waving.

I got in the car and drove back down the mountain. The first thing I knew, I was honking the horn. It sounded like wailing. A whole other part of my life was dead.

The first house I got to, the people were already out in the driveway wondering what happened. They hadn't even seen the smoke. They were inside watching TV till they heard me coming. Then they ran out to see what it was. I told them to call an ambulance. There was a man dying up on Blood Mountain. One of them ran in the house and called the hospital, and I went back and stayed with Tom till the ambulance came. I didn't want to leave him alone with those Mexicans. They were all busy anyway packing up, throwing everything they had into a couple of old beat-up cars and tying the mattresses on top.

When the ambulance got there, I started to climb in the back with Tom, but the Mexicans all came running up, crowding in, smiling and jabbering. The old lady was still trying to hold my hand, and the old man took a patch of cloth from around his neck and gave it to me. It was tied on a greasy loop of string and looked like it had been scorched in the fire, it was so old and full of sweat and Mexican bear grease. The edges were lace, but they were all brown and curled. On one side was a picture of Jesus. The other had a heart with flames coming out of it. The old man put it around my neck, and they all started smiling, nodding their heads.

"Well," I said. *"Adiós, amigos,"* and climbed up in the back of the ambulance.

That got them to laughing and jabbering again, and I looked at them and almost started crying I was so mixed up thinking about Tom and those Mexicans both. If we could have talked, we might have been friends. I never met a bunch of people who seemed to like me so much. They thought I was some kind of hero, and I never did know if it was because I went in after Tom or because he went in after that baby.

A couple of kids were climbing around in the back of the ambulance, and their mothers were busy pulling them out when all of a sudden it started moving. The ambulance was parked on a slant, heading uphill, and the doors were still open. Tom was on one of those stretchers with wheels on the bottom. It wasn't chocked, and as soon as the ambulance started moving, the stretcher came rolling out the back. The Mexicans saw what was happening and ran up and caught it just about the same time the driver heard me yelling and stopped. He came around and pushed Tom back in. Then he slammed the door, and that's the last I saw of the Mexicans.

17

We got Tom to the hospital, and the doctors said they couldn't treat him there. He had to go to a special burn unit down in Marietta. I asked a neighbor to keep the dogs and went down there with him and stayed three weeks sleeping in chairs and doing what I could to help. The doctor said he might not die of the burns. They covered 30 percent of his body, but his heart was good, and that might pull him through. The real danger, he said, was infection. They gave him morphine to kill the pain, and after about ten or twelve hours of that, they let me in to see him, but he wouldn't talk.

He was like that a couple of days. Then they started in on the grafts. That went on a week or so, but the grafts wouldn't take, so they gave him more antibiotics, and he got better. His temperature fell, and he was almost normal except for the morphine. He was either sleeping or getting his grafts checked all day. Then at night after supper he watched TV or talked to me. The better he got, the more he talked, all about Kate and his days in the army.

The best time of all was the second week. He'd settled in a little by that time. The grafts were over, and he seemed to be at peace. It may have been the morphine, but he was real easy to be with. It was quiet in there, and he'd talk about this and that. There was no hurry and nothing to do but sit there and talk, and after a few days he covered it all—his whole life. He laid it all out there in that room, and what it came to was that he wished he could have been a radio announcer. That's one thing he figured he would have been good at. That or an engineer. He wished he'd had a chance to go to school and learn how to be an engineer. If he had, it might have been different. He talked about Kate and said he loved her more than his wife. He was ashamed of that, he said, but it was the truth. She was the finest woman he ever knew, bar none. That's how come he didn't want me marrying her. I told him she was wasted on me, and he agreed. He didn't deny it. He said she could have married the president of the United States if she wanted to. She was that perfect.

The only one who came to visit was Benny. He came in one day, I was laying on a vinyl couch in the waiting room, taking a nap. I wasn't able to sleep at night. The couch I was napping on was too little. The biggest one they had was a two-seater, and I could hardly fit. I slept there and in a chair sometimes. I was sleeping real good when Benny came in and hit me on the sole of the foot. I had my shoes off and didn't know what happened at first, I was so startled.

I looked up and Benny said, "How is he?"

I said, "All right, considering."

He said, "Well, at least it got rid of the Mexicans."

I said, "What happened to them?"

He said, "Packed up and gone. I don't know what the hell happened to them. That's the last Mexicans that'll work around here. It ain't worth it. We got our own folks to look after. Where is he?"

I took him to this closet they had with a bin full of masks and hospital gowns. We put them on and went in to see Tom, and I was real pleased we did. I never saw a happier man. It might have been the Holy Ghost descending on him in tongues of fire, the way Tom was acting. I never did see what he saw in Benny, or what Benny saw in him for that matter. But I wasn't from around there. They shared something in common the same way Tom and I did. They had things they remembered together.

"Take care of him," Benny said to me when he was leaving. "There aren't many left that remember the old days." He said, "Tom, you're a good old son of a bitch but a hell of a man to have working for you."

"Why's that?" Tom said. I could see his eyes jumping and sparking. It was almost worth being burned up in a fire to have Benny joking with him like that. He took it as a real compliment.

"Well," Benny said, "you burned up two houses. That makes you a dangerous man. Good thing I had insurance."

I said, "You had insurance?"

I hadn't even thought about that.

Benny said, "Of course I had insurance. You might say I specialize in insurance. I'm saying the Mexicans did it themselves, cooking in the fireplace. Anyone comes around asking about it, you tell them that."

That's how come he drove down, I figured. To get the story straight for insurance. We were out in the hall by then. Benny was leaving, and I said, "So nobody's going to prefer any charges."

I could see that with the insurance it wouldn't be in his best interest to do it.

"That's right," Benny said."Unless Tom dies. Then it's a whole different story."

I said, "Why's that?"

"That's going to escalate it," he said. "A man dies, they send out investigators. It ain't just the sheriff's word anymore. Or the fire chief's. It's the investigators'. And they're going to find out what did it."

I said, "What happens then?"

He said, "In that case, you leave. Get out, disappear. As soon as he dies, you keep on going. They won't even know where to look."

I said, "I might want to stay a while. I was thinking about settling here."

Benny smiled and said, "I know. But we don't always get what we want."

I was thinking of those Mexicans. I had more in common with them than I did with Benny. How come I was working for him? I thought about what Benny said, and it seemed to me that some folks always get what they want, and other folks hardly ever do. It didn't seem fair.

"It's in your best interest," Benny said.

I said, "You mean yours."

Benny said, "That's right. It's not my fault, of course. I didn't tell you to burn down that house. But I wouldn't want it creating suspicions. I'd want a conviction right away. Of course, I'm just talking now. This is pure speculation. Old Sarge might not die. He's a tough old bird. He ever tell you a dog chewed his ear off? That's what I mean. I'll see you, boy. You sleeping good? You don't look like you're sleeping too good to me."

I said, "I'm not. I worry too much."

"That's a failing," Benny said. "That's a sin against God Himself."
He put his arm around my shoulder. "He's looking after you, son.
This is a little old piss-ant place. There's nothing here. With Tom
gone, what's keeping you? You wouldn't even want to stay."

I said, "I might. I'd like a choice."

Benny said, "I would, too. But that's the problem. Insurance fore-
closes on choices around here." He put his hand on my shoulder and
squeezed. "You take care of old Sarge, you hear? See he don't get hurt."

Then he was gone.

A few days after Benny left, the fever came back. Tom rejected most
of the grafts, and the doctor said he was worried about him. So was
I. He could hardly talk. All he did was sit and stare at the TV.

Then one day we were watching *Days of Our Lives,* and the doctor stuck his head in and said he wanted to see me. Tom was so sick
he didn't even know the doctor was there.

I went out in the hall, and the doctor said he didn't think Tom
was going to make it. There was nothing he could do. He said he
was sorry.

I said, "I am, too."

I went back in the room and watched *Days of Our Lives* and
thought about my life and Tom's and how they were ending and
what sense they made. I tried to figure out why that was. What were
we supposed to do? I kept feeling there was something or else we
wouldn't have been thrown together. But I didn't know what it was.

I sat there with Tom and thought about all that. I thought about
how much he meant to me and how well I knew him. We were wo-

ven together like vines in a thicket. There was no way he could die without taking a part of me with him. I thought about him being dead and what that was like and if he was going to get to see Kate again or if he was just going to go to sleep and never wake up. Just go off in the dark of a dark night and not be anything anymore the same way he was before he was born. Something called Tom into existence and made him what he was, and I couldn't forget him as long as I lived. We were both inside one another in ways we couldn't even imagine. It was like a seed planted in me. It kept on growing.

I didn't know what I meant by all that, and I don't now. I was just grieving and trying to make sense out of the fact that I knew Tom was dying. I thought about dying as hard as I could, trying to figure it out, but I never could. It didn't make sense. When Tom was still healthy, before he was burned and the infection started taking his life, I used to wish I didn't know him. I ended up spending half my time looking out for him, seeing he wasn't forgetting something, and I was getting tired of that. But then when the doctor said he was dying, all I could think of was how much I loved him and how much I'd miss him when he was dead. Maybe that's one good thing about dying. All the human failings are gone. All the lies. All the corruption under the skin. The worm that eats at the heart is gone. And it's better that way. I actually told myself it was better.

I sat in that room and realized finally that I wouldn't have to remember him as he was. I'd just remember the good things about him. I mourned him, of course. But if the doctor said he was getting better, I could take him home tomorrow, I'd probably be sorry. The only reason I loved him so much is I knew he was dying.

Then I got to thinking about Kate. Maybe she was like that, too. Maybe the only reason I loved her is that she was gone. She was already dead. Maybe if she was still alive, I wouldn't even love her now. Why do people have to be dead before you know you loved them so much?

And what about Laurie? It seemed like I couldn't love her if I was still in love with Kate. It would be like losing her again, except forever. And I didn't want that. I didn't see how I could live without Kate—or Tom. They meant too much to me. They were too much a part of my life ever to lose them. I might as well cut out my heart or lose my eyes and walk in the darkness.

I kept thinking of something over and over. It didn't have words. It was more like just wanting Tom to be with me. Not like he was the last few years, but like he was when I first knew him. He was about the same age then as I am now, and I loved to be with him. We used to sit around and drink beer. Kate was alive, and he wasn't old, and we were all happy. I always wondered what that meant, but now I look back and think of those times, I know that was it. We were all happy. That's what I was praying for. For Tom to be thirty-eight years old again and Kate and me to be still married and all of us together on a Sunday afternoon, laughing and talking and having a good time just being together.

I kept saying, Give them back, Lord. It was like an ache in my body, a flame rising up from the tip of my mind like a tongue of fire. I said, Give them back, Lord. I'm nothing without them. What do you expect me to do with my life?

The feast was over, and I looked at my plate, and it was like garbage. I wasn't smart. I didn't know how to play the piano. I couldn't paint pictures. I didn't have a regular job. If I was a doctor, I could have done some good in the world. But God didn't give me the talent for that. The only thing He ever gave me were Kate and

Tom, and I finally figured that was it. They were like a gift from God, the only one I ever had. Sitting there in that dark room all day watching *Days of Our Lives*, I finally figured out who I was and what I was supposed to be doing here. And then God took it all away. He took Kate, and now He was taking Tom, and all I had left was this sickness in my heart, longing to see them again.

My whole life was like a disease full of longing and desire eating me up. It didn't make sense. It was just darkness. If God didn't put the desire in me, what was it there for? Where did it come from? What did it mean?

Every morning the doctor would come in, leaving a trail of something behind him. Inside the room, it smelled just like a hospital. The odor of piss and medicine, strong soap and disinfectant. But the doctor brought in something else, and I don't mean the aftershave he was wearing. I mean the smell of something far off, like rain in the distance. The smell of something different from death.

As soon as the doctor checked Tom out, the nurse came in and gave him a shot. It knocked him out in a couple of minutes, and I'd get up and go for a walk on the roof. They had a kind of garden out there. It was nothing but a few concrete planters full of flowers. The whole thing was squared off, and all the flowers were the same. There wasn't a tree or a bush in the place. But there were benches and pigeons looking for handouts, and there was the sky, and I could see the trees in the distance. It felt just like visiting another planet. I couldn't believe it was so bright and sunny. I thought about Lazarus. I knew just how he felt. I didn't ever want to go back in the dark. I just wanted to sit there all day and feed the pigeons pieces of breakfast.

* * *

The doctor said it was septicemia. That meant that bacteria got in Tom's blood and was sending infection all over his body. The doctor said it was like a shower of seeds. The infected burns seeded his blood, and his heart got infected, and that seeded the rest of his body. He was burning up. It was like a tree of fire burning inside him. Wherever the veins and arteries branched, the fire followed till his whole body was burning up. The doctor said his blood was on fire. Think of it that way. The case was desperate. They'd reached the point where the antibiotics were becoming toxic. I asked what that meant, and the doctor said, "Poison." The medicine was poisoning him. They had to back off and let the infection take its course or else the medicine was going to kill him. That's the kind of choices they had.

After a while Tom quit talking. He'd answer a question, but that was all. Then he quit doing that. It got where he wouldn't even watch TV. He just stared at the ceiling. Sitting there in the dark with the shades drawn, I didn't know if it was day or night or yesterday or twenty years ago. It was real peaceful. Tom looked at the ceiling like it was a movie, and I looked at him and wondered what he could have been thinking.

They say to look for a sign of election. You'll see on their face when Jesus appears. I kept thinking maybe that's what he was doing. Or maybe he was already on top of Mount Pisgah, waiting to cross over from Egypt into the Promised Land. No matter what his life was like, I'd say he was saved. The threads that tied him to life were loose, and the lion was laying down with the lamb.

Then one day he surprised me. It was around seven or eight o'clock in the evening. The sun was just going down. I had the door cracked a little to let in some light, and all of a sudden I saw Tom turn his head toward me. It was like on a pivot, it moved so slow. The light from the hall shone on his face, and his eyes were like mirrors, casting it back.

I said, "Tom, are you all right?"

He didn't answer.

I said, "What is it?"

He pointed at the door and said, "Who's that?"

I turned and looked. Nobody was there.

I said, "What do you mean?"

He said, "That man in the doorway."

I looked again, but I didn't see him.

He said, "Ask what he wants."

I said, "What's he look like?"

He said, "A colored man. In white clothes."

I said, "Hospital clothes?"

He nodded his head.

I said, "You mean an orderly? How long's he been there?"

He said, "All day."

I figured it must have been the morphine, so I said, "Hey, buddy. Why don't you come back a little later?"

Then I said, "How's that?"

He said, "You want to close the door?"

I said, "Okay."

I got up and closed it. The room was dark and Tom said, "Al! Al!" like he was excited.

I jumped up and turned on the light, and he was gone. I could see his mouth hanging open and his eyes fixed on the door. The spark of light, the fire God put in him, was gone. There was no life, no lasting life, unless he went to life everlasting.

I don't know what happened. I couldn't be certain. If it was an angel who came and got him that night, it could have been a sign of election. The white suffrage, like it says in the Bible. The seal on the forehead for those who are saved. Who knows? Tom saw it, I didn't. All I saw was an empty door. I got up and closed it, and he died in the dark just like Kate.

I might not have known exactly what happened, but I knew I'd never see him again. Not in this life. He was gone forever. Whatever Tom was and whatever he meant to me and Kate had disappeared from the face of the earth forever.

W e buried him at Doublehead Gap. The church is right on top of the Blue Ridge Divide. The waters on one side flow north into the Tennessee River and then into the Mississippi. On the other side of the Gap, they flow south into the Chattahoochee, straight down to the Gulf of Mexico. I knew where the waters went, but I didn't know where Tom had gone.

The preacher was the one who sold me the grave plot. He said he'd let me have it for thirty dollars. He said I could pay it out of the estate.

I said, "What's that?"

He said, "Sale of the trailer, such as that."

He already knew all about it. He even arranged to have the grave dug. I saw the backhoe skulking around behind the church. The driver was standing there with his hat off, waiting till we got through with the service to fill it back in. Benny sent flowers, and they took them out there and propped them up on a dirty green carpet that looked like grass. The flowers said, GONE BUT NOT FORGOTTEN.

The only ones there were me and Benny and some people I didn't know and Laurie. She went with me. And that was it except the men from the funeral home. The ones I didn't know were the pall-bearers. They all had big ears like Tom and red faces and blond hair like him and a nose with a crease in the middle just like he did. They were all different ages from twenty to fifty, and when they lined up on either side of the coffin, they looked like they might have been his sons, if he ever had any.

After the service, Benny took me aside and said, "They already started."

I said, "Started what?"

He said, "Checking that fire. You know what they found? They haven't been at it but a couple of days, and you know what they already found?"

I said, "What?"

He said, "One of those Mexicans. You know where they found him?"

I said, "No."

He said, "Right here in town. You know what he's doing? Working for me. And you know what else?"

I was tired of him asking me questions and answering them himself.

I said, "Listen, Benny. You got something to tell me or not?"

He said, "Yeah. I got this Mexican working for me, painting houses. The rest of them packed up and left, but this one stayed. He knows all about it, and not only that, he's ready to testify. He speaks pretty good English, enough to paint houses and testify."

I said, "What's he going to testify to?"

He said, "He might not. That's what I'm saying. There's no need to testify. That fire was set. That's a known fact. But they don't even know you were there, except for that Mexican."

I said, "I didn't set that fire."

Benny said, "I don't see that matters much. One, you're what they call an accomplice. And two, you already got a record. Who's going to believe you?"

I said, "That Mexican's illegal. He can't testify."

Benny said, "Not this one. He's got a green card. That's how come I hired him. I wouldn't have hired him if he was illegal."

I didn't know if he was lying or not.

I said, "Benny, how come you're doing this?"

He said, "Because I like you, boy. I don't want to see you go back to prison. I just want you to leave the county. No reason for you to stay. Old Sarge is dead, and you don't belong here."

I said, "Well, I'll think about it."

Benny said, "I wouldn't do that. There's no way here to make a living. This is a depressed economy. We got enough jobs for our people, but we don't need folks like you coming in, trying to steal what's rightfully theirs."

I said, "It's a free country."

He said, "Of course it is. But look at it this way. There's this old boy that lived here all his life, and his momma and daddy and cousins and uncles and all his kinfolks, they all live here and always have for as far back as anyone can remember, and he needs a job. He got a wife and family maybe, and he got to find some way to support them. And then there's you. You aren't from here. You're from somewhere else. The only one that knew you is dead. Killed himself in a fire he set. And not only that, you got a record. You're a bad risk. You know that. Nobody wants to hire ex-cons. So what about it? Which one are they going to pick if there's a job somewhere, which there ain't—you or him?"

I said, "All right. I'll think about it. I got some things to do."

"I understand that," Benny said. "A man got him some unfinished business, he just can't pick up and go. I know that. I'm a reasonable man. Just as long as we come to an understanding about it. That's all I want. A week or two. That ought to do it. A month, maybe. Take your time. I'm not trying to rush you."

I said, "Well, I'll think about it.'

18

After Tom died, I lived with Laurie, and it was a lot like being married to her. She wanted to know about my momma and daddy and where I was from and what schools I went to and the names of my teachers and all such as that. It's like she couldn't get enough. And then when she finally ran out of that, she started talking about what she wanted to do this year and the next and the year after that. She told me all her hopes and dreams, and I told her mine—what I had of them. Then if we ever got tired of that, we'd go into town.

Sometimes Laurie would get real restless, and we'd get in the car and drive all day, up to Ducktown and Copper Hill or down to Atlanta or over to Murphy or Dalton or Chattanooga, just looking around. We'd go in the malls and walk up and down and eat somewhere and get in the car and keep on going. It was a lot like killing time. I didn't know what she was wanting to do or how come she was feeling so restless.

One time we were going to Copper Hill. She liked to go up there, but I don't know why. It's an awful place. They mined a lot of copper up there, or used to. They closed it down now. What happened was, they smelted the ore and drove off the sulfur, and it mixed with the rain and turned into hydrochloric acid and burned the whole place up. Every tree, every bush, even every blade of grass. There was nothing there but dirt and rocks. It was worse than Arizona, parts of it, anyway, the ones that look like they were burned with a blowtorch. But at least there's cactus and mesquite. There's something growing in Arizona. But at Copper Hill there's nothing at all. The government's trying to reclaim it. The company was having to plant some trees. But that was just where the acid already leached out. In other parts it was still too strong, and that's where Laurie liked to go. She said she liked it lonely like that. It was mostly just rocks and dirt and broken glass and pieces of wood left from the mining.

We were messing around there one day, enjoying the scenery, when all of a sudden we went over a hill and came on a car down in a gully. It must have been sitting there fifty years. The paint was all stripped off by the weather, and it was rusted as red as dirt.

Laurie saw it and said, "Come on."

She ran down and got in the car and pretended she was driving.

I opened the door and got in with her. The upholstery was rotten, and the floorboard was rusted out. I could look down and see the dirt. I closed the door, and it was real hot. I tried rolling down a window, but it was stuck.

She said, "Where do you want to go?"

I said, "Nowhere."

She looked at me and said, "How come?"

I said, "I'm getting out." As soon as I did, I felt like I could breathe again. Laurie was still inside the car. I bent over and said, "You want to get out? It's too hot to stay in there."

But she was still driving. She had this fixed look on her face like she was going somewhere, somewhere far off in the distance. She might not have even known it herself, but that's what the whole thing was about. Sometimes we'd be making love, she'd get that same look on her face, and I could see how lonely she was. Laurie was going somewhere, driving that car. I didn't know where, and she didn't either, but she was still going, and she wasn't going to stop till she got there.

Other times we'd be driving around, she'd say, "Keep on going. Don't look back. We aren't ever going back." But she didn't mean it. We'd get to Murphy or Franklin or Chattanooga, and that was far enough for her. She'd come to the end of the rope she was tied to and say, "This is it. This is far enough. Turn back."

There was something bothering her. We'd go and turn around and come back. She wanted to leave. She wanted to stay. She couldn't seem to make up her mind one way or the other. It wasn't like that for me. I could have done what we were doing the rest of my life and not looked back and regretted a minute. But Laurie was always looking somewhere off in the distance without even knowing that's what she was doing or what she was going to do when she got there.

One night we were sitting on the sofa like that, side by side, watching TV. I had my hand on her thigh like you do, and Laurie was playing around with my fingers when all of a sudden it exploded.

Pieces of something were flying all over, and I started moving. I was already halfway out the door before I heard Laurie screaming. I turned back and grabbed her. Then it took out a piece of the wall. I fell over on her, and we rolled off the sofa down on the floor.

"Stay there," I said.

She looked at me, and her eyes were wide open, but she didn't see me. She was staring at something behind me.

I turned around and saw two lights. They looked like eyes. Inside the room it was still light, but out there on the other side of the wall where the hole led out, it was dark except for the eyes moving around.

Laurie was still screaming. I put my hand over her mouth, but she kept on trying to fling it off like she thought maybe I was trying to leash her. Her head was flailing around in my arms, and her hair was flying. I finally let go and started to crawl across the room, but she wouldn't let me. She grabbed my legs and held on.

I said, "Let go. I think they're going."

I could see the lights on the road. They flashed in the trees. It was kind of like blinking that might have been stuttering if it was a sound. Then it went around the curve and was gone.

Laurie was still screaming. It didn't seem like her. It seemed like something they threw in there with us running around, trying to get out.

I went back and held her, and after a while she got limp. I stroked her hair and whispered to her. I don't even know what I said. I wasn't thinking too good myself. I finally realized I could hear us breathing. It sounded real strange. I could feel her breath, her breath and my breath, coming and going inside my arms. That's when I knew we were alive.

I said, "You all right?"

It was like I just woke her up. She didn't know where she was at first. She said, "What was it?"

I said, "A shotgun. Somebody shot a hole in the wall."

She said, "What for?"

I said, "I don't know. Sorry-ass sons of bitches."

She nodded her head. Then she started trembling. Her hands were cold, and her lips were blue, and I tried wrapping her up in a blanket, but that didn't help, so I took her to the bathroom and turned on the water in the tub real hot and took off her clothes and put her in.

She laid back and closed her eyes. I sat on the seat of the toilet and held her hand, and she didn't say anything. She just kept breathing. That was good enough for me. I kept thinking about how they could have killed us.

After a while her hand was warm, and I said, "I'll be back."

She opened her eyes and said, "Don't go."

She started to climb out of the tub, but I pushed her back in.

I said, "I'm just going to see where they were."

She said, "They might still be there."

I said, "You saw them leave."

She said, "They could have killed us. They were trying to kill us."

I shook my head and said, "I don't think so."

She said, "How come?"

I said, "Because they'd have done it."

She didn't say anything. She just started crying. Her shoulders shook, and her arms looked loose, she was crying so hard. Her breasts were heaving.

I said, "It's all right. I'll be back in a minute. You want to get dressed?"

I touched the water. It was getting cold.

She shook her head, no. I went to the front door and turned on the floodlight. Then I went and checked out the yard. I don't know what I was looking for. There were no tire tracks because of the gravel. They must have parked beside my car. I picked up a couple of shotgun shells and started to go back in the house when I heard Laurie scream. Then I heard the phone ring. I ran in the bathroom. Laurie was standing up in the tub, trying to get out.

I said, "It's all right. You want a towel?"

The phone was still ringing.

I started to leave, but Laurie said, "Where are you going? Don't go."

I said, "I'll be back in a minute. I'm just going to answer it."

She said, "Don't do it! Leave it alone!"

I went out in the kitchen and picked up the phone.

A voice on the line said, "You get my message?

I saw a face come floating up and said, "Benny?"

He said, "That's right. You get my message? Quit screwing around. I told you there's going to be an investigation."

I said, "Screw the investigation. I already told you I can't leave. I got all Tom's stuff."

He said, "That's all taken care of. You don't have to worry about that."

Just then Laurie came out and said, "Who is it?"

I put my hand up to tell her to wait, and she sat down at the table beside me. It made me feel a whole lot better just having her with me. I reached out and touched her shoulder. Then I slid my hand down her arm. It seemed all right. It made me real happy.

Benny was still going on about me having a record and how much he liked me and how he was just looking after my own best interests and how that trailer belonged to Tom's sister and she was a poor widow near Chattanooga and I might think I had a claim on it but I was wrong about that. I might have a bank account with him, but he didn't deed me his property. That stayed in the family. Benny already looked into all that. There was nothing holding me there.

I finally cut in on him and said, "Listen, Benny. I'm tired of this shit. I already told you, I'm not leaving."

He didn't say anything for a minute. Then he yelled, "Get out! You and that goddamn whore of yours! I want you out! Not next week, not tomorrow, the day after tomorrow! I want you out now, you son of a bitch!"

Then he hung up.

I put the phone down.

Laurie said, "What is it? What did he say?"

I told her some. I didn't tell her the whole conversation.

She put her head down on the table and started moaning. I couldn't tell at first. It might have been crying. I couldn't console her. I just stayed there and patted her back till she quieted down. Then she looked at me and said, "They ain't ever going to give me my baby. Even if we go to court, they won't let me have her. I'm unfit."

I thought to myself, we're both unfit. Neither one of us fits in. I didn't tell her that, either. I just said, "I know how you feel."

She said, "Shit! You don't know how I feel! Nobody knows unless you're a mother and your husband left and all you got is a baby girl they took away from you! Then you know!"

I said, "I know."

She might not have believed it, but I'd been through all that before. Not the same way exactly, but it was close enough to know what she meant.

I said, "Well, it's getting late. The whole damn house is full of bugs. Pretty soon the bats'll be coming in. Let's go to bed. We can talk about all that in the morning."

Laurie said, "What did he say? He wants you to go?"

I said, "Yeah. He wants us *both* to go."

She said, "Don't leave me. Please don't leave me. I need you to help me."

I said, "I won't. I told him that."

She said, "I didn't hear you."

I said, "Well, I did. I told him we weren't leaving till you got your baby."

She said, "You told him that?"

She knew I didn't. She was right there beside me, listening to me.

I said, "Yeah. I told him that."

Later on we were laying in bed staring holes in the dark. Neither one of us could sleep. I could hear her tossing and turning.

I finally said, "Are you all right?"

She said, "Are they coming back?"

I said, "No. I don't think so. Benny's going to give us some time."

She said, "How do you know?"

I said, "I just know. That's how he is. Benny moves slow."

I didn't tell her he keeps on coming. That's what I should have said, but I didn't.

She said, "He might kill us."

I didn't say anything. I *knew* he might kill us. I had to start figuring out what to do. The only thing I knew for sure was that baby. She had to have it. I didn't want her spoiled on me, and she'd be spoiled without that baby. She was a wild, crazy woman. That's why I loved her. She was real bold. But that baby was different. She couldn't leave it any more than a ghost could the place that it haunted. I wanted Laurie, and she wanted that baby, and I was going to have to get it for her.

She put her arms around me and said, "You scared?"

I said, "Yeah. A little."

She said, "Well, they can't kill us."

I said, "Is that right?"

She said, "Yeah."

I didn't believe her.

I said, "Why's that?"

She said, "They don't have the balls. Say they kill us and we're dead—what have they got?"

I said, "Us. Benny don't care. He'd just as soon kill you or not if he has to."

She was smiling like she didn't believe me.

I said, "Listen. I know about Benny. I've been with men like that in prison."

She said, "Prison?"

I could see a little doubt creep in her eyes.

I said, "Lesson number one about Benny. He'll go at you real slow at first, trying to show how it's better for you and better for him and better for everybody concerned to do like he wants. Benny's a real politician. That's how politicians do. And not only that, it isn't just him. That's the most important thing about Benny. He isn't doing it just for himself. That's what makes him dangerous. He's doing it for the good of the people."

Laurie started laughing.

I said, "Don't laugh. It isn't funny. That's what he thinks. He wouldn't want to. Stealing and doing favors for folks and having them love him—that's what Benny's all about. He doesn't like setting fire to houses and killing folks in them. He doesn't like having to deal with that. Running folks off, that's all right. People like us blow in like pieces of trash on a fence and blow out again. We're real easy."

She was looking at me serious now, taking it in, and I figured she ought to. It was time she learned something about it.

"Riffraff," I said. "They don't mind us working for them, but they don't want us being a burden. You go on welfare?"

She shook her head, no.

I said, "How come?"

She said, "My husband was going to support me. Then they came and took my baby, and then I wasn't eligible. Dependent mothers— that's what it's for. Children and dependent mothers."

I said, "That's what I mean. Welfare's for them. Hard times. Good people, fall on hard times—that's what it's for. It isn't for whores and Mexican drifters and old hippies off in the woods living in tents, dealing dope. They got a nice place here, and Benny'll do whatever he got to keep it that way. I mean whatever. And they're going to back him. As long as he's doing it for them, he can do whatever he wants to."

She said, "I know all that," real snippy. "Don't tell me something I already know. What do you think I been doing out here, watching TV?"

I got out of bed. I figured she thought I was giving a sermon.

She said, "Where you going?"

I said, "Get me some breakfast."

She said, "I haven't finished talking yet."

I said, "I have."

I went in and took a piss, and she came in and put her arms around me. I just finished washing my face, and it was still wet, and she rubbed her cheek against mine and said, "You all right?"

I said, "Yeah, I'm all right."

She said, "What do you want for breakfast?"

I said, "What have you got?"

She laughed and said, "Sardines."

I said, "Sardines? I don't want sardines."

She said, "Of course not. Nobody wants sardines for breakfast except Mexicans, maybe, and they'll eat anything you got."

I said bullshit to that and went out and looked, and she was right. There was nothing there but five cans of Maine sardines—three in oil and two in mustard.

She said, "What'll you have, oil or mustard?"

I said, "Both. You got any crackers? How about some coffee?"

We made instant coffee and sat down and started eating. She had cracker crumbs on her tits—it looked like dandruff—and a spot of oil where it fell off a sardine.

I said, "I wouldn't eat naked if I were you."

She said, "How come?"

I said, "It might spoil my tits."

That got her to laughing. She kept on saying, "Spoil my tits," like that was the best thing she ever heard. But I meant it. That's one thing I'd never do, sit at the table like that and eat naked.

We ate up all five cans of sardines and a good part of a box of saltine crackers. Then she reared back and put her tits on the table and said, "You want some?"

I said, "Sure."

That landed us back in bed. After we finished making love, we laid there, holding each other. Then I heard her breath slow down, and I knew she was sleeping. It was just like holding a child, she seemed so young and innocent, sleeping. It was almost like she never grew up, never had a husband and child. She was still just dreaming about it. I kept turning my head to look at her. It was like a mystery. I was holding her in my arms, but I knew that no matter how much I loved her, I'd never know what she was thinking. It was like another world—like standing on the edge of the ocean and seeing the thin line of blue off in the distance where the sea and the sky come together and not being able to see the great schools of fish and the giant whales gliding around under the surface. Every now and then she'd twitch, and her whole body would shudder. She'd lay there awhile. Then she'd say something, a word or something. One time her lips started to move. She was saying whole sentences without making a sound. I tried reading her lips, but the only thing I made out was, *Gone.* She kept saying, *Gone . . . gone . . . gone.* Then it was like a curtain came down. She went underwater again. The surface was smooth except for the little swirls on top where the words were forming.

My arm was asleep, and I eased it out from under her. She said something like *Freaky, freaky.* It sounded like the cry of a bird off in the woods. Then she rolled over on her side, and I could see the soft white, almost invisible hair swirling around the small of her back.

I thought about Kate. I told myself I didn't love her because she was dead, and I had this other woman now who seemed to love me, and it looked like we could make a life together. Not the kind of life I had with Kate. But a *kind* of life. All I had to do was get around a few things like not loving Kate anymore and not being true to her like I promised.

The first night Kate died, I kissed her lips, and they were cold. I took her hand and held it, but her fingers were stiff. They wouldn't curl. I kept thinking about what they looked like before and how many times I used to watch her doing things with them. She was the most precious thing in the world, but I couldn't talk to her. She couldn't hear me. So I prayed to God, and that's when I promised.

I told God if He answered my prayer, I'd never forget her. I'd wait all my life if He'd just give her back. I took a solemn vow to be faithful to her the rest of my life if we could be together again.

And I kept that promise all those years. The rest of it would come and go—jobs, cities, people I knew and people I didn't. The only thing that didn't change was that promise that I was going to wait till Kate and I were together again.

And then I gave up. I went back on my promise. I still loved Kate, but I couldn't remember. I don't mean the big things. I could remember all that just like it was yesterday. What I couldn't remember were little things like the way she smelled and how her skin felt in my hand and how she laughed and talked about things. I still loved Kate. I knew I traded her in for a whore. I knew I betrayed her. I was with another woman. Every time I slept with Laurie, it made me feel guilty. Then after a while I didn't care. I couldn't quit. I figured I'd probably just have to lose her. Laurie was too much to resist.

I looked at her laying naked beside me and thought about how beautiful she was and how all I had to do was reach out and touch her, and she'd turn over and open her eyes and be right there with me, and it made me kind of sick at heart, thinking about it.

I felt her stir and looked over at her. She had her eyes open looking at me.

She said, "You okay?"

I said, "Yeah. You sleep good?"

She closed her eyes and nodded her head, and I couldn't keep my eyes off her. The room was still full of early morning light. It was pouring in through the window. The sheets were so bright, they were like water. The sunlight hit them and bounced off on the walls like reflections.

I rolled over on my back and closed my eyes. I didn't want to think about how beautiful it was.

19

The next few days I fixed up the trailer with sheet metal screws and roofing tin and replaced the window with glass from the hardware store. The TV was gone, and I didn't want to get a new one, so I went into town and rented one from Curtis Mathis. I figured two weeks. I'd know what to do inside of two weeks. Then I went by the bank and closed the account I had with Tom. The girl at the counter didn't want to give it to me in cash. She said she didn't have that much in her drawer, and besides, it wasn't safe. I told her I didn't care what she had in her drawers, I wanted my money. That got her real huffy. She called the manager, and the manager went back and got me the money. I told him I wanted it in hundred dollar bills. I didn't want too big a stack. Then I went back to Laurie's and hid it in the light fixture. I figured it was safer there than in the bank where Benny might try to get at it. It was Tom's life savings. Laurie and I could live on it a year or two if we had to.

The first week or so, it was real quiet. Nobody called. Nobody tried to wreck the car or set us on fire. The sheriff didn't come out

and try to evict us. Then one day I decided it was time. I still had a
lot of stuff at Tom's. He died without making a will, and Benny had
it tied up in court. He found that sister of Tom's in Ringgold—full
or half sister, I don't know which—and he was fixing to run it
through probate and give it to her.

There were some pictures I wanted to get at Tom's and things of
his to remember him by, and then we could go.

Laurie and I were just sitting there drinking coffee like you do,
watching the *Today* show on TV, when I got up and turned it off.

Laurie said, "What's the matter?"

I said, "You don't want to hear that shit."

It was some rock star in his underwear and a red bandanna
around his neck and a rag tied around his head like a bandage and
a two-day growth of beard.

I said, "I've seen better than that in jail."

She said, "Turn it back on!"

I said, "It's just a bunch of shit," and turned it back on.

Laurie said, "Hush up! I'm listening to it."

The rock star said he loved a man, and he loved a woman, and if
there was something else in between, he'd love it, too. He said love
is all there is. It doesn't matter who gives it to you, be grateful. It got
him off drugs. The only way he quit was love.

He went on like that for a while, and Laurie sat there and listened. I'd try to say something, and she'd wave her hand and tell me
to hush.

After the rock star got through, they had a commercial, and I
said, "What's that all about?"

She said, "Love. I wanted to hear it."

I said, "Shit. You call that love?"

She said, "Yeah. Look what happened. He couldn't even get out of bed."

I said, "Damn right. I heard that. Men *and* women."

She said, "No. I mean before that. When he was on drugs. He almost died. Love was the only thing he had. Love was what saved him. He'd be dead now if it wasn't for that."

I said, "I don't call that love."

We went on like that for a while, arguing back and forth. She said I was prejudiced. I told her I reckoned I was. She said in that case I ought to shut up about it.

I could see we weren't getting anywhere with that, so I told her I was going over to Tom's.

She said, "All right. I'll come with you."

I said, "No, you stay here. I want to get some pictures and stuff."

She nodded her head like she knew what I meant. I told her it might take a couple of hours, but she said she'd be all right. She had a new Harlequin romance. She'd read that and watch TV.

I said, "Don't get yourself too excited, reading all that sexy stuff."

She said it wasn't sexy exactly, but it was kind of interesting. It opened the pores.

"About like a soap opera," she said. "Some of them open the pores."

I went to the door and looked back. She was sitting there on the sofa drinking a can of Coca-Cola and waiting for the news to get over.

I got to Tom's and turned in the driveway. The grass in the middle had grown up and scraped the underside of the car. It sounded like

I was driving through water. The blackberry bushes snatched at the windows, and I had to roll them up to keep from getting torn to pieces. Wherever there was a sunny place, the blackberries were real thick. I got in the woods, they thinned out, and the road was wider. I turned the last bend and came out of the woods into the clearing.

The first thing I saw was the front door hanging open lopsided on one hinge. Somebody had taken a wrecking bar to it. I pushed it aside and went in. The pillows from the sofa were ripped and torn open and thrown on the floor. The stuffing was all over the place. There was food everywhere. Oatmeal and flour and Rice Krispies and saltine crackers and rotten apples and broken eggs and catsup and mustard. Somebody wrote *shit* with a mustard squirter on top of the table and made a mark that looked like an M on top of a W. I figured that must have been his initials. The floor was almost a foot deep in places in paper and garbage and broken glass. Everything put up in the cabinets or drawers or under the bed or in the closet was thrown out on the floor. The whole place was a wreck. It looked like a tornado or a hurricane had gone through it from room to room. I searched for the TV, and it was gone. The recliners were gone, the mattresses, most of my clothes and Tom's, and everything in the medicine cabinet. I started to call Laurie to tell her about it, and even the telephone was gone.

I walked around from room to room, looking at it. I wasn't surprised. I don't know why. I wasn't upset. I wasn't much of anything. Tom was gone, and it didn't matter. It was just junk anyway. I walked across it, and it kept crunching—broken glass or Rice Krispies. That's what I remember the most, walking across it and hearing it crunch.

I went outside and sat on the steps. I looked at Tom's car, and the hood was up. I went over expecting to see the engine gone, but it was still there. Most of it. The wires and plugs and air filter were pulled out, and there was a stick crammed in the grill straight through the radiator.

I went over to the shed where Tom kept his tools and gasoline, and that was all right. They hadn't messed around in there. I went back to the house and sat down on the steps again, thinking about how we get all this stuff and then we die, and the things we love—the chair we sit in and the food we eat and the bed we sleep in and the pillows that still carry the shape of our heads—all that's still there. But what good is it? I kept thinking of generation after generation coming in like waves on the shore, each one leaving a line on the sand full of seaweed and broken shells and dead fish and rotten oranges and wood and garbage and broken glass.

The dogs were still down at the neighbor's. You wouldn't think it looking at them, but they were real valuable dogs. The man that had them liked to hunt. I figured I'd call and give them to him. He'd be happy to have them. He already tried to buy them off Tom two or three times.

I finally got up and went back in the house. I lifted up all the clothes on the floor and kicked at the blankets and opened the drawers and looked on the top shelves of the closet and under the bed, and the only thing I found was a picture of Kate when she was just a little girl. It looked like a school picture Tom might have kept in his wallet. That's the only thing of value I found except for one picture of Tom. He was wearing a suit and holding a baby. It must have been Kate, but you couldn't tell. Tom's wife was with him. She was about the same age in the picture as Kate was when she died. I was surprised to see her looking so young. Her life had gone sour when I knew her, and it showed on her face. But in this picture she was still a girl. Nothing had happened to her by then. She had a husband in a felt hat. She had a baby her husband was holding. She had a new dress and high-heel shoes and somebody to take their picture together. You could see the shadow falling on them like the shadow of time and death. I ripped the picture in two and kept Tom and the baby and threw the other part away.

The only other thing of value I found was Tom's old shotgun. It was a single-barrel Stevens, hidden on the top shelf of the closet. Tom had a lot of guns in his life, but that was the one he loved the best. He kept it in an old pillow slip that smelled of grease. I opened it up, and the gun looked brand-new. The bluing still had fire in it, there were so many different colors. The stock was made out of walnut, and it was so old and had been oiled so many times it was almost black. The hammer and trigger guard were trimmed out in silver, and there was engraving on the side—a wreath of flowers and Tom's name and the date when he got it. There was also a box of shotgun shells. The Stevens was twelve gauge, and the shells were all buckshot. There were about ten or twelve of them left. I didn't know how old they were or if they'd even fire or not.

I put it all back in the pillow slip and got a towel from the floor in the hall. It just had some toothpaste on it. I wiped that off with a pair of trousers and wrapped the pillow slip inside that so it wouldn't get me greasy. I had the pictures I found in my pocket. I looked around for a clean piece of paper. I couldn't find one, so I tore off a piece of grocery sack and wrapped the pictures up in that and put them in my shirt pocket.

I was already in the car fixing to leave when I thought about the gasoline in the shed. I sat there a minute thinking maybe I'd burn down the trailer. Then I went on. I had gone back to say good-bye, but Tom wasn't there. Nothing was there. There wasn't anything to remember him by except a couple of pictures that didn't even look like him and a gun he bought when he was a boy and loved all his life because it reminded him of a time before he joined the army and started getting drunk and living rough, losing his wife along the way and even his daughter. Tom loved Kate as much as I did, but he didn't know her. She was everything he wasn't. That's what he loved. Tom said a man can have a daughter, and they're sweeter and gentler and kinder and softer and what you might have been yourself if you weren't what you already were and had to be since you were a man. It was like the shadow in that picture of her as a baby. He loved the shadow. It wasn't Kate. He came cranking in on it himself with the sun at his back casting him forward across the lawn, the top of his head touching the tip of her shoes.

I thought about how I wasted my life. If Kate hadn't died, we might have lived together a while and drifted apart. I couldn't tell. The fact that she died is what gave her to me. If she was alive, I might not have had her. I might have been a drunk anyway and drove her off just like her daddy. She was living in me like a poisoned white mushroom growing inside the dark of a cave. I needed her so much, I just made her up. It was like a vampire or something. They look real. They feel real. They talk like a person and act like a person, but they aren't real. Put them up in front of a mirror, there's nothing there. All you see in it is yourself.

I wanted Laurie. That's all I thought about driving back home. How much I wanted to reach out and touch her. If I had her, I'd have something real, I'd have a real life. I kept saying that over and over. I could hardly wait to tell her about it.

It was like being wrong all your life and all of a sudden getting the answer. I felt like a man coming back from the doctor after just being told he had six months to live. I knew what to do. I had it all figured out. I knew just what I wanted.

I knew exactly what it was.

The next morning I got on a chair and started taking down the light in the kitchen. Laurie was still laying in bed. She heard me rattling around out there and said, "What are you doing? Come here a minute."

I told her I was getting my money.

She said, "What money?"

I went in the bedroom and showed her the money. She wanted to know how much it was. I told her how much, and she couldn't believe it.

She said, "That's almost a whole year's pay!"

I said, "That's right. It's Tom's life savings plus a little we'd been adding to lately."

She said, "What are you getting it now for?"

I told her it was time to go. We were getting out of there.

She said, "When?"

I said, "Right now."

She said, "What about my baby?"

I told her we were getting her baby. *Then* we were going.

She said, "Where?"

I said, "This place I know. Tuba City."

She laughed and said, "Tuba City! Where's that?"

I said, "Arizona. They won't think of looking out there. They don't care, anyway. The only one that cares is Benny."

"And that other son of a bitch," she said, meaning her husband.

I said, "That's right. And his momma and daddy when we go out and get that baby. They'll make up a warrant and put out an all-points alert. But we won't be here. We'll be gone. Sell that car and get another and drive on out to Tuba City and start a whole new life out West. You're going to love it."

She said, "I am?"

I could see she didn't believe it.

I said, "That's right. You know where it's at?"

She said, "How would I know?"—real disgusted.

I said, "The Painted Desert."

She said, "The Painted Desert!" That got her real tickled again. She started laughing and said, "What's that?"

I said, "This desert. Got rocks in it look like they're painted."

She said, "Painted with what?"

I said, "Painted with paint. They're all different colors."

She said, "Is it pretty?"

"It's beautiful," I said. "The sun gets on it, it's the prettiest thing in the world. There isn't a blade of grass in the place. Just rocks. Whole hillsides and landscapes of rock with the sun shining on it, bringing all the colors out. There are so many colors you can't even count them."

I told her how I used to get drunk and go out and watch the sun set on the desert. All that time Kate was dead and I couldn't figure out what to do with myself, that was the only peace I had, getting drunk and going out and watching the sun set the rocks of the Painted Desert on fire and seeing the shadows creep across the face of the earth. I told her about that and the Petrified Forest.

"It's like a land of dreams," I said.

I couldn't tell her what I meant.

I said, "You just got to see it. You just got to see it before you believe it."

She said, "I already saw it. In the movies."

She meant the Westerns.

I said, "No. It isn't like that. You know it's real, or else you couldn't be walking around in it. But it's like a dream. It's like you're making the whole thing up."

She said, "Maybe you are."

I could see she didn't believe me.

I said, "No. We're really going."

She said, "When?"—still looking funny.

"As soon as you get out of bed."

She said, "In a minute. Come here." She rolled over, and I got in bed, and she scrunched up in my arms. That's how she did. She believed in getting real close. She'd talk to me, and I'd have to back off to see her. I couldn't even focus my eyes. We'd get in the car, I couldn't even shift the gears with her sitting on me. But I didn't mind it. I wasn't used to it exactly, but I got where I liked it. I got to where I loved it, in fact.

I was just about to fall asleep when I felt her stir like something inside me, shifting around.

She said, "All right! We're going to do it, come on, let's go do it!"

She jumped up and grabbed my hand and pulled me sideways out of bed. She hugged me real tight and got up on tiptoes and whispered, "I'm getting my baby, and then I'm going. I ain't ever coming back." Then she put her tongue in my ear—I could hardly breathe for a minute—and said, "Come on, I'm ready"—the way she did when we made love.

I said, "You don't look ready to me. Go get your clothes."

She started to go, then stopped and came back and grabbed me again and held on real tight.

I said, "What's the matter?"

She said, "What if they stop us?"

I said, "Who?"

She said, "The sheriff."

I said, "The sheriff's not out there. Who's out there?"

She said, "Nobody. His momma and daddy."

I said, "Well, then. We'll just go out and pick up the baby."

She said, "Then what?"

I said, "Keep on going to Tuba City."

I kept thinking about how empty it was. You could do anything you wanted to out there.

She said, "I wish I didn't grow up where I did and do all that stuff."

I said, "What stuff?"

She said, "All that stuff I told you about."

She didn't tell me.

She said, "You're the only one I ever loved. You know that?"

I didn't believe her, but it didn't matter. It wasn't her nature to love me like Kate.

She said, "You believe me?"

I said, "Sure."

She said, "It's the truth. I never loved anybody but you. I might have been with them, but I never loved them. I dreamed about you all my life."

I didn't know what to make of that, and neither did Laurie, most probably. She'd get going on about something, and there weren't any edges. It all ran together. She'd say whatever popped in her head because it seemed like the truth. Loving Laurie was like loving a river.

She wasn't the same from day to day. There was no real, abiding truth in her the same way there was in Kate. But she wasn't boring, I'll say that for her. The only way to get tired of Laurie was to get tired of being alive. She changed about as much as the weather, but that was all right with me. I didn't want her to stay the same. I loved her to tell me things like that and think in her heart she was telling the truth because who knows?—maybe she was.

20

There wasn't a whole lot to do to get ready. I took my clothes out to the car and threw them in the backseat. Laurie took the clothes for the baby and the shotgun and the box of shells and threw them in. And that's how we left. Laurie wouldn't even go back in the trailer, not even when I told her to get some toys.

She said the toys were ruined. She threw them all out in the yard after the sheriff came for the baby. I asked her how come she wanted to do that, and she said she didn't know. Something came over her. I told her she was crazy to do that, and she said she knew it. She was just mad.

We were about halfway there when all of a sudden she said, "O my God!"

I said, "What's the matter?"

She said, "You reckon she'll know who I am?"

I said, "Who?"

She said, "My baby."

I said, "Of course. You're the mother. A baby knows its own mother."

She started crying and said, "What if she doesn't?"

I said, "How long's it been?"

She said, "Two hundred and twenty days."

I said, "How long is that?"

She didn't answer. I had to figure it out myself.

I said, "Seven months. That's more than seven months. You haven't seen your baby in seven months?"

She said, "I saw her, but I didn't hold her. They wouldn't let me."

I said, "Well, as long as you saw her, she knows who you are. They don't forget."

She was still crying, and I couldn't stand it. I tried to console her.

I said, "How old's this baby, anyway? What are we talking about?"

She said, "A year and a half. A little more."

I said, "Well, then. That baby won't forget you in that time. A baby don't forget in a year."

She said, "You sure?"

I said, "Damn right."

I didn't know what I was talking about, of course, but I didn't want to tell her that. Then I thought about the clothes.

I said, "You sure those clothes'll fit?"

She said, "O my God!" and started crying. It was like losing the baby all over again, realizing the clothes she had wouldn't fit.

I kept telling her it didn't matter.

"Seven months," I said. "That's nothing. What's seven months?"

But she didn't listen. She stared out the window and chewed on her knuckles and cried a while. Then she said, "Half her life. Seven months is half her life."

I said, "So what? Look at it this way. In twenty-five years, seven months won't matter a bit"—and so on and so forth, trying to make her feel better about it. I knew what it was to lose the only thing you ever loved, but nothing I said seemed to help. I kept on talking anyway till all of a sudden she said, "Turn here," and pointed left at a gravel road that went up a little hill through some pines. We went down that road six or eight miles till Laurie told me to turn again, and we went down a road that opened up into a pasture. The house was on the far side of that, and the road went straight to it. There were fences on either side of the road with weeds grown up in them and cows scattered around, eating the weeds. They lifted their heads and looked at us passing. Their eyes were as big as dinner plates.

I said, "Those cows are real interested, aren't they? You reckon they ever saw anybody?"

She said, "What do you mean?"

I said, "Look at them looking."

There were a couple lined up on her side of the road, and I pulled over to let her get a good look at them. One of them tried to stick its head in the window. It had a mouth full of weeds it was chewing, and that got her to laughing.

I said, "Cows are all right."

She said, "Yeah. I love cows, don't you?"

I said, "Yeah."

And I did at the time. I don't usually, but it broke the spell. Laurie quit crying, and I was grateful for that.

After we looked a while, I said, "How about it? You seen enough?"

The cow was still staring in the window like it couldn't get enough. It acted like it knew who she was, the way it was looking.

She said, "I reckon. I hate to leave it."

I said, "I don't blame you for that. I wouldn't want to leave it either if it was admiring me like that. You sure it ain't a bull?"

She said, "Not with that titty."

I put it in gear and said, "That's funny."

She said, "What?"

I said, "One titty."

She said, "I don't know. It all depends."

I said, "On what?"

She laughed and said, "On if you're a cow."

By that time we were about at the house. There was a gravel parking lot half as big as a football field. It had big old white oaks scattered around it, casting their shadows. I pulled up beside a truck and cut off the engine and sat there a minute. It was real peaceful. It looked like it might have been underwater, it was so shady.

I said, "This is nice, isn't it?"

She said, "Yeah. There she is."

I looked at the house. There was a big boxwood fence between it and where we were sitting. The house was old. It was two stories high, painted white with a tin roof and a porch that ran across the front and down one side. It was a real substantial old place, which was unusual for that part of the country.

Laurie said, "See her? Look over there."

I could see an old woman sitting on the front part of the porch and an old man sitting off by himself on the side. Neither one of them acted like they knew we were there. They didn't get up or wave at us. They just sat there.

Laurie said, "That's her. Come on."

I said, "No. Wait a minute. Let me talk to her."

She said, "What for? You got a plan?"

I said, "Yeah."

I figured they knew who Laurie was, and as soon as they saw her, that old lady was going to start yelling, and that would set the old man off, and he'd run in the house and get a gun and I don't know what all. But they didn't know me. I could go up there and get them to talking, and before they knew it, I'd grab the baby and get out of there before they even knew what happened. That was my plan.

I said, "Let me handle this, all right?"

Laurie said, "All right, but you better hurry."

That didn't make much sense to me, but I got out of the car and went through the gate in the boxwood hedge. It was like going through a wall. I just about made it to the porch when the old lady said something, but I couldn't make it out. I kept on going, and she said it again. I was close enough by then to see that she was shelling beans. They looked to be speckled runners to me.

I said, "What are you doing there, lady?"

I figured I'd let her know I was friendly.

I said, "Looks like speckled runners to me."

She said something else. I still couldn't make it out, and that kind of upset me. I was close enough by then to know what it was—if it was words.

But it wasn't words.

I was climbing the steps by then and said, "That's all right, lady. You're all right"—the way you do when you're calming a dog. "I'm not going to hurt you."

She set the pot of beans on the floor and stood up just about the same time the old man came around the side of the porch and said, "What the hell's going on around here?"

I said, "Damn if I know."

The old woman went and grabbed his arm and pointed at me. He said, "I see him." Then he said to me, "What do you want?"

I said, "What's the matter with her?"

He said, "She had a stroke. She can't talk."

I thought a minute and said, "You got a Bible?"

That's all I could think of.

He said, "What?"

I said, "A Bible."

He said, "Of course. You selling Bibles?"

I said, "No, sir. I'm a Jehovah Witness. . . ."

And that's about as far as I got.

I thought at first it was the old woman. She had her mouth open and looked like she was saying, "O my God! O my baby!"

I turned around and looked at the old man. I thought for a minute maybe he'd know, but he just looked at me and said, "What's that?"

I said, "Damn if I know."

I was just about to say something else when all of a sudden the old woman started across the porch. The screen door exploded. It hit the wall of the house and bounced back, and Laurie was halfway across the porch struggling with the old lady, trying to keep her from grabbing the baby.

She saw me standing there gaping at them and said, "Do something!"

I said, "What?"

She said, "Hit her!"

I said, "Hit her?"

That kind of caught me by surprise. I never hit a woman before. The old man touched my arm and said, "Don't hit her."

I said, "I won't."

I just thought maybe I'd hold her a minute when all of a sudden Laurie got loose and said, "Come on!" and ran down the steps.

I turned and followed as fast as I could. I was already off the porch, going through the gate in the boxwood, when I looked back and saw the old lady standing at the top of the steps like she was frozen. She had both arms stiff at her side, and her mouth was open like she was yelling, but there was no sound coming out. Then she started leaning and fell headfirst down the steps just like a board. I started running as soon as I saw her start to go. I thought maybe I'd be able to catch her, but she was already laying at the bottom of the steps like a heap of old clothes. Her dress was pulled up around her waist. She had on brown stockings that came up to her knees and a pair of white panties. Her legs were white and chunky-looking. I started to pull down her dress when the old man said, "Leave her alone!"

I looked up and saw him grab a post to steady himself and start to come down the steps. Then he stopped and said, "You son of a bitch!"

I said, "What?"

He said, "Stay there. I'm calling the sheriff."

He turned and went back on the porch. I could hear him stomping around up there, so I yelled, "Call an ambulance!"

Just about that time Laurie came running up. I was still trying to see about the old lady when I heard the baby screaming. That's how I knew it was her.

I looked up and Laurie said, "Come on! Let's go! We got to go!"

The old lady's face was turned toward me. She had her eyes open, one of them, anyway. It didn't have any life in it. It was just staring. Her mouth was open, and she was drooling on the gravel. I could see a little patch of saliva underneath her lips. Her teeth had come loose, and they were more or less outside her mouth. I thought her jaw was broken at first. I looked for her glasses, but I couldn't find them. They were probably up under her somewhere.

"Leave her alone," Laurie said.

I looked up. The baby was like an octopus on her.

I said, "I can't. She might be dead."

Laurie didn't say a word. She just turned and started running. She looked knock-kneed, running and trying to hold the baby.

I figured I couldn't leave the old lady. I had to see if she was still breathing. I put my hand flat on her back, but it was like trying to feel a feather move in a breeze or a bird heart beating in its breast. I tried breathing for her. I turned her over and held her nose, and it was like going down in a cave. Her whole body was full of darkness. Then I heard the screen door bang, and the old man came stomping across the porch.

I quit working on the old lady. I looked up and said, "I don't know if she's dead or not."

He said, "You goddamn son of a bitch!" and lifted the gun.

I saw the barrel catch in the sunlight. It flashed like a mirror just about the same time I started running. I went along the boxwood hedge like a rat running along the base of a wall. Then I cut out in the open.

I got to the car, Laurie slid out of the driver's seat. I jumped in and she said, "Where are the keys? You still got the goddamn keys!"

I said, "What do you want the keys for?"

Then I knew.

I thought of Jackie Kennedy climbing over the back of the convertible after they shot her husband in Dallas and the Secret Service man on the bumper pushing her back in. I didn't figure Laurie would go off and leave me, but there it was. I was real upset about it at first till I realized she wasn't in her right mind. She probably just didn't know what she was doing.

I said, "What you want the keys for, Laurie?"

I was still fishing them out of my pocket when she said, "Come on! He's fixing to kill us!"

I told her to cool it. I didn't see him.

She said, "That don't mean he ain't there!"

Then I saw him come through the gate and said, "Oh, shit!"

I was already trying to crank the car when Laurie saw him, too. The old man was standing there leveling the gun when she started yelling so loud I couldn't tell if it started or not. I crammed it in gear and let out the clutch and the car just sat there a minute, spinning its wheels. Then it caught and started skittering forward and sideways both at once.

We were heading straight for the house except for an oak tree in the way. Laurie reached over and grabbed the wheel. We veered to one side of the tree and started heading straight for the old man instead. I thought for a minute she was trying to kill him. We were just about to run him down, but he was holding his ground. I'll say that for him. Others might have tried to run, but he was just standing there fixing to shoot us when I grabbed the wheel and drove straight through the boxwood hedge.

We circled the house and were heading back on the road through the pastures when I yelled, "What happened? You see what happened?"

I meant to the old man. I was afraid he might have got hurt.

She said, "I don't know. Who gives a shit? You almost killed us!"

She already climbed in the backseat by then and was sitting there holding the baby, rocking it back and forth in her arms. The baby was crying, and I said, "Why don't you get it to hush? It's making me nervous."

She said, "What do you think I'm doing?"

I said, "I don't know, but whatever it is, it's not working."

She said, "It's not like a car. You don't just cut it off."

I watched my driving for a while. The baby kept crying.

I said, "I just figured you'd know what to do."

That got her attention.

She looked at me in the mirror and said, "What do you mean?"

I said, "It acts like it never saw you before."

Laurie said, "O God!" and started crying. I could see her shaking all over. Pretty soon they were both crying, Laurie and the baby both. She was still rocking it back and forth, getting it all stirred up.

"She doesn't even know who I am," Laurie said.

I checked her out in the mirror again. She had her head thrown back on the seat. She was still holding the baby, but she wasn't rocking it at least. It wasn't struggling. It was just laying there on her chest face down, whimpering a little.

I said, "Well, at least you got it quiet."

She said, "It's worn out, poor thing."

That got me thinking about the old man. I asked if she saw what happened to him.

She said, "No. He just went down."

I said, "*Went down?* You mean he fainted?"

She didn't say.

I said, "What do you mean, 'went down'? What happened to him?"

She said, "I don't know."

I said, "You think he's dead?"

She didn't answer.

I said, "You think both of them are dead?"

She still didn't answer. I looked back, and it was just like a picture. Mother and child. If I didn't know what had just happened, I'd have thought it looked real peaceful. But I kept seeing the old lady laying face down in the dirt looking at something that was too close to see. And I didn't even know about the old man. It might have been a heart attack.

I wiped my eyes and tried to quit thinking about it. I had to figure out what to do. The first thing we'd need for that baby was food. That and some place to stay. I figured I'd drive over to Dalton. That was about fifty miles away over the mountains, on Interstate 75. They had a lot of motels over there. We'd check into one and leave the next morning. Go south to Atlanta, then keep on going west after that, through Anniston and Birmingham. We'd probably get to Meridian that night, trade cars the next day and get a powder-blue Cadillac convertible. Laurie said she always wanted one, and I didn't see how I could refuse her. Then we'd get in and keep on going, the top down, the wind blowing the hair in our face, watching the country coming up at us and flinging on past till the trees thinned out and dried up in Texas, and keep on going beyond that, where it turned into desert, and beyond that, where the seeds ran out, and there were just grains of sand with the pitiless sun beating down on them, grinding them up, trying to make it where something would grow if it ever had water, and then even beyond that, to where it was nothing but slickrock and canyons—all the way to Tuba City.

I figured we'd get married as soon as we got there and buy us a trailer or even a house and settle down on a permanent basis. I had good friends in Tuba City. Around there and Moenkopi. I figured they'd help us get a job. I wanted to work for the government in the

Adolescent Alcoholic Rehabilitation Program. I like young folks. They're full of promise. And most of the time it's not too late. You can still do something with them. I had a lot of experience drinking and a few good years dried out in the Program. There aren't a whole lot of folks walking around Tuba City sober enough for them to be choosy. I figured I'd make a good counselor, sharing my experience, strength, and hope. I wanted to do some good in the world to make up for all the time I wasted. Barring that, I could always get a job with the Department of Interior, Bureau of Indian Affairs, painting on the reservation.

I figured we already had us a family. Pretty soon it would start growing. Laurie and I'd probably have two or three of our own, boys and girls all mixed up together. And that's it. That's all I wanted.

I wanted Laurie and me to be happy just like everybody else. I wanted us to love one another. I wanted us to grow old together. That was all the hope I had. It was everything I ever wanted or needed or ever wished I had with Kate.

21

The road ran along a lake, but I didn't know what it was for a minute. It looked like a pasture covered with frost. The trees around it were mostly all pines, and I'd see something flash through the needles. Then it was gone. We'd go down a hill or around a curve, and the whole thing would disappear, and all of a sudden it would rise up again. It didn't seem like it could be water. It was too bright for that. It was more like a pool of light with the moon shining in it. Then we came out on the edge of the water, past of a row of dark houses, and all of a sudden we were heading right at it. Then the road turned, and we climbed a hill and climbed another, and little by little we left it behind.

It was just about dark. We'd come to a curve, and the woods would rear up like a wall, and just before we hit it, we'd turn and glide on past, and the road would open up again, and I could see down it as far as the headlights. It was like a dream I kept having.

After a while we were back on the pavement. I picked up speed and started thinking more about driving. We went through the town of Etowah. There was nothing there but a pickup truck and a couple of boys on the hood drinking beer. They waved and yelled something, and I blinked my lights.

Laurie reared up in the backseat and said, "What happened?" She must have been sleeping.

I said, "Etowah. We're at the red light."

She was leaning forward touching my ear and stroking my neck and saying she loved me. She never loved anybody but me.

She said, "Listen. You hear that? I can hardly breathe, I love you so much."

It's like she was running. Her voice was thick from breathing so hard, but I couldn't think about what she was doing. My mind wouldn't work. It was like a puzzle. I was trying to put the pieces together, and Laurie kept on messing it up. I'd get a part, and she'd come along and scatter it on me.

We went on a couple of miles, past Thriftown and the Dairy Queen, heading to Dalton, when I saw a convenience store and one of those blue telephone booths that look like a hair dryer stuck on a pole. I pulled over and called 911. I told them I wanted to report an accident.

The man on the phone said, "What kind of accident?"

I said, "A woman fell down some steps. She might be dead."

He wanted to know where it was, and I told him, and he said he'd send an ambulance. Anything else?

I said, "Yeah. There's another one."

He said, "Another what?"

I said, "Another person. He might have had a heart attack."

He said, "Goddamn! How did that happen?"

I said, "I don't know."

He said, "What are you, a neighbor or something?"

I said, "No. I was just passing."

He said, "You saw them both?"

I could see he was getting suspicious.

I said, "That's right," and hung up.

I got back to the car, Laurie sat up and said, "Where are we going?"

I said, "Dalton. But first we got to get some food for the baby."

She said, "That's right!"—like she forgot all about it.

We were going back over the mountains by then, and they were like dark waves in a dream. We were driving the switchbacks, swaying back and forth in the curves all the way to Chatsworth.

We pulled into town, I saw a Red Dot Grocery and turned around to Laurie and said, "You know what that baby eats?"

Laurie said, "Of course I do. I'm the mother"—like that made her know.

I pulled in front of the store and stopped. As soon as I cut off the engine, the baby rose up and looked around. I thought it was going to start crying again, but it just sucked its thumb and went right back to sleep.

I said to Laurie, "You know what you look like?"

She said, "What?"

I said, "A picture."

She said, "What kind of picture?"

I said, "Mother and child."

That got her laughing.

She said, "Don't get me laughing. You'll wake up the baby."

I said, "I mean it. Just like a picture in a book."

That seemed to make her real happy. She smiled at me like she had a secret.

I said, "You happy you got your baby?"

She said, "Yeah. The son of a bitch thought he was going to keep it."

I said, "Well, you got it now."

She said, "That's right. Just what I wanted—ain't it, sugar?"

She was squeezing the baby and kissing it, and it looked at her and started crying.

I said, "Well, what do you want to get it to eat? You're the expert on babies around here."

She told me milk and soda crackers and baby food.

I said, "What kind?"

She said, "All kinds."

I went in, and by the time I came out, I had two whole sacks full of baby food. I got to the car and looked in the window, and I couldn't believe I had them in there.

Laurie saw me looking through the window and smiled. It was that same smile again. I felt my heart thump in my chest and the blood rush to my face. Then the baby lifted its head and started crying.

"Look what you did!" Laurie said. "You got it to crying."

I didn't say anything one way or the other. The baby was snuffling and sucking its thumb. Laurie was trying to get it to go back to sleep, so I just I put the groceries in the car and started driving. I got to I-75, and a truck passed, roaring by, then another, then a whole string of them. The baby woke up, and Laurie started rocking it, singing it songs like "What a Friend I Have in Jesus" and "Whispering Hope."

I hadn't heard either one of them in years.

When she got finished with "Whispering Hope," I said, "Sing something happy."

She said, "Like what?"

I said, "I don't know."

I thought for a minute.

I said, "'The Marine Hymn.'"

She laughed and said, "That isn't happy."

I said, "All right. What about 'Wayfaring Stranger'?"

She said, "I don't know it. That's not for babies."

I said, "Neither is 'Whispering Hope.'"

She said, "It is, too. Babies love it. Don't you, honey?"

She went on singing "I'll Fly Away" and "Lead Kindly Light" and "Jesus I'm Coming" and I don't know what all till finally the baby was sleeping again. I don't know where Laurie got it all. The Balm of Gilead and Rivers of Babylon, Fountains of Blood and the Beautiful Shore—all that kind of stuff. She was about as bad as Tom.

Laurie finally went to sleep herself, and it was quiet after that, considering the traffic. I drove along thinking about all those trucks carrying all those loads of precious cargo through the dark, abysmal night. It sounded just like one of those songs. The words kept running around in my head till all I could think of was the sound of the tires slapping the seams in the concrete pavement and the words of that song about carrying loads of precious cargo through the dark, abysmal night, pounding along like that mile after mile.

We got to Dalton, I stopped at a motel called EZ-REST. It was all lit up with strips of pink neon, but it seemed like an old-fashioned place. About ten rooms in a line and an office at one end. It wasn't on the interstate. That was one of the main reasons I stopped. The ones on the highway cost more money and would probably be too noisy for babies. There was a big sign that said, FREE MOVIES! KITCHENETTES! REASONABLE RATES! CHILDREN FREE! ANY NUMBER! FIFTEEN DOLLARS!

It looked like a family place to me, so I pulled in and went to the office. There wasn't anybody at the desk, but it had a sign that said, RING THE BELL. It was a little dinner bell, and I picked it up and rang it, and nothing happened. I rang it again, and a big, fat woman came shuffling out from behind a pink curtain. She had on a blue flannel gown and was carrying a little gray miniature poodle. She set the poodle up on the counter, and it started trembling.

It looked at me, and its muzzle was white, and its eyes were running. I thought it was crying before I remembered dogs don't cry.

The woman didn't say anything. She picked up the dog. It quit trembling and licked her hand, and she finally looked at me and said, "You want a room?"

I said, "Yes, ma'am. That's what I'm here for."

She give me a card to fill out. I got through, she turned it around and said, "Apalachicola, Florida. You from there?"

I said, "Yes, ma'am."

I figured I'd better start lying about it.

She said, "How come it's a Georgia tag?"

I hadn't even thought about that.

I said, "It's near. I *live* in Georgia."

She nodded her head like she didn't believe it. The dog was just sitting there, looking mournful.

I said, "That dog's eyes are bad."

I figured I'd better change the subject.

She said, "Yours would be, too, if you saw what it saw."

I didn't know what she meant by that, so I said, "Yes, ma'am."

She said, "I've been to hell and back."

I said, "Yes, ma'am. I reckon you have."

She said, "I mean it."

I said, "Yes, ma'am. I know you do."

She said, "You got any children?"

I started to say no, when she looked down at the card I wrote and said, "One child. How old is it?"

I said, "Two or three. Something like that."

She said, "Don't let it grow up to be like mine."

I said, "I won't."

She said, "An ungrateful child, you know what they say? It's sharper than a serpent's tooth. You believe that?"

I said, "Yes, ma'am. I know that's the truth."

She said, "My child's in jail."

I said, "That's bad. That's a bad place to be."

She said, "I'm the one that turned him in. I had to do it."

I didn't know what to say about that.

She said, "You love your mother?"

I said, "Yes, ma'am. She's dead, but I love her."

She nodded her head.

She said, "I wish my child was dead. He don't love his mother."

I was getting real uneasy.

I said, "That's bad. That's real bad, ain't it?"

She started crying. The tears were running down her face.

She said, "Loving somebody's a terrible thing. I wish I wasn't born sometimes."

That's the first thing she said that made sense all evening.

I said, "Listen, lady, that's the truth. Loving's the painfulest thing there is."

She said, "You poor man. You poor, poor man."

I said, "Yes, ma'am. I got to go. They're waiting on me."

She went to the window and peeked out the blind.

She said, "That's them in the car?"

There wasn't but one car in the place.

I said, "Yes, ma'am. That's them."

She gave me a key. Room seven.

She said, "That's a good one. Everything works."

I drove over to room number seven and opened the door. Laurie got out of the car and was standing there holding the baby. I said, "Come on. I'll carry you in."

The baby turned and looked at me, and Laurie said, "What?"

I said, "I'll carry you over the threshold."

She started laughing and said, "That's if you're married."

I said, "Well, we're fixing to be."

She said, "What?"

She put her head sideways and looked at me like she was trying to figure me out.

I said, "I always thought we were. Come on."

I started to pick her up, she said, "Watch out, you'll drop the baby."

I said, "You hold the baby."

I carried them both in the room and dropped them on the bed. They bounced on the mattress, and Laurie started laughing. That's the sort of thing she loved. The baby was so surprised it started laughing, too. They both laid there on the bed laughing together. Then the baby started bouncing around, and Laurie grabbed it and kissed it all over. The baby was trying to pull away, but Laurie held it and started bouncing up and down, and the baby started laughing again.

I went out and got the groceries. I heard the toilet flush in the bathroom, and Laurie came out. The baby was wrapped up in a towel.

"She was wet," Laurie said. "She was wet all afternoon, poor baby."

I said,"What's her name?"

She said, "Lucy."

I said, "Well, Lucy, how are you doing?"

I held out a finger. I thought maybe she'd reach out and grab it the way they do, but she just looked at it like she never saw a finger before. I eased forward and touched her with it, and the baby looked down at it and smiled.

"See there," Laurie said. "She likes you already. You know they got a kitchen in here?"

I said, "That's the main reason I got it."

She said, "Come on. Lucy's hungry."

And that's how we did—just like a family. I went out and got us some burgers and fries, and by the time I got back, Laurie was sitting there, feeding the baby.

I said, "How much you feed it already?"

Laurie said, "Three jars. This is the fourth. Ain't it sweet? Look at her looking."

The baby was doing two things at once—opening its mouth eating and looking at me. I didn't know which it was more interested in. Then Laurie wiped the baby's mouth with a towel and gave her to me. It was like holding a sack full of groceries. I didn't know what to do with it.

Laurie set out the hamburgers, and we took turns holding the baby and eating. She already had on the news, and the baby was sitting there watching it like she knew what it meant. I kept waiting to see if they found the old lady yet, but it was only about Washington, D.C., and space shuttles and people protesting the government.

I said, "When they going to get on some news?"

Laurie and the baby both looked at me. Laurie was sitting there, feeding it bits of hamburger. The baby would eat about as much as you gave her. She was like an owl, she looked so serious sitting there being fed.

I said, "She's going to eat up your food."

Laurie said, "Then I'll get me some more. She don't much like baby food. She'll eat it, but she's too old. She got all her teeth."

I said, "Is that right?"

It didn't surprise me. I figured she would. I didn't know they grew them from scratch.

I said, "She sure is eating a lot."

Laurie said, "She was hungry. Weren't you, Lucy?"

The baby looked at her and said something.

Laurie said, "That means food. She's already talking."

I went over and laid down on the part of the bed that didn't already have cracker crumbs on it and watched TV. The baby finally went to sleep, and I put my arm around Laurie and held her.

I could feel her breath rising and falling. It was like standing on the edge of the ocean, seeing the waves coming in all the way from Africa. It was like a mystery, seeing her breath coming in from somewhere so far off I couldn't even imagine where. And not only that, it kept on coming.

I turned my head so I could look at her better. I wished I knew what she was thinking, but all I could see was the breath moving through her. The baby was sleeping. I laid there awhile and stared at the ceiling. The neon light outside the room came in through the blinds and made it look as red as fire.

I don't know how long I laid there like that. It was real peaceful. It felt like a hand holding us up, giving us the breath to breathe, and that's what I prayed to. I said, Hold us up, Lord. Keep us safe. Protect us all like innocent children. Then I prayed for love. I asked Kate to give it to me. I didn't ever want to lose it again.

That baby felt like a whole new life stirring in me. I laid there, tears running down the sides of my face, and I thanked God I wasn't drunk and I wasn't dead. I felt like I had a new life. I could feel it growing in me like a seed.

Flesh of my flesh, I kept thinking. Bone of my bone.

Then I must have fallen asleep because the next thing I knew Laurie was whispering my ear.

She said, "Listen. You awake?"

I said, "Yeah. I am now. "

She said, "I want to tell you something."

I said, "What?

She said, "You're a real good man. I'll always be grateful."

I said, "What for?"

She said, "Getting my baby. I'll never forget it. I want you to know that, no matter what happens. Remember that."

I said, "What?"

She said, "Promise me you'll always remember."

I said, "I will."

I didn't know how I could forget it. I didn't even know what it meant.

Then she kissed my ear and said, "Go on to sleep, now. You got a lot to do in the morning."

I laid there a while staring at the neon light on the ceiling, worrying about what Laurie said. I couldn't figure out why she said it. Then I worried about Benny and the old lady and the old man and Tom and Kate and Laurie and Lucy. I could still hear them breathing beside me, and that gave me some comfort.

Then I fell asleep myself.

22

When I woke up the next morning, I didn't know where I was for a minute. I'd been lost in the dark of a dreamless sleep, and all of a sudden there I was in the blink of an eye like it says in the Bible: *The trumpet will sound, and the dead will rise up in the blink of an eye, and they will be incorruptible.* And I thought to myself, That's right. There isn't a knife edge of difference between them. I might have been dead a hundred years, a thousand years since Kate died, and all of a sudden there I was in the blink of an eye. I laid there awhile thinking about that till I got tired of speculating and rolled over and reached for Laurie. But she wasn't there. I felt around, but I couldn't find her.

I sat up and looked.

Laurie was gone, the baby was gone. The bed was empty. The room was dark, but the air was red and smoky-looking. I could see the door to the bathroom was open. I thought maybe she was in there. I called out, but she didn't answer. So I got up and went in the bathroom and looked. I even pulled back the shower curtain.

No one was there.

I went back out in the other room and turned on the light. The baby clothes were still on the dresser. There were chewed-up pieces of hamburger meat the baby spit out and greasy, wadded-up hamburger wrappers and paper napkins and skinny yellow fingers of French fried potatoes and dried-up smears of mustard and ketchup and little white grains of salt and cracker crumbs all over the top of the table. It didn't look like a meal, exactly. It looked more like garbage.

I checked my watch. It was 5:54. I went to the window and pulled back the drapes. The car was gone. I opened the door and went out in my underwear just to make certain. Then I went back in the room. That's when I saw the clothes were gone—I mean the ones Laurie was wearing. I checked the floor around the bed. Her shoes and socks were gone, too. I looked on the dresser. My wallet was still there, sitting on a pile of loose change in the ashtray. The key to the room was right beside it, chained to what looked like a sawed-off piece of broom handle. I opened my wallet and counted the money. It was all there. I counted it a second time just to make certain. Three twenties, a ten, and a couple of ones. Seventy-two dollars, plus change. I figured Laurie had gone to get breakfast, but I didn't see how she could have done it. She didn't have any money on her. A couple of dollars, maybe. Why didn't she take any of mine? Why didn't she wake me? Then I thought about the baby. Why didn't I hear it crying and carrying on? Why didn't it wake me? It was like one of those scenes in a movie where someone goes deaf, and you see people walking around talking to each other and cars passing on the street and airplanes taking off at the airport, and there isn't a sound. Just silence. It was like somebody stole them from me while I was sleeping, or Laurie went and got herself lost and wasn't ever coming back.

Then I thought about the money. There was an old Bible in the drawer of the dresser, one of those old Gideon Bibles they put in motel rooms, and I took it as soon as we checked in the room and put the envelope with Tom's money in it inside the Book of Psalms and set it on top of the valve in the toilet. Then I put the cover to the toilet tank back on. Laurie was standing there watching me do it. She said that was a damn peculiar thing to do, hiding money inside the toilet. I told her it was either that or the light fixture, and I didn't want to get electrocuted just for one night. The valve in the toilet was easier.

As soon as I thought about the money, I went in the bathroom and lifted the top of the tank to the toilet. The Bible was there just like I thought. I picked it up and looked. The money was gone. I slid down on the floor and sat there beside the toilet, holding the Bible. It was like being in a wreck. After it's over, you sit there like that, feeling the blood rush to your face, pounding inside your head like a drum, and the skin prickling all over your body and the hair raising up on the back of your neck till after a while you realize it's over, you aren't dead after all, and you begin to check yourself out to see if you're hurt and if the car's going to catch on fire and how you're going to get out if it does.

I just sat there like that and let it all sink in for a while till I was sure it really happened. The money was gone, and Laurie was gone, and she wasn't ever coming back. The first thing I remember thinking about was what it said in the Bible about planting the seeds, and how some fell on rocks and some fell in weeds on the side of the road. Some were eaten by the birds of the field and the fowl of the air, and some fell on good soil and grew. The more I thought about those seeds, the more I realized I wasn't surprised. I didn't know Laurie. I knew the story of her life. I mean what she told me. But I didn't know what she was thinking when I'd see her looking so sad and lonely. I didn't know why she was always so restless. I couldn't trust her. I knew that. She wasn't true. She wasn't loyal. She just wasn't that kind of person. There were things about Laurie that bothered me, little bits and pieces of things that stuck in my mind like thorns and nettles. But I couldn't figure out what it was till that very minute, and then I knew. It was like her heart's desire. I mean her secret, inner heart like it says in the Bible: *Do not lay up for yourselves treasures on earth, where moth and rust consume and where thieves break in and steal. But lay up for yourselves treasures in heaven. For where your treasure is, there will be your heart also.* That's what she was thinking about when I'd see her staring off in the distance. That's why she was always acting so restless. *For out of the abundance of the heart the mouth speaks.* And her mouth spoke when she stole all that money.

I don't know how long I sat there like that. It's like I was blank. I didn't want to get up and go anywhere. I didn't have any plans anymore. I didn't even have any dreams or ambitions. I was right back to where I was after Kate died, except it was worse because I already knew what was going to happen. I thought about when I was drinking the worst. I'd stay in the trailer till it got too hot. Then I'd get out of bed and go down to Nogales and look at the tourists and count the buzzards in the trees by the river and get drunk and wonder, What happened? What next? And I wouldn't know. I was like those seeds in the Bible. There were rocks, but there was no water, there was no soil, nothing to grow on.

I was like that a couple of days. I finally figured I needed some money, so I went down to the union hall and hung around in the yard outside under the trees, talking to people. I told them I had a card of my own, but it expired when I was in prison, and I needed some money. I was robbed by the woman I loved and didn't have but a few dollars left to buy groceries and pay the room rent at the motel, and I'd be grateful for some kind of work even if it was only at half the regular union scale if that's all I could get. I was a real professional painter, twenty years on the job, and not only that, I was a union man myself—just lacking a card, that's all. And finally one of them took me on like Bubba Jones, same kind of deal, except he was white and didn't have a coffle of others, and I worked for a him a couple of months, saving my money.

After that, I went back to the motel and worked another deal with the old lady that owned it. I told her I was down on my luck, which she already knew from Laurie's leaving. I told her I'd paint the place for her in the evenings and weekends if she'd buy the paint and let me live there for free while I did it. She said she'd be glad to do it, so we went to the store and got the paint—pink to go with the strips of neon. She said she always wanted it pink. Pink was her favorite color, she said. But she never had the nerve to do it till her son got in prison, and what did it matter—why not? The motel needed painting real bad. It was flaking and peeling like the bark on a tree. That's why she did it. That and wanting to change the color to pink. But that wasn't the only reason she did.

I'd come home in the evening, and she'd fix us some dinner in back of the office, and I'd help her wash up. Then I'd go out and start in to painting, and she'd drag a web chair off of what she called the veranda and sit there with the dog in her lap, both of them looking old and gray, commenting on this and that like Tom—for the company, mostly—all about all the hard times she had and how nobody ever loved her, but dogs—she didn't know why. She kept saying I reminded her of her son except he was in prison, and she wished he was dead. He wasn't good company like me. And I didn't mind. It was important for somebody to listen and let her unburden her heart to them. And it was important for me, too. I didn't much want to hear what she said, but I wasn't as lonely as I might have been if I hadn't done it.

It went on like that. Days passed. I was saving my money and finally had enough to buy a car. After that, I'd lay up in bed and count the money, watching it grow, thinking about all the good times I could have for a while, getting drunk on it, raising hell. Except I didn't want to. I don't know why. I'd think about it, maybe even dream about it a little. But I just wasn't interested. It seemed like another life.

I kept asking myself, What next? What was I going to do the rest of my life? Then one day a couple of weeks later, I was inside a house painting the trim on a window, looking out at the sky. There wasn't a cloud. It was empty and blue and went on and on, clear as a thought, and all of a sudden I thought to myself nothing had changed. Laurie left and took all my money and all my hopes and expectations. But I was still there. That hadn't changed. I could go out to Tuba City all by myself if I wanted to do it. There were lots of good folks out there. I might even be able to help some of them, sharing my experience, strength, and hope. I didn't have to do it with Laurie. That was a new idea to me. I must have thought about it two or three days, turning it this way and that. Then one night I had a dream.

I dreamed that the sun was going down in a thick grove of pines on top of a ridge. The needles were silver and broken like glass. I could see a woman walking uphill into the flaming red ball of the sun. Her hair was electric, glowing like a halo of glory. Her clothes were on fire. A thin line of flame outlined her body, and inside that, like the heart of the fire, a circle of darkness, moving inside her. The sun kept dropping lower and lower. Inside the woods it was already dark, while down below, where the woman was walking, the sun was still shining. I thought at first the woman was Laurie, leaving me in my dreams. She finally got to the edge of the trees and turned around. I could see her full in the face, and it wasn't Laurie. It was Kate. She smiled and waved. Then she turned and took a few steps into the shadows. She took a few more and disappeared. She was swallowed up in the darkness, and I knew in my heart I'd lost her forever. I would never see her again.

I always thought this was a love story, and it is in a way. But not about Laurie. It's about Kate. I loved Laurie—or thought I did. But there were things about her that made me uneasy. Like all those men and how she was going to go off and leave me if she had the car keys that time, not to mention the fact that she finally did it. That's when it all caught up to me, and I knew for a fact that I never loved her. I missed her, all right. I missed making love to her. But I didn't miss all the rough edges. I didn't miss wondering what she was thinking and if I was ever going to be able to trust her. The only reason I thought I loved Laurie was that I missed Kate so much I tried to find a substitute for her, the same way I did with Tom till little by little, living with him, I finally realized he wasn't Kate no matter how much I saw of her in him flashing out sometimes. And Laurie wasn't Kate either. And all the while, under all that, there was something else going on—some dark current flowing in me, carrying me forth out of the darkness.

I was almost forty years old. I'd lost everything I ever wanted. The people I loved were dead and gone. I didn't have a regular job. I didn't have any money to speak of. All I had was a motel to paint and a dog and an old woman who couldn't tell me from her own son, she missed him so much. And the funny thing is, it didn't matter. That's what amazed me. Not only that, I was pretty happy, all things considered. I finally figured I had a plan. I had a place I was going to go and a pretty good idea of what I was going to do when I got there. I didn't want to go back to drinking. I knew what that was like, dragging yourself down every night in a dark, black sea of regrets and having to start all over again in the morning, cold sober and sick at heart, till after a while you're all used up. You don't have the strength and energy for it. Living doesn't seem worthwhile, and you end up more and more alone, wanting to end it.

But it's like I had something else now. I don't know where it came from. I can't even describe what it was. But it's like I was ready. I don't know what I was ready *for*. It wasn't like that. I was ready *for* anything. I was just ready. I didn't want to be somewhere else or with someone else or even doing something else. It was all right like it was. I didn't need it different from that. The main thing was feeling I had a future. I didn't have to spend the rest of my life looking back, yearning for Kate. She wouldn't even want me to. I'd always miss her. I'd never forget her. But I knew I'd never see her again. Not in this life. Not till we were together again on the other side of the veil.

We lived in the country when I was a boy on a little old piece of land that wasn't much good for anything except to hold the rest of the world together. In the summertime, night would come on so gradual it felt like you were going blind, and all the bugs in the world would start singing, filling the dark with their songs and rejoicing, and I'd sit out on the porch by myself hearing my momma washing the dishes and singing the words to a song she knew called "Kingwood." It was her favorite. She sang it whenever she did the dishes because of what it said about *endless deeps*.

> My days, my weeks,
> My months, my years,
> Fly rapid as the whirling spheres
> Around the steady pole.
> Time like the tide its motion keeps
> And I must launch through endless deeps
> Where endless ages roll.

My momma used to talk about hope. She used to say that's all we have. God smiles on His children. I didn't know what she meant, of course, because I wasn't old enough yet. You got to lose hope to know what it is. But I remember sitting out on the porch hearing my momma sing that song and all the bugs and stars in the world making a racket, and the whole world felt just like a promise. That was the closest I ever got to it. I was just a young boy then. I had my whole life in front of me. I'd sit there and think about all the wonder and glory to come, and something rose up in my heart like a bubble, I loved it so much. I was so grateful.

I still am.